PAGAN'S SPY

Matt Eaton

ONE

Tuesday November 18, 1952

President-elect Dwight Eisenhower had been sure they were leading him toward the Situation Room. He was surprised to find his Secret Service man instead taking a different corridor, past the White House Mess to a dead end.

One of the agents tugged on a panel in the wall; it opened a well-hidden door, revealing a dimly lit spiral staircase leading down to a rough concrete tunnel. There were pipes hanging from the ceiling. The tiled floor looked like it hadn't been swept in years.

"Is it safe in here?" the President asked hesitantly. "It looks like a construction site." Ike was wondering whether this might be Harry Truman's idea of a practical joke.

Secret Service agent Elmer Deckard stepped into the tunnel, immediately followed by fellow agent Jim Hipsley.

"It's quite safe, sir," Deckard assured him. "It always looks like this."

"Did Harry run out of money or something?" Eisenhower wondered aloud.

"The tunnel is a well-guarded secret, sir. President Truman ensured it doesn't appear on any of the official White House plans," Hipsley replied.

Harry Truman had gutted the White House in 1948 and expanded upon FDR's underground air raid shelter (hurriedly constructed after the bombing of Pearl Harbor) to accommodate a nuclear-age concrete bunker directly under the East Wing. The tunnel was the most direct route to the bunker from the West Wing, allowing the President to cross from one side of the White House to the other without being seen — never an easy feat for the most-watched man in America.

The agents led the President down the tunnel and around a bend, to the door of what looked like a large bank vault.

"We seal you inside in the case of an emergency," Deckard explained. "The bunker has its own air supply and you are safe from all forms of attack."

"Save a direct hit," said Eisenhower.

"Well, yes, I guess that'd be true, sir." Deckard threw a switch just inside the vault door, and the space flickered before his eyes as fluorescent lights blinked into operation.

"I hope you're not planning on sealing me in there today."

"No sir. But I will wait here at the door while you're inside. Agent Hipsley will go back now to bring down your guests."

Officially, the bunker was known as the President's Emergency Operations Center (PEOC). As he entered, Eisenhower noted the wartime feel to the place. Cots lined a hallway that led to a large open meeting room, containing a long table and about twenty chairs. One or two smaller rooms branched off the main area, but there was nothing much to the place. A spartan and dire hole in the ground to bury the Commander in Chief, as the world outside went to hellfire and damnation.

Ike pulled out one of the chairs and sat down. He hoped like hell he would never have to come down here again. He couldn't bring himself to imagine that even Joseph Stalin might be mad enough to wage nuclear war against his former ally. But then again, the war had shown Ike that men of power often acted out of spite, instead of reason or good intent. After being sworn in, he hoped to avoid any such catastrophe.

He wondered if Dick Nixon knew about this place. He figured it was unlikely. Ike relished the idea of keeping this one to himself, having some time ago decided to tell Vice President Nixon only what he needed to know and nothing more. They would never be friends, and Eisenhower suspected they would never work closely together while in office.

"Hello sir, sorry to keep you waiting." Admiral Roscoe Hillenkoetter carefully placed a folder down on the table and took a chair diagonally opposite the President-elect. "It's an odd room this one, don't you think?"

"That'd be putting it mildly," said Ike, shaking the Admiral's hand.

"I've only been down here once or twice. Never liked it."

"Well, putting our venue to one side, I must say I'm intrigued, Admiral. A secret room for a secret briefing. What could possibly be of such critical import?"

Hillenkoetter opened the file in front of him. "Sir, I am a member of a Top Secret group known as Majestic-12, or MJ-12 for short. My designation is MJ-1, being the first appointed to the group shortly after becoming the Director of the CIA in 1947."

"Majestic," said Ike. "Sounds auspicious."

Hillenkoetter placed a briefing paper down in front of Eisenhower. "I've been directed to bring you up to speed with our work. This document, which I must insist on taking with me after our meeting, will explain to you what we're about."

Hillenkoetter sat patiently in silence for the fifteen minutes it took Ike to absorb the contents of the briefing paper. The front page set the tone with a warning:

"*This is a Top Secret – Eyes Only document containing information essential to the national security of the United States. Reproduction in any form or the taking of written or mechanically transcribed notes is strictly forbidden.*"

The briefing paper named all members of the Majestic-12 group. According to the document, this group managed a research and development intelligence operation, answerable only to the US President and established under classified executive order.

It detailed the retrieval operations undertaken to gather wreckage from several crashes of disc-shaped objects, dating back to 1947. Including how four small humanoid bodies were recovered from a crash site in a remote part of New Mexico, and taken to Roswell Army Air Base (now Walker Field).

"A special scientific team took charge of removing the bodies for study. The wreckage of the craft was also removed to several different locations. Civilian and military witnesses in the area were debriefed and news reporters were given the effective cover story that the object had been a misguided weather research balloon.

"A cover analytical effort organized by Gen. Nathan F. Twining (MJ-4) and Dr Vannevar Bush (MJ-2) acting on the direct orders of the President, resulted in a preliminary consensus that the disc was most likely a short-range reconnaissance craft."

The paper pointed out that while the bodies found were human-like in appearance *"the biological and evolutionary processes responsible for their development has apparently been quite different from those observed or postulated in homo-sapiens".*

"Since it is virtually certain that these craft do not originate in any country on Earth, considerable speculation has centered around what their point of origin might be and how they got here.

"Mars was and remains a possibility, although some scientists, most notably Dr Donald Menzel (MJ-10), consider it more likely that we are dealing with beings from another solar system entirely."

For some time after he had finished reading the words on the page, Eisenhower continued to stare at the paper, evaluating their implications. He'd heard about the crash at Roswell in 1947 when he was Army Chief of Staff. But this was the first time he'd seen or heard any mention of alien bodies. When Ike finally looked up, Roscoe Hillenkoetter was watching him patiently. "Who else knows about this?" Ike asked the Admiral.

"Only people with a Majestic clearance level."

"What about the CIA?"

"Well sir, as you will have noted, CIA Director Walter Smith is a member of MJ-12. As to who else at the agency knows, I can't say for certain but I believe it would be a handful of people at best."

"There are more than twelve people in the loop."

"President Truman also placed Dr Menzel in charge of another group that maintains Majestic access. It's known as the Verus Foundation. Verus has Majestic-level clearance."

"Never heard of it," said Eisenhower.

"Which is precisely the point, sir. Verus was created as a clandestine storage hub for Majestic and all other highly classified matters, with a view to it being a library of critical data for future generations."

"And you're sure this level of secrecy is warranted?"

"We are, sir," Hillenkoetter replied.

Ike couldn't help but notice a pause before the Admiral said those words. Like he didn't truly believe it. He saw the shadow of doubt that swept momentarily across Hillenkoetter's face. "It says here Majestic is a research and development group. How far have you got with that?"

"Not very far at all, I'm afraid. We are dealing with technology far in advance of anything yet devised by our own scientists. It could take decades to make sense of what we have here. It's one of the reasons for secrecy — there are too many questions that remain unanswered."

If he'd been free to speak his mind, Hillenkoetter might also have mentioned a Top Secret project called FS-1 — which had deliberately been omitted from the presidential briefing paper. A project in possession of working alien technology, which aimed to turn it to America's strategic advantage. But FS-1 was also way behind the eight ball; it would be years before they knew what they were dealing with.

Perhaps even longer than Eisenhower himself would be in office. As such, Majestic-12 had voted by overwhelming majority to take FS-1 out of the presidential approval process. President Eisenhower, they had decided, didn't have a need to know.

TWO

Tuesday November 18, 1952

Eisenhower and Hillenkoetter emerged from the POEC vault to find a woman waiting dutifully alongside Agents Deckard and Hipsley. Seeing her caught the President-elect off guard; she was younger than he expected — and her face was familiar.

"Hello," he said.

Edna Drake saw the look of recognition in his eyes and smiled appreciatively as Hillenkoetter made the introduction. "Hello again, sir."

Ike turned his head slightly and frowned. "I'm afraid you have the advantage over me, Miss Drake. I must admit I can't recall where we met. Where was it again?"

"To be honest, sir, I'm surprised you remember me at all. It was on Utah Beach at Normandy."

"Good God, I do remember that. You were helping that brave medic, what was his name?"

"Waverley Woodson, sir."

Woodson — a black medic — had been forced to work single-handedly to save a score of critically wounded men at a makeshift medic station. Edna and two other nurses were rushed in from their hospital ship to help him on June 8th. The rest of the 24th Evacuation Hospital didn't arrive until four days later.

Edna had volunteered to go on ahead, not realizing those four days would come to feel like an eternity of hell. She had arrived to find the medic station a bloody shambles. In her first moments of the war, she was almost overwhelmed by panic, pain, and terror.

A day later, while touring Omaha Beach, General Eisenhower had thanked them personally for their service. "It was one of the bravest things I'd ever seen," said Ike. "A remarkable act of compassion. Now here you are again."

"I've been wanting to congratulate you on your election win," she said.

"Very kind, thank you," said Ike, glancing briefly in Hillenkoetter's direction. "But why weren't you in that meeting with us?"

"I'm not cleared to Majestic level just yet," Edna admitted sheepishly. She hoped the President didn't think less of her for it.

"Miss Drake is replacing Bill Donovan as the Verus Foundation security consultant," Hillenkoetter explained. "She's been reviewing material already in the foundation's possession. We haven't yet cleared her to take part in ongoing operations." This was at the behest of Donald Menzel; given the nature of her entry into Verus, he was yet to be convinced of her loyalties.

Ike shook his head. "That needs to change, Roscoe."

Hillenkoetter nodded. "Of course, Mr President."

Eisenhower laughed. "Bill Donovan. That old fox told me nothing about any of this, you know."

During the war, Donovan had headed up the OSS: the progenitor of the CIA. Inside the agency and out, he was known as America's spymaster. He'd never had a direct hand in agency affairs post-war, because Truman didn't like Donovan so much. But it was a mark of Truman's grudging respect for the man that he'd placed Donovan in charge of security for MJ-12 and Verus.

Ike and Donovan had been good friends for years; Bill had even worked closely on Ike's campaign. But Donovan kept his affairs strictly compartmentalized. Since the Washington saucer flap the previous year, Ike had strongly suspected Donovan knew more about aerial phenomena than he'd ever let on. Yet no amount of probing or prodding had brought forth anything from Donovan on the topic.

"Truman thought he'd told you everything," said Hillenkoetter. "But Bill knows how to keep a secret."

With the Secret Service agents leading the way, they began walking back along the sparse corridor toward the West Wing basement proper. "This place gives me the creeps," Ike told them.

"It's the lighting," Edna decided. "It feels like we've left the whole world behind."

"Too much has already been forgotten in this place," said Ike. "But I do like the sound of this Verus Foundation. A keeper for the secrets. Yes, I like that. My door is open to you, Miss Drake, if you ever need anything."

She smiled. "Thank you, sir."

"Big shoes you're filling. Bill Donovan is one of the greats. A real-live American hero."

Edna swallowed hard, reluctant to reveal she didn't hold the same lofty view of Donovan's character. "I'll do my very best."

"I have no doubt of it," Ike assured her.

She wondered how Ike would react if and when he discovered Donovan was responsible for bringing the FS-1 flying saucer onto American soil. At great personal and physical cost, Donovan had flown the spacecraft halfway around the world from right under the nose of the Russians. It struck Edna as perverse in the extreme that MJ-12 was keeping this from the new President, but she too was a keeper of secrets. To break that vow by speaking out of turn would endanger her life and liberty; it was a risk she dared not take.

They emerged above ground near the Cabinet Room, inside the West Wing. Eisenhower looked both ways, but didn't move. "I'm lost — where to now?"

Deckard led the way, taking a right turn along a corridor that led them to the West Wing lobby. "Just head out through the portico, then turn left to West Executive Avenue," Deckard told Edna and Hillenkoetter.

Ike waved them farewell. "I'd better look in on Harry before I go. Until the next time. A pleasure to meet you, Miss Drake."

Edna noticed two men in conversation near the building entrance. She was certain one of them was President Truman's right-hand man, John Steelman. She didn't recognize the other fellow, but he had the look of a typical Washington bureaucrat. Edna didn't think much about it. She noted that he'd caught Hillenkoetter's eye, and though the Admiral made no attempt to greet the man, she was sure they knew one another.

CIA counterintelligence chief James Jesus Angleton did indeed recognize Roscoe Hillenkoetter; the man was his former boss. Angleton watched their departure with interest. "Who's that with Hillenkoetter?" he asked Steelman.

"I have no idea. His secretary, perhaps?"

"Yes, I suppose so," said Angleton, though he didn't believe that for a moment. He could tell Steelman was lying. Angleton left aside the more pertinent question of what business Hillenkoetter could possibly have with the President-elect; Steelman wouldn't give him a straight answer. But Angleton knew then and there he absolutely had to find out more. With a new administration came new opportunities, and there was nothing that opened doors like insider knowledge.

Eisenhower had called her Miss Drake. Angleton would make it his business to find out what she and Steelman were hiding.

THREE

Friday December 5, 1952

A shiver ran up Edna's spine as she turned her shiny new Ford Crestliner coupe onto the dusty track that wound its way to Lee Tavon's farm. Trees had been planted along the roadside, making it harder to see the farm from the edge of the drive. The place felt far less menacing in daylight hours, particularly given the military was now nowhere to be seen. But the memory of being kidnapped at gunpoint was still vivid, and unsettling to say the least. Edna Drake had borne witness to a level of strangeness so detached from everyday reality that all these months later, her recollections had become hard to reconcile. Her life had taken a sharp turn that night, and it would never be the same.

She half expected to walk into Tavon's barn and find nothing but animals and farm equipment. Not because she doubted what she'd seen here with her own eyes, but because there was still a part of Edna that suspected Verus and Majestic-12 would one day cut her loose and leave her in the cold. After weeks of being immersed inside the greatest secret in human history, she remained painfully aware that the men who had brought her into the fold still saw Edna as an outsider.

Donald Menzel had made it plain that he was reserving judgment on her loyalty; it left her wondering what they expected from her. When Hillenkoetter told President Eisenhower Edna Drake was replacing Donovan as a security consultant, it was the first she'd heard of it — security was hardly her field of expertise. Trouble was, she didn't really know what she was supposed to be doing, other than serving as some sort of internal troubleshooter, or agitator, by calling them out on their own lies.

Verus was a storage house for sensitive information. It received files classified Top Secret or Above Top Secret. Information that might not make its way to the National Archive. Even so, it required sifting through the vast quantity of paperwork generated by the bureaucracies of the intelligence services. The foundation had an entire staff of people set to the task — retrieving weekly drop-offs of files from locations hidden ingeniously in plain sight, in stationery storage cabinets or forgotten janitorial cupboards, moved about by people who had no idea of the sensitivity of the material in their grasp. Verus needed to remain unseen by the people whose secrets it collected, lest awareness prompt a filtering of the information flow. The source of this river mouth was the office of the Director of Central Intelligence, who had been tasked with the job by President Truman — on the proviso it would not be released to the public for forty years or more.

But it was far from the only source, as Edna had come to realize. Verus was also closely associated with several Top Secret operations, all of which functioned outside the purview of the official intelligence apparatus. There were no restrictions placed on this information — officially it didn't exist. This was the area in which Edna had focused most of her time; it was what had prompted her invitation to return to Tavon's farm.

Edna was fairly certain Menzel didn't know she was here. That was unlikely to do anything to improve her relationship with him once he did find out, but the chance had been too good to pass up.

A brief, handwritten request had been poked under the front door early one morning at Verus HQ. By sheer luck or impeccable timing, she'd been the one who had found it first. On any given weekday, the

Verus foyer was busy with researchers moving documents, walking between the basement and the ground-floor kitchen for coffee or food. There were usually six to eight other people in the building conducting hush-hush Verus affairs; any one of them could have found the note. But the Outherians could read minds; it would be easy for one of them to wait for the exact moment Edna Drake was walking past. After reading the note, she'd quickly pulled open the front door (something frowned upon by Menzel, who preferred people use the rear entrance), but whoever had delivered it was long gone.

On face value, it was simply an invitation to spend a quiet weekend in the country. No names. The location itself was enough. Anybody perusing the note who wasn't hip to what had gone down there the previous year would have no reason to suspect a thing.

The farmhouse looked just the same as she remembered it; the barn loomed ominously as Edna drove closer. In reality, it was a hangar in convincing camouflage. She turned off her engine and checked herself quickly in the rearview mirror. Her dark hair still had that Sofia Loren tussle to it, that bed-head allure men found so disarming. Her red lipstick was in good shape and she was showing just the right amount of cleavage.

On cue, an unfamiliar face appeared from nowhere. A young man, hair cropped short, dressed in dirty brown overalls and covered in grease like a mechanic. He was wiping his hands clean. "Can I help you, ma'am?"

He sounded friendly enough, but she didn't buy his act for minute. "I'm here for the weekend to stay with Mr Tavon and his family. I'm Edna Drake."

"Oh yes," the young man said, staring her straight in the chest, "I've been expecting you."

"And you are?"

"White's the name. John White."

She raised an eyebrow. "As in brother of Snow?"

"Something like that," he said. "Hey, I like your car."

"Thank you," she said. "A perk of the job." She didn't say what job. He didn't ask.

"I take it you have some ID on you?"

She pulled out her letter of invitation. "This good enough for you?"

"How about a driver's license?"

"Who are you, the farm police?"

He stared back at her nonplussed, as if to say, "try me and you'll find out soon enough."

Edna hopped out of the car and flashed her license. White smiled at her long legs without even realizing he was being so obvious; he nodded his approval and waved her in through the hangar door. She was relieved to find he left her to find her own way, but wondered how he'd gotten his hands so dirty. Had it all been for show?

Inside was no mechanic's workshop, but a hive of activity nevertheless, just like she remembered. The same feeling returned — like she was stepping into a dream, awake and asleep at the same time. As if anything was possible, yet the outcome was predetermined. The rules of this game were different, and remained tantalizingly elusive.

The large hatch in the heavy concrete floor slid open, revealing all of the subterranean chambers with their Escher-like twists, existing in utter contempt of Sir Isaac Newton's laws of gravity. It sent a chill down her spine; this time she would be descending into that world. She had never been permitted this far.

Yet she knew it was where they wanted her to go.

Tavon was marching across the hangar's concrete apron, smiling. "Welcome, my dear. I'm very happy you could make it."

He too was in overalls, but his were clean and baby blue. He held out his clean hand for her to shake; his easy cheerfulness brought Edna back to herself. There was genuine warmth in his big brown eyes.

"It's good to see you, Lee," Edna said. He held her gaze for a long time, untroubled by the extended eye contact. It was both hypnotic and slightly disturbing. "Donald sends his apologies," she added.

Lee pursed his lips in a stifled smile. "You didn't tell him you were coming, did you?"

She grinned. "Nope."

"You are always a breath of fresh air, Edna Drake."

"Looks like you're busy," she said.

"Always." He turned and walked toward an area near the edge of the cavernous floor opening. Directly in front of him, an elevator rose through the concrete, as if by magic. It had no doors, but was massive inside; big enough to take a vehicle. She walked into the middle of the elevator car figuring this was the safest place. Edna saw no buttons, but as soon as they were both inside, it began to descend into the subterranean depths.

Entry points appeared fleetingly like windows as they fell through different levels, and she quickly felt dizzy as the world twisted and turned like a kaleidoscope. Each successive floor was rotating 90 degrees anti-clockwise — vertical, then upside down, then vertical again, before returning to normal. On each of these floors, people walked about normally, untroubled by their strange orientation.

"Why do you do this? Defy gravity like this?" she asked.

"It saves floor space," Lee explained, like it was the most normal thing in the world.

"And how did you make this elevator work? Are you controlling it with your mind?"

Tavon nodded, but he was looking distracted. "They've been visiting me, you know." She didn't know. She had no idea what he was on about. "To be fair," he said, "I've been visiting them too. We speak to one another."

"Who, Lee? Who's visiting you? Do you mean Majestic?"

He shook his head. "Others. They live here, you see. Underground, like us. But their home is buried deep in the forest. Impossible to find unless you know where to look. They visit me quite often."

She realized he meant alien visitors. Edna made a mental note to ask him more about it later. Right now, there were more immediate questions.

FOUR

Friday December 5, 1952

They stopped at a floor Edna was relieved to find was already the right way up.

"The lift knows, you see?" said Tavon. "It adjusts your perspective to your destination before you arrive."

Edna stepped out of the elevator cart to a room in which all the other Lee Tavons were already waiting. They didn't bother greeting her — one of the peculiar consequences of being carbon copies of one another. What any one of them experienced was known to the others. They were one person, and yet many. Away from one another, they lived separate lives. Together like this, they were a single entity.

They were all dressed in the same jumpsuit. She realized now it was like something a pilot might wear. The room was plain white. The floor curved seamlessly into the walls and again into the ceiling, one single shell.

The Tavons looked excited.

"What's going on, guys?" She mustered a smile in the hope it would mask her unease.

"Teleport," they told her, all at once.

So much for a quiet weekend in the country. "Does that mean what I think it means?" she asked.

"A device to transfer physical objects between two points in space-time," they replied.

"We want to show you," said the Lee who had greeted her.

"By starting small," said the others.

They unfurled a black rubberized mat onto the shiny white floor. It was about one foot square. There were no wires attached to it, nor could she see any sign of power. But she could sense its presence in the room, like it was alive. Subtly vibrating the space around it. There was one just like it on the other side of the room.

They started with a baby doll in a blue jumpsuit, its hand in the air like it was waving goodbye. One of the Tavons threw the doll in the direction of the mat.

It disappeared.

"Success!" they yelled together, pointing across the room.

She saw then the doll was lying on the floor — thirty feet away near the second mat. It hadn't been thrown hard enough to cover that distance, but it was there just the same.

"You didn't tell me that was going to happen," she said.

"We wanted it to be a surprise," they said, smiling in triumph like seven Houdinis.

"Are you telling me you transported the doll from one mat to the other?"

"Exactly!" they cried.

It was a remarkable feat. It might have been even more impressive if she'd known to watch for the doll's arrival at the other end. "Can you show me again? I'll watch more closely this time."

"Stage two," they said together. One of them was now holding a tabby cat, like a rabbit that had been pulled from an invisible hat. He placed the cat on the floor and waved it in the direction of the black square.

Never before in her life had Edna seen a cat obey instruction without food being involved. This one did as it was told and walked directly to the mat, but changed its mind at the last moment and sat down. Typical damn cat. It stared into space, as if it could see something in the air just ahead, then leapt onto the mat and vanished. Instantly, the cat reappeared beside the doll on the other side of the room.

"Success!" the Tavons yelled again.

Edna laughed in delight. "That's unbelievable."

"Nothing really," said one.

"A window through space-time," said another.

"A tunnel beneath reality turning two places into one."

"Now you've lost me," she admitted.

One of them grabbed her by the hand and swung her around to face him. "Human beings have long considered other dimensions of reality. Like heaven and hell. Olympus. Valhalla. But those are just ideas. There is another universe where space is in inverse proportion to our reality. Our device is a gateway through that universe. It works as a shortcut. In this world, the distance between those two places may be great. But by traversing through this other world, we move through a doorway that links two destinations into one."

She nodded. "I think I understand you. But where is this other world and how does it connect to both places? Neither heaven nor hell, I take it."

"Maybe it's both," said Tavon. "It's connected to all places at once. Our devices at either end are merely anchoring points."

"Now for the moment of truth," the Tavons exclaimed. "One of us."

The Tavon furthest from her had, by that time, picked up the tabby cat and was cradling it in his arms, stroking it gently. The cat appeared to be enjoying the attention. The Tavons exchanged knowing glances, and Edna figured they were trying to decide which of them would be first.

But the elevator arrived in the room at that moment, though Edna hadn't even noticed it leaving. It brought a young girl into their midst; she was no more than six or seven years old at best.

"Perfect timing, Faye," they said. "We're ready for you."

Edna somehow knew at that moment Faye was their daughter. She watched in horror as the child stepped up to the mat. How could they be so reckless as to needlessly endanger the life of a child?

"There is no risk," said Tavon, reading her thoughts.

"Then do the test yourselves," said Edna, not bothering to hide her irritation. Having them inside her head felt like an invasion of privacy.

"We will, in time," the nearest Tavon told her. "But for the purposes of scientific testing, we are progressing more gradually. It is a matter of scale. You might do, Edna, if you prefer."

Edna did think this might be a preferable alternative and was about to say so, but the child looked up and shook her head with a sense of knowing way beyond her years. Her expression told Edna to back off, that she didn't know what she was dealing with. As Edna opened her mouth to object, the little girl took three quick steps and launched herself at the mat, reappearing instantly on the other side of the room, still running. Faye managed to avoid stepping on the head of the doll just in time, its maiden test flight already long forgotten.

Edna rushed across the space between the mats to take a closer look at Faye. She touched the girl's face and ran her hands down her body to check for injury. Everything was where it should be. "Are you feeling OK, sweetheart?"

Faye was untroubled. "You don't need to treat me like a child," she told Edna. "I'm smarter than you are."

Edna laughed, "No doubt." She turned to the Tavons. "Who else knows about this?"

"Nobody," they said in unison.

"You haven't told Lockheed?"

As three of the Lees crouched down to speak further with Faye, another stepped forward to answer Edna's question. "Donald was most insistent we keep it from them. This is a Verus project. He hasn't told MJ-12 about it either."

The implications of what she'd just witnessed had her head spinning in ever-expanding circles. "This will revolutionize transport." It would do a lot more than that, of course. It would turn their understanding of the universe upside down.

"Precisely why Donald insists we tell nobody," said Tavon. "We would send the transport industry to the wall in one swift movement."

"You're right. But it wouldn't stop there. What would religious leaders have to say about it, I wonder? Proof of god — or the devil's work?" Emboldened by the audacity of it all, Edna had made up her mind. "OK, my turn now."

"Be our guest," they said.

She stepped across the mat quickly, before her rational mind could tell her what a bad idea it was.

The sensation was like swimming through a dark flooded tunnel. There was a dreamy sense to it, a pleasing sensation she wished could have lasted longer. But it was gone in a fraction of a second, replaced by the far more disconcerting sensation of being spiritually ripped from one's own body. Then Edna was through to the other side. She'd felt no physical movement.

The Tavons were grinning madly. "How do you feel?" they asked her in chorus.

"OK, I think," she said. "No different."

"That's good. This is as it should be. It is the space around you that is being bent, you should notice nothing."

"I'm not sure I'd go that far. I definitely noticed something. A bunch of emotions, actually."

One of them stepped forward and touched her forehead. "The dream state, nothing more."

"How long before we can use this in the field?" she asked.

"The next step is to test it over a greater distance," said one.

"Tomorrow," they decided together. "It will be ready tomorrow."

FIVE

Friday December 5, 1952

It was night time when Edna emerged from the underground complex to bunk down for the night in the farmhouse. As Tavon led the way into the open air, she was gripped by the oddest sensation. It rather reminded her of going through the dimensional doorway. It was as if the barn interior was in another place entirely, in which all of life's basic assumptions were subtly yet fundamentally altered. Stepping back outside was a relief, a return to the familiar. Yet at the same time, she felt a certain sense of loss because of what she was leaving behind. Her visits here would be rare occurrences.

As Edna breathed in the evening chill, she realized she was exhausted. The night air was rich with the sound of crickets, and birds sang their final chorus ahead of nightfall. There was the smell of pot roast wafting from the farmhouse. A woman was waiting for them on the porch, smiling.

It wasn't Tavon's wife. At least, not the woman she'd met last year. The term wife had a different meaning to the Outherians.

"Hello there," the woman said, smiling warmly at Edna. "My name is Grace. It's a great pleasure to meet you." Reading the confusion on Edna's face, she offered an explanation. "It's our practice here on the farm to divide our time between a variety of partners. We have found this to be more fulfilling."

Edna started to laugh, half in shock and half in admiration. "You swap partners?"

Tavon twitched his nose and grimaced as he guided Edna into the house. "I wouldn't say swap is the right word. It's a little more complex than that. But we don't believe in your idea of marriage. It would be fairer to say we are married to many people at once. It's what makes us happy."

Who was she to argue? She'd yet to hold down a successful long-term relationship. "Wow, that food smells incredible."

"My daughter Rose prepared it for you," said Grace. "I'm not so good with human recipes and we don't eat a lot of meat," said Grace.

"You didn't need to cook it on my account," Edna said.

"We wanted to make you feel at home," said Grace, leading Edna into the sitting room. A beautiful pale green three-seater couch dominated the lounge. Matching single seaters on either side of it were spread around a neat little coffee table on a fluffy white rug. There was a compact cocktail bar in the corner. It looked like something off the cover of American Home.

"We put your luggage in our guest room upstairs," said Tavon. "First door on the left whenever you'd like to retire. Meantime, can I make you a Tom Collins?"

"Marvelous," said Edna. "Now please, both of you, tell me more about this lifestyle of yours. I'm intrigued. Don't you ever get jealous?"

Tavon chopped a lemon in half with the swing of a knife that looked powerful enough to butcher a calf. "Outherians got past that a long time ago," he said. He grabbed some ice cubes from a small bucket and threw them into a tall glass, squeezed the lemon halves into it, added a generous splash of gin and sugar syrup and topped it up with a squirt from a gorgeous silver mesh soda syphon.

"It's one of the benefits of being able to see each other's thoughts, you see," said Grace. "We never misunderstand one another."

Edna thought "seeing" was an interesting word to use for telepathy.

"Ours is a more collective form of love," Tavon continued, handing Edna her drink. "I don't want to sound overly critical, but the human state of marriage in my experience revolves around compromise, domination, frustration, and fear."

"Each of us is not one person, but seven, you see," said Grace.

"Even when we are apart, none of us is ever truly alone," said Tavon.

"Yes, but I happen to enjoy being alone," said Edna. "Not all the time, admittedly." She took a sip. "Oh wow, that's really good Lee, thank you."

"Our pleasure," he replied with a knowing grin.

"And can I just add, just so there are no misunderstandings — joining your carnal collective is not why I'm here," said Edna. She was starting to feel like the night could get away from her unless boundaries were quickly established.

"Relax," said Grace. "You're really not our type."

Edna laughed so hard she nearly spat her Tom Collins over the rug. "Where are your other selves, Grace?"

"One of me lives in New York. Another here. We also have a life in Chicago and one in Akron, Ohio."

"Everyone always feels the need to say 'Ohio' after Akron," Tavon added, "because nobody knows where the heck it is. I've got a house there too. I have funds invested in Firestone and B.F. Goodrich — and Akron, as they say, is where the rubber hits the road."

"Do you do the wife swap routine in Akron too?" Edna asked him. "I'd have thought that would raise a few eyebrows."

"It's not such a problem in Chicago and New York," said Grace. "But it's true that Akron requires a more subtle approach."

"It's why we move around a lot," said Tavon. "And that is about to get a whole lot easier."

"True," Edna agreed. "I can see now why you might be highly motivated to develop a quicker and more advanced method of getting around."

"Sex is the best motivator," said Grace.

"Though Americans treat desire as the devil's temptation," said Edna. "Like it's something dirty to be feared and shunned, or limited to brief acts of procreation. It was so liberating to experience European attitudes to sex, even if I had to do it in the middle of a war."

"You're right about that," said Grace. "Religion has been given too much latitude."

"If you ask me," said Tavon, "men in frocks should look in the mirror before throwing stones."

"Are you not religious in any way?" Edna asked them.

"No," said Tavon. "Humans cling to religion like an insurance policy. You treat God like an underwriter doing all he can to avoid a payout. We have a fundamentally different understanding of the ways of the universe."

A young girl appeared in the doorway. "Dinner is served," she said.

"Thank you, Rose," said Grace. "Edna, I hope you're hungry."

Without even needing to ask, Edna could tell Rose was not Tavon's child, but they all seemed more than happy together. Rose looked no older than Tavon's daughter Faye, though Edna knew looks were deceiving with the Outherians.

Lee and Grace filled their plates with vegetables, but didn't touch the meat. Rose, on the other hand, pulled the roast apart eagerly inside the roasting pan and filled Edna's plate with the tender beef and gravy before helping herself to a large serving of the same.

"She's having a growth spurt," said Grace. "She likes her food."

"A girl after my own heart," said Edna.

SIX

Saturday December 6, 1952

Tavon was swinging slowly back and forth on the porch rocking chair when Edna appeared bleary-eyed and half asleep to light a cigarette.

"Those things will kill you," he told her.

"You might be right," she conceded. "I find myself waking up with the craving. And I can't help but remind you of your views on the pleasure principle." She lit the end of her cigarette and drew back, sighing in contentment as the smoke hit her lungs. "Though I did change brands after someone showed me an old magazine advertisement claiming more doctors smoked Camels than any other cigarette."

"Camels are the worst of them all," said Tavon.

"Yeah. It's why I went for Lucky Strikes. Because, you know — they're toasted."

"I love this time of morning," he said. "Everything is so quiet. I can hear our neighbors' kettle whistling and their house is a mile away."

Following an eventful afternoon in the lab and a pre-dinner cocktail that had set her head spinning, Edna had hit the sack early. It was probably just as well; there were no curtains or blinds on her bedroom window. She woke as the room filled with light at the break of dawn.

She sat down next to Tavon in a chair of the non-rocking variety and took in another lungful of tobacco smoke.

"The pursuit of pleasure can never be an end in itself," he told her. "We take pleasure where it is freely available, but we also embrace the pain that comes with physical existence. I think you humans delude yourselves into thinking it's possible to live a life free of pain. That's a fantasy."

"Are you saying that's why I smoke?"

"You start off thinking of something as a reward. Once that pleasure becomes an addiction, you feel the need to reward yourself more and more often. Your mind and body trick you into thinking your happiness depends on it."

"Oh, for God's sake Lee, it's too early in the morning for psycho-analysis."

"I never used to like the sunlight," he said. "Not when I first arrived on Earth. The old Lee Tavon has always loved it, but the Outherian part of me still has a fear of sunlight."

"Because of the sun that destroyed your world?"

"Yes. But also because prolonged exposure to our sun was deadly long before our world came to an end."

"What did you call yourself on Outheria?"

"My name was Brynthalnak."

"That sounds suitably foreign. Almost Scandinavian."

"I sit here each morning to face the sun and, in so doing, face my fear. Embrace the pain," he said.

"How's that coming along?"

"A little better each day."

Edna took the hint, stubbed her cigarette under her heel and they sat in silence until the heat of the sun began to make her sweat. "When you've finished torturing yourself, do you think you could make me a cup of coffee?" she asked.

He headed inside and she marveled at the silence of the countryside. The city was never silent. Here it was quiet enough to hear your own heartbeat. Edna was deep in thought when he returned with a steaming mug. Feeling the first rush of a caffeine hit, she remembered she had questions about the previous day's events. "You said your doorway is a link to another world. Tell me more about that."

"We call it the dark space dimension."

"You mentioned that when I first interviewed you last year. You called it a sphere within a sphere."

"Dark space exists both here and there — it is in both dimensions at once. But in the dark space dimension its principles are reversed. Or more specifically, inverse. For us, space expands across vast distances. In the dark space realm, the opposite is true. There is almost no space between every point in the universe. It is a singularity. It is the place where a Big Bang will never happen and it exists to balance this world across the dimensional multiverse.

"This singularity is connected to all things here. By tapping into its power, we can bend space in this dimension to travel vast distances in an instant."

"I guess that makes sense, although I suspect that if I asked you the means by which you achieved this bridge between the two worlds, I would find the answer a lot harder to understand."

Tavon nodded. "It is enough for you to know that the bridge exists."

Edna stared at him with renewed admiration. "How long have your people known about this?"

"A very long time. But it's not just us. It is a touchstone of Indian mysticism. In Hinduism, Jainism, and Buddhism, it's called the Akasha. Hindus call this the essence of all things. Buddhists say Akasha is split into limited space and endless space."

"Are you telling me Hindus and Buddhists have been influenced by ancient aliens?"

He nodded. "They used to live here openly. They were worshipped as gods. They're still here, except they no longer wish to be known to humanity. These are the people whose blood is shared by the man who is half human and half alien, kept in hiding inside the Vatican."

"Paolo Favaloro. I've read about him in the Verus files. His people are called the Ryl. They built the flying disc that Majestic captured. They call it FS-1." She shook her head in wonderment. "So the Ryl are still here on Earth — are these the people who've been contacting you?"

Tavon shook his head. "They remain reluctant to show themselves."

"Then who are you talking to?"

"They are from a binary star system called Zeta Reticuli, which exists in the Milky Way galaxy and is about forty light years from Earth."

"They speak to you?"

"Not with words. They are inside my head," said Tavon. "They came again last night. They know you're here. They are very interested in you."

A cold chill ran down her throat. "What do you mean?"

"They want you to come with me to see them. They told me they live like us, underground. But their home is hidden deep inside the Monongahela National Forest in West Virginia."

"That's hours away," Edna realized.

"We won't need that long," said Tavon.

SEVEN

Sunday December 7, 1952

"Edna. It's time."

She sensed the silhouette outlined in the doorway of the bedroom before she was even fully awake. For some time, Edna stared at the door unable to move. She couldn't remember where she was. She knew it was Tavon speaking to her, but his voice seemed different. Her thoughts hovered in that zone between dreaming and waking until the recollection made her bolt upright in bed.

He was taking her to meet his aliens.

"Let me pull on some clothes," she told him.

"Be quick. I'll wait downstairs."

But moments after he left, another figure appeared in the doorway. Grace stepped silently into the room and sat on the edge of the bed. "He won't let anything bad happen to you. But if you'd rather not go, I will be happy to tell him." Her eyes were wide with concern. "He chooses not to see it, but I know this fear is real for you."

Edna stood up and grabbed a pair of trousers. "Is it the same fear stopping you from revealing yourselves to the rest of the world?" she asked.

"What you feel now is natural," said Grace. "To discover your most fundamental beliefs are founded upon a false premise is not an easy thing to confront."

"Which is why I'd be a hypocrite to sit here and give in to that fear. I just wish it didn't have to happen in the dead of night."

"This is the time the world is lost in slumber. It's when all things strange are possible. You remember this much from your nights as a reporter."

"That's true," Edna admitted.

"The hours between two and four in the morning are when the power of collective subconscious rises to its most potent."

Edna stepped slowly and carefully down the stairs. There were no lights on anywhere in the house and she didn't want to slip and break her ankle. He was waiting in the sitting room.

"Do we need to go back underground?"

"No," said Tavon. "But we do need to be standing on the Earth. We're still refining the parameters of the translation field. It remains unpredictable inside wooden structures. I don't want us impaled upon the floorboards when we return."

"No," she agreed, "that doesn't sound good at all."

He took her by the hand and walked out the back door, then unrolled the transport pad on a patch of grass. He had given another mat to his visitors the previous night. They had agreed to place it at their destination. Which meant neither she nor Tavon knew exactly where they would end up.

Tavon wanted her to go first. Trying hard not to think of herself as a human guinea pig, Edna took two quick steps and leapt directly into the energy field over the rubber pad. The same series of sensations fluttered through her head — pleasure and peace, quickly followed by dislocation — before she came out the other side into a clearing surrounded by tall trees, lit only by the Moon in the sky above. Edna stepped forward and then off to one side, knowing Tavon would be following her. He collided with her just the same, sending her sprawling to the ground.

"Sorry about that," he said, helping her up.

She gazed up again. "It's remarkably bright, isn't it? The Moon?" Then she realized there was another light above them, much brighter than a star, that appeared to be moving.

"Here they come," he said.

"I thought you said they live here."

"Maybe not right here. But close. They're secretive. Wary of us. Of you especially."

He meant humans.

The light quickly grew brighter and larger as it descended upon the clearing. It turned from white to orange, and then a deep red as it came close to the ground, stopping in the air fifty feet above them. A loud squealing noise erupted in Edna's head. She tried to block her ears with her hands, but found she couldn't move a muscle. Edna panicked, and for a moment she found it impossible to breathe.

Two orange lights shined down from the bottom of the ship, illuminating the ground in front of them, and from those beams two figures emerged. They were slightly shorter than she and Tavon, no more than five feet high at most. But as soon as they appeared, a sense of peace flooded through her body, and Edna found she could breathe easily again.

"Don't be scared. We cannot hurt you," one of them assured her. She couldn't tell if the words were spoken aloud, or simply implanted in her head. "We thank you for coming here."

She tried to open her mouth, but no words would come.

They appeared to anticipate the question. "We have lived here for a long time. The Shawnee called us the Star People. We call ourselves the Grar."

Edna tried to take note of the way they looked, though the more she tried to focus on them the more ill-defined they became. They were dressed in light blue clothing that covered most of their thin bodies. They looked mostly human, but their eyes were different, out of proportion with the size of their heads, far larger than any person she had ever met before.

"Always remember you are never alone," they told her.

It was an oddly imprecise message to impart, considering they had gone to such trouble to be here, but it was all they wished to say. They were back inside their ship and gone moments later.

"How odd," she heard herself saying, staring once more at the Moon and seeing it as she had never done before. Not as a disc, but as another world orbiting the Earth.

Edna knew beyond all doubt the Star People had been there too.

EIGHT

F riday July 3, 1953

It wasn't yet noon, but the wise men of Majestic-12 weren't holding back on the booze. The suite in the Hamilton Hotel wasn't as large as their former meeting place at the Mayflower — nor was the hotel management as liberal in providing complimentary food and drink — but on this occasion Vannevar Bush was picking up the tab as a business expense, and the bar had been well stocked.

Donald Menzel opted for coffee, because he wanted a clear head to lay out his plan. He needed to move quickly; consensus among these men was never assured. Several faces were missing. Many of those who were present looked to have aged significantly since their last meeting. Hoyt Vandenberg was with them, despite having retired from the Air Force earlier in the week. It was clear to them Hoyt was not at all well. His usual charisma seemed to have deserted him.

Wally "Beetle" Smith was here too, solemn as usual in a suit two sizes too big for him and looking a little lost; his usefulness to the group had come under question since President Eisenhower had seen fit to replace him with Allen Dulles as CIA director. That said, it had been Beetle's intelligence that brought them together today.

The alcohol had brought a certain lethargy to the room. There was a distinct lack of urgency, what with it being the Independence Day public holiday. Menzel found their festive mood irksome; he felt

MJ-12 had lacked a firm hand since Harry Truman had left office. They had unanimously voted to proceed in a different capacity under the new president, who had inexplicably acceded to their request to hold meetings without him, on the proviso they report back on a quarterly basis.

This meant that the Majestic-12 were making decisions without governmental oversight.

"Gentlemen, I really think we should get started," Menzel declared. Having gained their attention, he didn't bother to wait for them to sit down. "One or two of you will no doubt be aware of the turmoil in Moscow right now. The head of the Russian secret police, Lavrentiy Beria, has been placed under arrest."

There were various murmurs of assent and surprise around the table. Menzel handed out a briefing paper prepared by Verus researchers, in close consultation with the CIA:**USSR SITUATION REPORT**

TOP SECRET — MAJESTIC

Soviet leader Joseph Stalin died on March 5, four days after suffering a cerebral hemorrhage. He was kept alive by Kremlin doctors alarmed by the prospect of the consequences from not being seen to do all they could to save him. Nine of their colleagues —all Jewish — had already been imprisoned in the name of a fictitious "Doctors Plot" supposedly waged against the Soviet leadership. This was no more than an anti-Semitic purge that, in any event, was quickly called off in the days after Stalin's death.

Stalin suffered regular dizzy spells in the final weeks of his life. His personal physician, Professor V.N. Vinogradov, had advised him to stand down as the head of government for the good of his health. It was advice the Soviet leader ignored. Professor Vinogradov was himself arrested shortly thereafter and accused of involvement in the Doctor's Plot.

Neither Vinogradov, nor any other medical expert, could have done much to prevent the Soviet leader's death. He spent more than 12 hours lying paralyzed on the floor of his suite before he was found. His own security officers had been loath to check on him, having previously been ordered by Stalin not to enter unless summoned.

It took the senior members of the Communist Party Presidium four days to announce Stalin's downfall to the Russian people. They didn't dare do so until they were certain his death was inevitable. The delayed announcement had much to do with the members of the Presidium jostling for positions of power, as they sought to decide who would take on ultimate authority. In the end, three names arose and a form of collective leadership emerged. The man many assumed to be Stalin's successor, Georgii Malenkov, was appointed chairman of the Council of Ministers.

The second member of the triumvirate was Lavrentiy Beria, who had been Malenkov's close ally up to this point. He quickly began to scramble for power as if Stalin's demise meant nobody would dare stand in his way. Beria had been in charge of the MGB's secret police, the MVD. On March 5th, Beria was appointed First Deputy Premier and, with the support of the Council of Ministers, immediately removed Semyon Ignatyev from the post of Minister of the MGB. The MGB was absorbed into Beria's MVD. This put him in control of both the secret and the regular police, as well as a small private army of infantry divisions.

The third member of the power trio was Nikita Khrushchev, secretary of the Moscow party organization. Khrushchev was appointed the top secretary of the Central Committee. Initially, he was very much the outsider in this group. While opposed to the alliance between Beria and Malenkov, Khrushchev could do nothing to come between them.

That changed on June 16th, when an uprising against the East German communists arose in East Berlin. In the wake of the uprising, it quickly became clear Beria had little regard for East Germany as a genuine Soviet satellite state. He said it was only held in place by the force of Russian ground troops, and strongly indicated he would be willing to permit German reunification in return for a large injection of American aid money, given the cost of World War II remained a heavy burden on the Russian economy.

Within days, Khrushchev persuaded Malenkov and other party leaders that Beria's policies were dangerous and destabilizing.

On June 26, Lavrentiy Beria was arrested, accused of treason and spying for British intelligence. His arrest was kept quiet, while Beria's lieutenants were likewise gathered up to prevent any move by loyal MVD officers to rescue him.

Krushchev had taken care to enlist the support of popular Russian war hero, and Marshall of the Soviet Union, General Georgy Zhukov. General Zhukov was among the soldiers who personally placed Beria under arrest, before smuggling Beria to a bunker in the headquarters of the Moscow Military District. Beria is being held in detention and his execution is believed to be inevitable.

Gordon Gray was the first man around the table to look up from the briefing paper. He had a mind like a steel trap and, like Menzel, wasn't drinking. "How exactly is this a problem for us?" he asked.

"I believe it offers us a brief window to carry out an extraction in Rome," said Menzel. "As you're all aware, the 'man' we call Paolo Favaloro remains a guest of the Vatican, as per the agreement General Donovan reached with Stalin himself."

There were murmurs both of surprise and support for Menzel's intentions. Some of them would need more convincing.

Favaloro was a giant — a little over eleven feet tall — but he was also, at best, half a man. The other half was not human at all; his father was a member of the interplanetary race known as the Ryl. Thousands of years ago, the Ryl had lived openly on Earth as kings and gods in the city-states of ancient Mesopotamia. Favaloro, then known as

Utnapishtim, incurred their wrath by obtaining a Ryl spacecraft for his own purposes, without sanction. Rather than kill him, the Ryl condemned him to an eternity locked inside a sarcophagus in a state of frozen animation — hoping to force him to relinquish the "stolen" saucer. But the Ryl were jealous gods and Utnapishtim had reason to believe the Ryl would kill him once he gave them what they wanted. Trapped for millennia, he might have quickly gone insane if not for his ability to detach from his body and roam the world as a living ghost, taking vicarious pleasure as a Watcher of humanity.

Thousands of years later, the sarcophagus that had kept him trapped was unearthed by an archaeologist and later found its way into the hands of British Cardinal Arthur Hinsley. As Hitler had begun his assault on Great Britain, Hinsley delivered the relic to Bill Donovan for safekeeping on US soil.

Within weeks of the war ending, a priest named Clarence Paulson stole the sarcophagus from Donovan's New York storehouse at the behest of Pope Pius XII. Donovan, a devout Catholic, was at first incensed but ultimately forgiving of the crime. Years later, when Donovan offered Favaloro the prospect of release from his state of captivity, Favaloro revealed the location of the spacecraft — still fully functional and hidden deep inside a stone monument in the Lebanese town of Baalbek. Donovan beat the Russians to the saucer by a matter of hours. Thus, the craft was stolen again, this time under heavy Russian fire.

The Baalbek Incident might have sparked open nuclear conflict between the two superpowers, if Donovan hadn't moved quickly to secure a deal with Stalin himself. Donovan had given his own personal assurance that America would never use the craft for its own strategic advantage. Nobody believed it, least of all Stalin. For more than two years, Majestic had been partnered with Lockheed's Skunkworks in a research program dubbed FS-1, seeking to unlock the spacecraft's mysteries. The Russians, suspecting FS-1 would go nowhere without

Favaloro, struck a deal with the Americans. Paolo Favaloro would remain in Rome, a "guest" of the Pope. The US would allow Russian agents to visit Favaloro in his Roman cloister. It was the sort of deal that could blow up in everyone's face if it ever went public, so church and states had happily kept their dirty little secret.

"I would argue that deal became null and void the day of Stalin's death," Menzel now told the men of MJ-12. "But more to the point, instability in the Soviet leadership and an uprising in East Germany has their attention focused elsewhere."

"We want to get Favaloro out of Rome and bring him here," Vannevar Bush added. He and Menzel had discussed the situation ahead of the meeting. Bush, ever a man of pragmatism, was frustratingly noncommittal from the start, pointing out espionage and counterintelligence operations were not within his field of expertise. But Bush had finally agreed it was probably a risk worth taking.

"Do we know what we're dealing with?" asked Admiral Hillenkoetter, a man who had all too often been let down by faulty intelligence.

Wally Smith nodded. "According to our most recent intelligence, two female Russian agents visit Paolo on a weekly basis. They trade sexual favors in the hope he will offer them information about his flying saucer."

"We're concerned it's only a matter of time before Mr Favaloro does let something valuable slip," said Menzel. "Furthermore, we believe once we get him here, we can persuade him to be of greater assistance with FS-1."

"Which he has refused to do up to now," Hoyt Vandenberg pointed out, his voice thin and drawn.

"Paolo knows the arrangement we have with the Russians," said Menzel. "Once we show him that deal is dead, I think we'll be able to talk him around."

"You're talking about an extraction operation," said Smith. "That's CIA territory."

Menzel shook his head. "We can't do that without the backing of Allen Dulles, and he's not in the loop. There's no time to bring him in. We need to move quickly. I want to get someone over there within the next seven days."

Looks of surprise and apprehension flickered across several faces. But Menzel wasn't about to let these old men slow him down. "I believe I'm right in saying it's now or never, gentlemen. What resources are we able to bring to bear?"

"Donovan's your man," said General Nathan Twining, who had just taken over from Vandenberg as Air Force Chief of Staff.

Again, Menzel shook his head. "He's just accepted the post of Ambassador to Thailand. I'm afraid Donald is done. Hoyt — your thoughts?"

Vandenberg offered a wan smile. "I'd offer to go myself, but I'm afraid those days are behind me. In fact, this will be my last meeting with Majestic. My health is not so good. I've got cancer."

The news came as a great shock to everyone at the table. It was a cruel blow to a man who, at fifty-five, had his best spent years in the service of his country. Hoyt deserved better.

"How bad?" Vannevar Bush asked him.

"The doctors say it's gonna get me before too long. I need to spend the time I have left at home."

"Of course you do," Menzel agreed. But his heart was sinking; he'd hoped Hoyt would lead the Rome operation.

"Beetle, you must still have agents at your disposal," said Vandenberg.

"Donald's right. That's not an option without going to Dulles first. Not without presidential sanction."

"Again," said Menzel, "time is against us." Menzel was starting to see there was only one option open to him.

NINE

Saturday July 4, 1953

All across Washington, bars and restaurants were festooned with American flags. The city's hardworking residents were making the most of the second straight day of Independence Day celebrations; the day itself had fallen on a Saturday.

Edna was silently ruminating upon being forced to remain indoors at Verus HQ, instead of making a day of touring all the U Street jazz joints — something she'd been looking forward to for weeks. She was invariably one of the few white faces in the crowd at Crystal Caverns and Republic Gardens, but she'd become well-known in the area, and always felt safe there when she ventured out alone.

"I've ordered pizza from Famous Luigi's," Menzel told her.

That put a smile on her face. "I hope you remembered the anchovies."

"Of course," he said, pouring two whiskeys.

Menzel was playing nice, and she couldn't help wondering why. Relations between them had been strained for months in the wake of her encounters with Tavon, even though Menzel had eventually been forced to admit that she had made a critical step forward in contact with the Grar.

The door to Menzel's study opened and Clarence Paulson entered the room, most likely drawn in by the sound of the ice hitting the crystal tumblers. "One of those for me?"

Menzel nodded, handing them their drinks.

"Not joining us, Donald?" Paulson asked.

"Maybe in a minute."

"Oh dear, it's like that is it?" said Edna, not at all sure she was ready for where the conversation was headed.

Menzel gave them a summary of his discussion with Majestic. "The MVD is in disarray right now. Beria's man in East Berlin, Colonel Danilov, is responsible for Russian activities in Rome, but Danilov will have enough on his plate trying to dampen anti-communist sentiment in Germany. He won't be paying close attention to events inside the Vatican."

Paulson knew at once what Menzel was intending. "You're sending me to Rome."

Menzel nodded. "You and Edna."

Paulson sighed. "I might be sending them lots of money, but I'm still not exactly high on the Curia's Christmas card list."

In recent months, Father Paulson had shown himself to be a remarkably insightful buyer and seller of gold. Funds left in his care by the Vatican had been increased tenfold. At the same time, he had been able to curate a profitable investment fund for Verus. But Father Paulson had not shown his face in Rome for nigh on two years. The last time he'd been there, moves had been afoot to have him declared insane and committed to a mental asylum. "And you want me to walk in there with a woman who doesn't speak the language, and who uses the word Catholic as a way to describe her taste in men."

"I've been to Rome," Edna pointed out. "During the war. Though it's true I didn't spend a whole lot of time with men in frocks. I prefer them in Fiats or Ferraris."

"Stop it, Edna," Menzel chided. "Look, the new Russian leadership is making overtures to the West. Khrushchev has indicated they're ready to pull back from the most hardline policies of the Stalin era. It was only after Stalin's death the Kremlin showed a willingness to enter negotiations to end the Korean War. Thanks to them, an armistice agreement is in place. For the next few weeks, the Russians will have their eyes on Seoul.

"This will be quick. You go in, grab Favaloro, and get out. With any luck, you'll be gone before the Russians even know you're there."

Menzel looked confident. Edna wasn't so sure. "What's my role in all of this?"

"Good question," said Paulson.

"Favaloro responds well to women," said Menzel. "Your job will be to talk him out of the Vatican archives and into a waiting car. That's all. Simple."

"It can't be as simple as that," she argued.

"The best operations are always simple," said Menzel. "Ask Bill Donovan. He's assured me you're up to it, by the way."

"Oh, well, in that case it's fine by me," she said facetiously.

"In Bill's words, you're a woman and an atheist — you won't let religious sensitivities hold you back."

"Donald, can I just point out that I'm not one of Wild Bill's former agents or saboteurs. I'm basically a reporter with some wartime nursing experience."

"Gordon Gray agrees with Donovan," Menzel told her. "He thinks you'll do fine."

Menzel could see the feedback from Gray hit home. Edna respected Gordon's opinion; Menzel was almost certain she'd fallen in love with Gray the previous year. Gray had broken off all contact with her shortly after the Washington saucer flap, not wanting the relationship to develop further. More recently, Gray had been consumed by his wife's critical illness.

"That's all very well," Edna said, "but are you seriously telling me there is no one else for you to call on? I mean, you guys are from the military and the goddamn CIA. There must be any number of people who are better trained to do this."

"She's not wrong, Donald," Paulson agreed.

Menzel sighed. "There is nobody else we can confidently trust in the time available."

"What if I talk to the President?" she said.

"No," Menzel said angrily, "you do not do that." He took a deep breath and tried harder to keep his temper in check. "I'm afraid it's down to you two. Look, I'm not going to send you in blind. We have some good contacts inside the Curia and the Swiss Guard, courtesy of General Donovan. And he's agreed to spend a few days with you next week to help you prepare."

Edna Drake rolled her eyes. Bill Donovan might be renowned as the great wartime spymaster, but the last time they were in each other's lives, it hadn't ended well.

TEN

M onday July 6, 1953

Edna knew the moment the maid answered the door she was several steps removed from the world she knew. She and Clarence Paulson were silently ushered inside the Georgetown mansion, and led along a burgundy-carpeted hallway replete with massive Georgian oil portraits to the door of Bill Donovan's equally luxurious office.

It occurred to Edna that she felt more at home among Tavon's Outherians, than she did in close quarters with certain members of the human race. Wild Bill Donovan topped the list of people she'd happily spend the rest of her life avoiding.

It had been almost exactly a year since the UFO sightings over Washington were repeated over two successive weekends. Donovan waved as they entered the room. "Hello there, Father Paulson. Good to see you again. You too, my dear."

Edna was ready to object to his tone of condescension, but Donovan put his finger to his lips. He mouthed the words "not here" and pointed at the door. She turned to Paulson, who merely shrugged his shoulders. It sounded odd hearing Paulson referred to as "Father"; she'd only ever seen him in plain clothes. She didn't think of him as a priest.

Donovan led them through his roomy eat-in kitchen and through two glass-paneled doors into the back garden. A table had been set up under the shade of a large umbrella with a pitcher of iced lemonade and three glasses.

"Please," Donovan urged, "sit down, pour yourselves a drink." He scanned the perimeter before taking his seat beside them. "I'm sorry to be so jumpy, but I'm quite certain my walls have ears. I doubt we'll be overheard out here though."

"Overheard by who exactly?" Paulson asked him.

"The CIA," Donovan replied matter-of-factly. "They still have somebody listening."

"Still?" Edna repeated.

"They took an interest in me last year, during the whole FS-1 farrago," Donovan explained. "I'd be doing the same thing now if I were them, knowing a man with my background and extensive overseas contacts is about to become the Ambassador to Thailand."

"Why wouldn't the CIA trust you?" Paulson asked.

Donovan laughed quietly. "They don't trust anybody — they're completely paranoid. They see reds under the bed everywhere."

"Good work, Senator McCarthy," said Edna, screwing up her face as if merely saying the name aloud left a bad smell into the air.

"Indeed," Donovan agreed. "But he's not alone. There are people inside the CIA these days who make Joe McCarthy look like a liberal."

Edna asked after Gordon Gray. She had been rather hoping to see him here.

"His wife died just a couple of days ago," said Donovan.

"Oh God," said Edna. "That poor man."

Donovan smiled apologetically. "Which means you get me as a solo act." He knew he wasn't Edna's favorite person.

"To think this time last year, you were holding a gun to my head," she said. "Why do I get the feeling it's happening all over again?"

Paulson chuckled sardonically. "Bill and Donald are good at that."

"Edna," Donovan replied, "here's the thing — your country needs you." Coming from almost anyone else, it would have sounded hokey.

"All right then, General, but let me warn you — I won't hold my tongue about the Catholic Church and Pius XII just to please you."

Donovan looked toward the heavens. "You won't offend me."

Edna didn't buy that for a moment. "Come on General, I need you to be honest with me."

"You think you're more intimidating than Truman or Eisenhower? Truman is a little man with a short temper," said Donovan. "Ike is a big man with big expectations."

Edna looked quizzically at "Father" Paulson and wondered where he sat these days on the Catholic spectrum.

In answer to her raised gaze, Paulson told her there was no love lost between himself and the Roman Curia. "I've been all but defrocked. They tried to have me denounced as madman and a heretic. I'd be happy to end my days with an ocean between me and the Vatican."

"Yet you're coming with me," Edna said.

Paulson offered a smile that came off as more of a grimace. "Because you need me."

"All right then," she said, staring at Donovan, "first off, let me say this: I believe your Pope is an anti-Semite who colluded with the Fascists. But you're going to tell me I need to keep my opinions to myself, right?"

Donovan could see she was spoiling for a fight. He let the words hang in the air for a moment. Edna expected him to blow his stack, but his response was much more measured. "Pius is actually nothing of the sort. Nobody has ever outsmarted the Vatican in secrecy or subterfuge; they've been at it for hundreds of years. That's why there's been no better place to hide Paolo Favaloro. Pius hid Jews and rebels a few doors away from the Nazis in Rome during the war, and the Germans never knew. You need to look past the surface. You're entering a world where things are not what they seem to be."

She nodded. "Play nice. I get it."

"You're not going to Rome as Edna Drake, reporter and truth-seeker. You want these men to see as little of the real you as possible. That means playing the role of a subservient woman. You are Father Paulson's meek and mild personal secretary, appointed to the position personally by me."

"Why subservient?" she asked angrily.

Donovan's face hardened. "These are men who see women as weak and fragile. Apart from their mothers and sisters, the only females in their lives are monastic nuns who do their bidding like indentured servants. You need to be compliant — be seen and not heard."

Edna stared back at him scornfully. "This is getting better by the minute."

"You're a spy," said Donovan. "You're playing a role. I'm just here to prepare you for it."

She sighed. "All right, misogyny I can deal with. But how hard is it going to be getting Favaloro out of the archives — I assume they're guarded?"

"Day and night," said Donovan.

"We know the head of the Swiss Guard," said Paulson. "I believe he'll help us."

"Am I right in saying you two both have the power to summon Paolo Favaloro's apparition?" Edna asked them. "Why don't we do that now and see what else he can tell us?"

"I don't think that's a good idea," said Donovan.

"Me neither," Paulson agreed.

"If we tell him what we're up to," said Donovan, "we have no way of preventing him from spilling the beans to one of his Russian harlots. I believe he's very much in their thrall. I'm certain he's been telling them about the saucer since they threatened to withdraw their favors if he didn't."

"Which is why we need to get him out of there," said Paulson.

"How do these women actually get to him?" Edna asked.

"Graft and corruption. Sleight of hand. Sparrow honey pot. All the usual tricks. We agreed to look the other way to make it easy for them — it was part of the deal I struck with Stalin."

"I'm starting to understand why you don't want the CIA listening in," said Edna. "You're making me very nervous."

"Good," said Donovan. "You need to watch your back all the time to look for anything out of place."

"We should be fine," said Paulson confidently. "Like I said, I know the head of the Swiss Guard, Leopold von Altishofen. He's a good man. He's also ambitious. The Vatican Archive is not under his control — it's currently under the control of the Vatican Gendarmerie. But I know for a fact Leopold thinks the Gendarmerie are undeserving of the task. I'm certain he'll agree to help us."

"Really?" said Edna. "You're saying this all hangs on persuading a 'good man' to turn a blind eye to a kidnapping?"

"She's got a point," Donovan agreed. "And I wonder if you're over-complicating things. Why not just pay off the men on the door?"

Paulson shook his head. "It's not wartime, Bill. If they refuse, we can't just shoot them. Leopold will help because it means he gets two birds with one stone. He blames the gendarmes at the archives who, after all, are the ones breaking the rules by letting in Russian spies. Plus, he gets rid of Paolo Favaloro. The priests in the archives are terrified of Paolo; they think he's demonic."

"What else can you tell us?" Edna asked Donovan. "I don't want to be walking in there blind."

Donovan smiled. She was starting to think like a spy. "Trust your intuition. If something is worrying you, don't ignore it. But above all, trust Clarence. He knows what he's doing."

ELEVEN

Monday July 13, 1953

Storm clouds were rolling in over Washington National Airport. It was still light outside, but much darker than normal for this time of the afternoon. The Lockheed hangar was some distance from the main terminal and it was lit up inside like the Times Square Christmas tree.

There was barely a soul to be seen on the hangar floor. This was by design; the fewer people who saw them leaving, the better. Donald Menzel's black Packard proceeded to pull up a short distance from Skunkworks chief Garrick Stamford, who was waiting at the front stairs of his beloved Super Constellation. Its silver hull gleamed under the spotlights.

Menzel shook Stamford's hand and introduced him to Edna Drake and Clarence Paulson. Stamford shook Paulson's hand and stared at Edna with a look that immediately creeped her out. He waved his hand at the uniformed air steward standing nearby, ordering him to ferry their bags onto the plane. The man leapt to the task like his future depended on it.

"The flight will take about sixteen hours, but you won't need to refuel," said Stamford.

Edna held up her passport. "Does anybody else need to see this?" she asked him.

"Not until you land in Rome," Stamford said. "My man on the ground there will look after you. He knows our third passenger won't have his papers. I await your return with great enthusiasm. In the meantime, sit back and relax."

The propellers started to spin. The pilot was wasting no time.

"This weather won't be a problem, will it?" Paulson asked.

"Not at all," said Stamford. "You will literally rise above it. The cabin's pressurized, which means you can fly higher and faster, above the storm."

"Well then," said Menzel. "I suppose it's bon voyage."

"Isn't that for ships?" said Paulson, giving a dismissive wave good-bye as he began climbing the stairs.

"Good luck, Miss Drake," said Stamford. "I'm sure I don't need to tell you how valuable Favaloro will be to our work."

"Hopefully luck won't come into it," she said, offering him a confident smile. "Thanks for the classy ride."

Stamford followed her up the stairs and shut the hatch once she was safely inside the cabin. They were the only passengers and had their choice of seating — there was the cocktail lounge up front, or their choice of a dozen leather recliners that lined the windows on either side of the cabin further to the rear.

Yes, this would do nicely.

Edna figured she might as well start in the lounge; she hadn't been in a plane since the war. This one beat the hell out of an Army DC-3. Returning from stowing their luggage in the rear, their steward welcomed them aboard. "My name is Richard. I'll be taking care of you on the flight to Rome. Would you like to start with a cocktail?"

"Why yes," Edna told him with a glint in her eye, "I believe I would."

Paulson opted for water.

Out over the Atlantic and well into her third Tom Collins, Edna was staring down at the water when she realized Paulson, sitting on the lounge chair opposite, had barely said a word since take-off. "Everything all right, Father? I see you're still out of uniform."

"I'll change when we land," he said quietly.

She continued to stare. He was quite handsome really, though he did his best to hide it. With a decent haircut and a good suit, Father Paulson could come off as dashing. She was starting to make herself uncomfortable; good looks were something she'd never associated with priests. As a child, the only men of religion in her corner of the world had been bitter old curmudgeons, spouting hellfire and brimstone. Her mother was a devout Catholic who attended church every Sunday, though her father didn't have a religious bone in his body. They'd been happy together nonetheless, a classic case of opposites attracting. But Edna had followed in her father's footsteps on questions of religious faith.

"How old are you, Clarence?"

"What does that have to do with anything?"

"Why aren't you drinking? Not having second thoughts, are you?"

"I'm forty-three," he told her.

"Christ — really?"

Clarence Paulson stared back at her disparagingly.

"Oh, sorry. But then again, is that really taking the Lord's name in vain? Using it as an exclamation? I'd argue that's neither positive nor negative. Besides, what I meant was you don't look that old."

"Clean living."

Edna laughed. "Now I know you're lying."

Something that might have been a smile lifted the corner of his lips. Father Paulson stared at her intently for a moment, before slowly shifting focus to stare at the clouds out the window beside her. Like he was seeing her for the first time, and trying not to pay attention.

"Tell me more about this alien friend of yours," Edna persisted. "I hear he's quite tall."

"About eleven feet at full stretch."

"Christ. I mean... Goodness, that is tall. So how does that work with the ladies? Is everything, you know, in proportion? He'd be splitting those poor Russian girls in half, wouldn't he?"

She was deliberately trying to embarrass him, but Paulson didn't take the bait. "Fornication is not my strong point."

"No, I guess not."

"But there's more than one way to..."

"Skin a cat?" Edna suggested.

"Something like that. And I'm not drinking because I hate flying and I want to be at full alert when we land."

"What's not to like? This is a flying palace. Heck, Richard says they're serving us lobster for dinner. I could get used to this."

"I hope it doesn't give Paolo ideas. He used to a be a king, you know. Long time ago. Wives, concubines, the whole nine yards."

Edna leant forward. She caught a whiff of his Old Spice aftershave and thought it suited him. "He looks like us then? I mean, he's not alien-looking?" she whispered.

"Well, he's the tallest person you'll ever meet in your life," he replied. "He's half human."

"Which half?"

"You know what I mean."

"Sure, I do. You mean he's hung like a donkey."

Paulson blushed. "You have a mouth like an open sewer, you know that?"

Edna smiled demurely. "Where are the rest of the Ryl now?"

"We're not sure," he admitted. "We believe they're somewhere close, though that might not be anywhere on Earth. Could be Mars."

Edna shook her head in amazement. In the space of a few short months, she had discovered a world within a world. It was a marvel how a veil of secrecy could so successfully mask the truth from the public. A veil that was not to be easily pulled aside. People liked seeing their world a certain way, Edna had learned, and didn't like it when their views were challenged. "Anything more you can tell me about how the Russians are getting in past the gendarmes?"

"Money. Favors," Paulson suggested. "To be a gendarme, you need to be in your early twenties and unmarried. I imagine an attractive woman could lead them around like obedient puppy dogs."

Richard pushed a silver service tray toward them, declaring "dinner is served".

As he placed a plate of the most delicious seafood in front of her, Edna asked, "What about you, Richard? What are your views on aliens and flying saucers and the like?"

"I'm sure I don't know what you mean, Miss Drake."

"Nothing to see here, eh? I guess Stamford trained you well. I understand. Now tell me, is there any chance you have French champagne on board?"

"Moet or Bollinger?"

"She'll have neither. Cold water will do fine."

Edna frowned. "I suppose you're right. We'll save the champagne for the flight home."

TWELVE

Tuesday July 15, 1953

They landed in Rome shortly after three in the afternoon. Stamford's man on the ground ushered them quickly through immigration formalities and had them in a cab within fifteen minutes.

It was a hot, sunny day, and the wind through the rear window was baking. Paulson had changed into his cassock shortly before they landed, knowing it would facilitate their journey through the city. Edna could see the sweat on his brow, and suspected it had as much to do with the job ahead as the warm weather.

Everything smelled and sounded different. The car horns, the taxi driver's cigarette, the odd aromas wafting out of the cafes and restaurants they passed along the way. She had been to Rome during the war and felt a certain distant familiarity with the place. It was incredibly exciting to be back; she wished they could stay longer.

The driver chattered away to Paulson in Italian. When the priest responded, his tone was somehow different. Not just because he was speaking in another language, but because he had assumed the persona of a cleric: wise, graceful, distant. She wondered whether it was an act, or if he was reverting to his own kind.

The driver delivered them just outside St Peter's Square on Via di Porta Angelica, near the entrance of the Swiss Guard Barracks. The street was thick with pedestrians. It was, after all, peak tourist season.

The office of the Commander of the Pontifical Swiss Guard was on the first floor; it was a wood-paneled suite that smelled like a church and felt like a courtroom. Edna was happy to keep her mouth shut while Father Paulson did the talking. She felt she had nothing of value to add to the conversation. In fact, she found herself struggling to stay awake.

Leopold von Altishofen listened intently as Paulson outlined the situation. In so doing, she was impressed by how closely Paulson stuck to the truth. He merely avoided certain facts that risked painting the story in a different light. Paulson came supported by a letter from General Donovan, which stretched the truth to breaking point by implying Paulson had been sent to Rome on behalf of President Eisenhower. Donovan was held in high esteem in Rome and his word carried weight. He had described Paulson's mission as a delicate matter of the utmost importance, but best handled outside of official channels. Under no circumstances, Donovan insisted, must Paolo Favaloro be permitted to provide technical assistance to the Russians.

When von Altishofen raised his head from the letter, his face was grave. "We have a plane on standby," said Paulson. "With your help, we can have Favaloro out of the Vatican and en route to America in twenty-four hours. You will be aiding the US President and dealing with Russian infiltration of the Gendarmerie Corps."

"Russians? You are certain of this?" he asked.

"I am, Commander."

Von Altishofen picked up his telephone receiver. "J'ai besoin de voir le Pere Morello." He hung up immediately and told them: "Father Morello is with the Secretariat of State. He is the liaison between the Swiss Guard and the Gendarmerie."

Edna felt a wave of panic shooting up her spine. She touched Paulson on the elbow and leaned over to whisper in his ear. "This is getting out of control."

Paulson nodded in agreement. "Is this absolutely necessary, Commander?" he asked von Altishofen. "I'd prefer not to complicate matters."

"Yet you present me with a problem that is already complicated," said von Altishofen. "We must do this my way. But as you will see, Father Morello will view this thing, how shall I say, avec pragmatisme. C'est un homme pratique."

There was a knock at the door and Morello was ushered in. He was a stern man with a thick Italian accent and an aggressive air. Commander von Altishofen made introductions in English, then proceeded to explain the situation to Morello in Italian. It never ceased to amaze Edna how effortlessly Europeans switched from one language to another, but she had no real grasp of what was being said. Morello was shown the letter, which he read in silence, before the two men conferred briefly once more, concluding their discussion with a mutual nod.

"It is agreed," said von Altishofen.

"A most delicate situation," said Morello, staring at Edna. "One best kept from the office of the Pontiff until its resolution." His eyes darted down at her cleavage momentarily, a mere flicker of a glance, but Morello saw that she was aware of it and seemed to take a wry pleasure from her discomfort. "Miss Drake, please to come this way. We have arranged for you to stay tonight in the Istituto Maria Santissima Bambina. If you would like to wait outside, Sister Mary Josephine will be here soon to show you the way."

He was telling Edna to wait outside and not worry her pretty young head about the men's business. Edna nodded politely and did as she was told.

The Commander's secretary, a young male officer who smiled at her like she was the first lay woman he'd seen in close quarters since taking on the job, chattered away at her incomprehensibly before pointing

Edna to an uncomfortable wooden chair; it reminded her of the seats outside the principal's office at her old high school back in Rockaway.

The nun arrived as quiet as a mouse two minutes later. "Miss Drake?"

"That's right. And you're Sister Josephine?"

Josephine nodded meekly, offering a hint of a smile by way of confirmation. "Please, you come this way."

"My suitcase is rather heavy, Sister, I hope it's not too far."

"I'd be happy to carry it for you," the nun told her.

"No, no, I didn't mean that. I just wondered how far…"

"We are just across St Peter's Square. Two minutes, no more."

Edna stopped herself just in time from saying, "Thank God."

St Peter's Square was thick with visitors gazing adoringly at the basilica and dancing through the colonnades. A queue of people waited to see the Sistine Chapel, their brows covered in sweat from the afternoon heat. Edna checked her watch; it was half past four. Most people in that queue were not going to make it before closing.

Sister Josephine walked fast, like she had somewhere else to be and was running late. "What's the hurry, sister?" Edna asked.

"My apologies," said Josephine, "I always walk too quickly. There are never enough hours in the day. Always more to be done."

"I'm sorry if I've taken you away from something important."

Sister Josephine laughed lightly. "As important as it can ever be to keep a tidy house."

"Tell me about your order," said Edna.

"We are sisters of charity. We provide labor for those who need it inside il Vaticano. I work for Commander von Altishofen as well as for Father Morello."

"Doing what?"

"Domestic support. Housekeeping."

As advertised, the Institute of the Blessed Baby Mary was in the exact opposite position across the square from the Swiss Guards' barracks. Sister Josephine guided her inside the ancient and austere Roman villa to a first-floor dormitory with about a dozen beds lined up in rows. The dorm was mostly empty, but the majority of the beds looked occupied.

"I've placed you in the bed next to mine," Sister Josephine told her. "Most of the women here speak little English, so I thought this would be of some help."

"Thank you, Sister, that's most considerate."

Edna placed her bag by her bed and Josephine led her to the nuns' dining hall. Sister Josephine opened the door to the kitchen, where two other young women in white tunics and aprons were busily sorting vegetables and scrubbing pots and pans. "There is always someone in the kitchen," Sister Josephine explained. "Meal times are strict, but if you are hungry and you ask them nicely, they will be happy to find you an apple or some biscuits. We can speak more tonight, after dinner. For now, I must go."

"I've been keeping you from something important, haven't I?" Edna realized.

Josephine smiled wearily. "A sewer pipe burst this morning in the Swiss Guard Barracks. There is still much to clean up. You have given me a welcome break. But now I must go back."

THIRTEEN

Tuesday July 15, 1953

Edna spent an hour playing tourist through the areas of the Vatican already familiar to her, until she remembered she needed to find her way to the Belvedere Courtyard, which was adjacent to the Secret Archives.

It was seven o'clock when she returned to Maria Bambina, and she was late for dinner. The nuns were already eating, but politely sat her down and brought her food immediately. They treated Edna like a welcome guest, but she couldn't help feeling like an interloper. The language barrier didn't make things easier. None of them had a word of English.

Dinner was a bowl of stewed mutton and vegetables. Very tasty, though the serving was not big. She mopped up the sauce with bread and wanted to ask for an extra helping, but thought it might come across as greedy. She didn't want to anyone else to go hungry.

Josephine appeared in the dining hall as the last of the nuns were finishing their meals. She sat down next to Edna and ate her food quickly, looking exhausted. Edna asked about her plumbing emergency.

"Don't worry, I showered before coming to dinner," Josephine said.

"Don't they have plumbers to fix the pipes?" Edna asked.

"Yes, but they do not clean up the mess."

Edna raised an eyebrow, but bit her lip. Josephine shrugged and smiled. "This is the task God has set before me," she said.

Edna thought she was just making excuses for the men who were clearly making her life a misery. "Where are you from, Sister? Your accent sounds vaguely familiar."

"I'm Polish. I joined a convent in Warsaw after the end of the Nazi occupation."

"You were after safety, is that it?"

"The nuns were helping so many women who'd been left with nothing. I was one of them. They were so kind, I knew I had to dedicate my life to service. To help save lives."

Edna told Josephine about her time as a nurse through the last months of the war, and then in Berlin as the Russians and the Allies divided up what was left. How she'd spent the first weeks after the German surrender treating women who were beaten and raped by Russian and allied soldiers.

Josephine nodded, understanding immediately and apparently untroubled by Edna's florid descriptions of the horrors. None of this was news to Sister Josephine. Though their lives had taken different paths and Edna didn't understand the choices that led any woman to being a nun, she couldn't help feeling an odd sort of bond between them.

It seemed like a good opportunity to gather some background. "How well do you know Commander von Altishofen?" Edna immediately regretted the bluntness of her question.

But Sister Josephine seemed happy to respond. "He is a good man. A devout Catholic and dedicated to his job. He treats his men well and he has been kind to me. More than some."

"Really?"

Josephine's eyes widened and she looked down, ashamed. "Everyone here is doing God's work. You too, I think, Miss Drake."

"Me? No..."

"But you work for Father Paulson, yes?"

"Well, yes that's right," said Edna quickly. "But I wouldn't call it God's work. I'm a personal assistant."

"But you're a servant of the church. If the Father requires an assistant, his work must be important. I know so little about what happens here. There is the church, of course, and all that goes with being a beacon of the faith. But there is so much more besides — business, politics... Of these things I know nothing."

"The Vatican is a sovereign nation. That demands money and diplomacy, as much as it requires adherence to the faith," said Edna.

"And security," said Josephine.

"Yes. Exactly." Edna wanted to ask more, but couldn't think of a clever way to do it, so she just came right out and asked. "Tell me about Father Morello — have you had much to do with him?"

"He terrified me the first time we met," the nun admitted. "He never looks happy. Always scowling like he is angry."

"Yes, I noticed that," said Edna.

"This is because he is charged with keeping il Vaticano running smoothly. A burden that must weigh heavily upon his shoulders, I think."

Edna became aware of footsteps crossing the dining hall toward them. She looked up to see Clarence Paulson had finally found her.

"I will leave you now," Sister Josephine said. "Please, make yourselves comfortable here, you will not be disturbed." She smiled politely at Paulson, directed him toward her chair, then left without another word.

"I'm afraid you're too late for dinner, Father," said Edna.

"I ate with Father Morello." Then in a whisper, "I'm sorry to take so long."

"Are we all set?" Edna asked.

Paulson nodded. "Before dawn tomorrow. Morello is sending in half a dozen of the Swiss Guard to arrest the gendarmes. We'll be able to walk in there unchecked. In and out in a few minutes. Father Morello will have a car waiting."

"Won't he tell the Curia you're here?"

"Yes, but he's agreed to hold off until later in the day. We'll be gone before they have a chance to do anything."

Paulson's confidence was reassuring, but she couldn't help having lingering doubts. "What about the Russians? Any sign of them?"

"Morello admitted he'd heard stories about women posing as nuns, but he seemed genuinely shocked when I told him they were Russian agents."

"Was it wise to tell him that?"

"We need his help. Without him, Paolo isn't going anywhere."

FOURTEEN

Wednesday July 15, 1953

Edna rose with the sisters before dawn. While they were praying in the chapel, she slipped out to meet Paulson on the edge of St Peter's Square. There was no sign of movement anywhere across the square, and they found their way quickly to the Belvedere Courtyard and through to the Pigna Courtyard.

Six members of the Swiss Guard were waiting. Their leader nodded to Paulson, before signaling to his men to enter the archive building. They emerged less than two minutes later with three gendarmes in handcuffs. With these men out of the way, it was a simple matter of taking the elevator underground.

Having spent many years himself locked away in the underground cloister of the secret archives, Paulson had no trouble finding his way in. Paolo Favaloro's suite of rooms was on the lowest level. It was quiet, and eerily shrouded in darkness, as Paulson led the way through the labyrinth of rooms and books stacks.

"Looks like they've given him more space," Paulson observed.

Favaloro was lying down and half naked when they found him. He leapt to his feet in shock and anger, apparently unconcerned by his state of dress. Seeing him in the flesh took Edna's breath away.

"Hello Paolo," said Paulson.

"Clarence. You surprise me. I take it you haven't brought the woman for me?"

"I'm Edna Drake," she said, tactfully ignoring the fact he had just suggested she was a prostitute. "We're here to get you out."

"You assume I want to leave. You've come right when I was expecting a visit from one of my Russian priestesses."

Enough said.

"They like the early morning because there is nobody else in here to see them."

"How do they get in?" Paulson asked.

"One fucks the gendarme on duty and the other comes to me," said Favaloro. "They are very good at their work. Most dedicated."

It dawned on Edna why he was calling them priestesses. "These women — do they wear frocks like the priests and have hoods over their heads?"

Paolo smiled. "The priests call them nuns. But I don't think that is what these women are." Edna's stomach hit the floor. Then she sensed movement behind them. "Here she is, right on time," said Favaloro.

"We come and go as we please," a woman said behind them.

Edna turned. A nun. Holding a gun. Her face was familiar — from dinner in Maria Bambina the previous night.

"They just told me they've come to take me out of here," said Favaloro. "But I'm not going anywhere." He opened his arms, beckoning her into his embrace.

She moved toward him, keeping her pistol trained on Edna and Clarence Paulson all the while. What happened next was a blur. Paolo moved so quickly, snatching the gun from her with one hand and snapping her neck like a twig with the other. The Russian woman was dead before her body hit the floor.

Edna gasped in horror. "Jesus Christ!"

"You didn't have to kill her," Paulson yelled.

"I just saved your lives," Paolo said. "Lead the way. We still need to deal with her friend."

"Just a moment," said Edna, alarm bells sounding in her head. "She walked in here with her gun raised. She knew we were here. How?"

"Let's not hang around long enough to find out," said Paulson.

Edna picked up the Russian's gun, figuring she was the only one of them likely to use it. They crammed into the elevator, Paolo on his knees so he could fit. Edna hit the ground floor button.

The lift rose slowly. She listened intently for any sign of trouble as they arrived back on ground level. Hearing nothing, Edna pulled open the door and signaled to the others to wait while she went first.

She was two steps into the foyer when the bullets started flying.

Edna dove back inside the elevator cage. A bullet pinged off the metalwork inches from her head; the ricochet caught her on the arm.

They were pinned down.

"There's only one way out of here," a woman yelled at them, "and it's this doorway where I'm standing. You have nowhere to go but back down."

Edna's worst fears were realized. "Josephine? It's you, isn't it?"

"No, no," said Paolo. "That's Nina."

"I answer to both," the voice said.

Edna's arm was starting to bleed badly, but she wasn't going to give up without a fight. She knelt down and fired two shots out of the elevator in the direction of the front entrance. One thumped into the wall, the other hit the wooden door.

"If you had the slightest idea of how to use that gun, I might be worried," Josephine yelled back.

"She's right about getting out of here," Paulson whispered. "That's the only exit."

"Any ideas?" Edna asked him.

"Let me go out there," said Paolo, who was still stuck on his knees inside the cramped elevator car. "She won't shoot me." He began to shift one of his legs in a bid to get out.

Edna grabbed his arm. "If she thinks it's me coming out, she might start shooting anyway."

Paolo frowned. "A hunter never mistakes a lion for a kitten."

Before she had a chance to reply, Sister Josephine walked into view a few feet away, still dressed as a nun but with a Russian Tokarev pistol pointed straight at them. Startled, but still determined not to give in, Edna quickly raised her gun. A look of relish passed across the Russian woman's face. She was enjoying herself.

"Nina!" Paolo yelled, "It is you!"

"Polish my ass," said Edna. She couldn't help feeling Paolo's enthusiasm was misplaced.

"My name is Nina Onilova. I will kill you all on the count of three if you don't do as I say."

Edna believed her. "Unless I fire first."

Onilova's eyes narrowed. "In you I do not see this level of commitment, Edna Drake."

They both knew she was right. "So, what's the play here?" Edna asked.

"I will allow you and Father Paulson to walk out of here alive. But Paolo must stay."

"What if we call the gendarmes?" Edna asked her. "Tell them about your little plot? Or Leopold?"

Nina Onilova smiled. "Be my guest. You will be the ones they throw in prison. Since you're holding her gun, I assume my agent is dead. Murdered on holy ground. And on the matter of Paolo Favaloro, the Pope is on my side. This is why he knows nothing of your plan, am I right? You are out of your depth, Edna Drake."

"She's probably right," said Paolo. "The Vatican still hasn't forgiven Galileo for saying the Earth orbits around the Sun. Pius won't let me walk out of here. It puts the church at too much risk."

"Yes," said Edna bitterly, "we can't have people knowing the truth now, can we?"

"Come," said Nina. "You need medical attention. Don't make me kill you."

Edna lowered her gun. Nina stepped up and snatched it from her grasp. The Russian walked Edna and Paulson outside. She opened the rear door of a white Mercedes that had pulled up at the door.

Paulson groaned as he saw Father Morello behind the wheel. "You're not Russian."

"No, I'm Sicilian. But Russians pay well," said Morello.

Onilova leaned through the open rear window. "Remo will take you to your plane. If I don't hear back from him that you are in the air and on your way back home, I put a bullet in Paolo Favaloro's head." She tossed a field bandage into Edna's lap. "You're a nurse, you know what to do with this."

"What about Commander von Altishofen? He'll know," said Paulson.

Nina Onilova merely smiled. "Leo does what I tell him to do." She tapped the car on the roof and they started moving.

"Jesus, she's sleeping with the head of the Swiss Guard," Edna realized.

"This place," said Paulson in utter exasperation. "It's a pit of vipers. Are you even a priest, Morello?"

"I could ask the same of you," Morello replied. "Let's just say I'm well-connected."

"I see," said Paulson.

But Edna didn't understand at all.

FIFTEEN

Friday July 17, 1953

Donald Menzel was yelling at her and turning purple with rage. "I suppose I should blame myself for sending a woman to do a man's job." But he wasn't blaming himself at all, not one little bit. "It was amateur hour. What a complete and utter mess you've made of it all."

Edna had heard more than enough of it. "This is a failure entirely of your own making, old man. You didn't want to trust the experts; you threw me to the wolves with no preparation and no credible intelligence." She held up her arm, bandaged where Onilova's bullet had grazed her. "And you dare to blame me for this?"

Menzel just shook his head at her. He was nowhere close to accepting any of the blame. "Who did you tell?"

"I told no one."

Menzel laughed incredulously. "Well, somebody talked and it wasn't me."

"They knew we were coming," said Paulson.

"Maybe there was no leak," said Edna. "Maybe they were just two steps ahead of us. They knew we'd see Beria's arrest as a strategic opportunity and try to do something."

Menzel considered this. "It's possible, I suppose."

"Which is why you should have taken this to the CIA in the first place," said Edna.

"You need to move out of here," Menzel told her. "Right now. I can't have you in this building a moment longer."

"You're kicking me out?"

"Find yourself a hotel. We'll pay for it. Nothing too extravagant — and for God's sake, stay away from the Mayflower. The last thing we need is you tripping over Hoover and his boyfriend on one of their luncheon dates. Take some time to get your cover story straight. You were on a fact-finding trip for Senator Ives. Work out your cover story so it sounds convincing if anybody asks."

SIXTEEN

F riday July 17, 1953

Edna Drake checked into the Hotel Commodore on Union Station Plaza, insisting upon a room on the first floor so she could take the stairs and avoid the elevator.

She'd been tempted to book a suite, but they were on the top level, which brought the elevator into play. And she didn't want to give Menzel any excuse to renege on his promise to pay. She didn't trust that mad little scientist. If she'd learnt one thing in the wake of her catastrophic Roman holiday, it was that Donald Menzel would not have her back when the chips were down. His primary concern was covering his own ass. It deeply disappointed her; she had believed him to be a better person than that.

Clarence Paulson came calling an hour after she checked in. He had ditched his black frock in favor of slacks and a blue shirt and had a bottle of Irish whiskey under his arm; he declared it was an olive branch from Donald who had, by the way, empowered him to sort out her hotel bill. Paulson was probably lying about the whiskey, but Edna appreciated his attempt at rebuilding burnt bridges.

"He was spectacularly hard on you," Paulson said. "He's well aware it should have been the CIA going in there, not a jaded priest and an investigative reporter."

"Retired investigative reporter."

"You're not retired," he said. "It's just that now your work will never see the light of day."

"Do you really think that's true?" she asked, watching as he poured two doubles. "You think all this stuff will stay secret forever? There's ice in the bucket, by the way."

Paulson threw two cubes into each tumbler and thrust one in her direction. "I think you and I will be old and grey before the world finds out what's really going on."

She took the glass and held it in the air. "To abject failure."

"To better times ahead," he said.

"Yes," she agreed, "much better. And I must tell you, I prefer you out of uniform." It sounded lewd, but she let the words hang in the air as she threw open a window to hear the buzz of the city.

"It did confirm one thing for me," he said. "I'm never going back. I'll quit the church before I return to Rome."

"No, you won't. It suits everyone to keep you playing your part."

"That's all it is to me now, truth be told. A performance."

"Don't tell me I'm witnessing a crisis of faith?"

He shrugged and swallowed a mouthful of whiskey. "It's my cross to bear."

"I'm serious."

He smiled. "I still have faith, of sorts. It's more a question of losing my religion. Dying and rising from the dead? Turning water into wine? With everything we know now, it all sounds like children's fairytales, don't you think?"

"Well, come on now," she said, "you're sitting there watching me turn whiskey into wee-wee. Aren't we all our own little miracles?"

Paulson exploded in laughter and it was like he was unleashing something that had been bottled up tight inside. He poured again and they drank. Then again. He kept matching her drink for drink. It started to loosen her tongue. "Come on Clarence, don't you wish we could end all this secrecy? Isn't it high time the Verus secrets were brought out into the open?"

He reminded her she wasn't a reporter anymore and suggested it might be the booze doing the talking. Edna wasn't so sure. Her thoughts on the matter hadn't changed a whole lot since she'd been forced to leave journalism behind.

"These secrets are about control," she said. "They're holding us back. Don't you think it would be a chance to start working with the Russians? I mean, we have this incredible technology in our midst. We could change the world."

Paulson's face darkened. "You need to be very careful, Edna. This is thin ice you're walking. You mustn't say such things."

"We could stop all this mistrust and violence, and just get to work," she said.

Paulson stared at her long and hard, chuckled quietly and shook his head. "You really are quite drunk."

She pouted, concerned he wasn't taking her seriously.

But what happened next caught them both by surprise.

SEVENTEEN

Saturday July 18, 1953

Clarence Paulson wasn't what Edna would have called a great lover, but he was tender, attentive, and eager to please. He was shy about his body, insisting on turning out the lights before he let her undress him. He followed suit and explored her body like it was a fine work of art, and he needed to follow every curve.

It was only afterwards that he admitted to her that this was his first time.

She could see he was telling the truth, but given the visceral hunger she'd seen in his eyes, she found it hard to believe she had been the first woman to tempt him.

"I'm a Catholic priest, Edna. We take a vow of celibacy."

"Yeah, but I didn't think people actually held you to that. Do you really think there are many priests who remain celibate all their lives?"

"That's a very good question. I, for one, spent far too many years doing so."

She caressed his cheek. "This feels like a big deal."

"All these rules, all these vows and promises. Eventually they start to ring hollow."

"You really are losing your religion."

He nodded. "It's dead and gone. Never to rise again."

"Jesus."

Paulson shook his head. "He's gone. And I don't think he's coming back."

She got out of bed and walked to the window naked, staring out at the city from the cover of darkness. "We all love to hide in the shadows. We're all pretending."

"All that holds our world together is a thin veneer of faith and civility," he said.

"Not faith in God, surely."

"No, I mean faith in institutions. Belief that we are the ones in control." He moved to get out of bed and then checked himself, remembering he was naked. He wrapped himself in the bedspread and joined her by the window.

"Are you embarrassed?" she asked.

"No."

She laughed.

"Well, all right then, yes, maybe a little."

She touched his face, then lifted his hand slowly to touch breast. "No need."

He wrapped the bedspread around her, and she wasn't sure if it was to keep her warm or to cover her up. "I understand the fear of what could happen if we lose faith in things. Once it's gone, it could be gone forever." He kissed her gently on the lips. "Now, will you come back to bed?"

"Aren't you tired?" she asked.

Clarence shook his head, "I've never been more awake."

EIGHTEEN

S aturday July 18, 1953

They woke late. Her head was a little sore, but she felt surprisingly happy and ready to face the cold light of morning.

There was no way of knowing what to make of the previous night. While it felt like this might be a profound strengthening of the bond she had with this man, experience told her there was a good chance that shame could eventually get the better of him.

Talking about that right now wasn't likely to help either.

Clarence was still dozing when she called room service and ordered a full cooked breakfast for two. Edna grabbed some clothes and dived into the shower, aiming to look as good as possible when they sat down to eat. She figured a man in his forties, waking up in a woman's bed for the first time in his life after a night of heavy drinking, needed to be spared an early morning horror show.

Feeling much more human with her game face on, Edna accepted the food at the door and dismissed the busboy's offer to serve for them.

Clarence had made a break for the bathroom the moment he heard the knock on the door; he emerged fully dressed and groomed for breakfast. She could tell he was making an effort. Just the same, he downed two black coffees before managing to utter a word.

"Thank the Lord for caffeine," he said finally, placing his hands together in a mock prayer.

"My mother always made us say grace before eating the evening meal," said Edna. "Never at breakfast though. Which is odd, now I think about it. I'm usually much more thankful for breakfast."

Paulson groaned in agreement. "Me too." He took to his bacon and eggs with gusto, noticing after a couple of mouthfuls that she was watching him. "What?"

"How's the head?"

"It hurts when I think."

She poured him a glass of water and placed a tablet down beside it. "What's that?" he asked.

"Aspro. Good for headaches and housewives' blues."

"Can I have two?"

"Sure. You never lived at Verus HQ, did you Clarence?"

"No. At one point, Bill Donovan let me have a room at his place, but his wife began to get uncomfortable having a priest in the house all the time. Lee Tavon found me an apartment in Columbia Heights."

"Colorful part of town. I rather fancy it myself, actually."

"I like the diversity," he said. "It's a neighborhood that seems to welcome interlopers."

Clarence might have offered her a place to stay, if he'd felt confident that she'd take him up on it. There was a pain in his chest that was entirely new and, oddly, not altogether unpleasant. He took this to be love. Though utterly inexperienced in romance, Clarence was old enough to know that pain was a powerful sign his love was unrequited.

"I've been thinking about our conversation last night," she said.

"I won't hold you to anything said under the influence of Old Schenley."

"I mean what I said about secrecy," she told him. "When I think about what we did in Rome — we're lucky we weren't tossed in jail. And if that had happened, how would the US government have reacted? The President didn't even know we were there. Ditto the CIA. Donald sent us on what could have been a suicide mission. He could have simply washed his hands of us. This secrecy is a cancer eating away at good intentions."

Paulson frowned. "I'm not sure I like where this conversation is headed."

"The only way to get beyond it is to take the FS-1 project — and everything we know about the alien presence on Earth — into the public domain."

"You tried that already, remember?" he reminded her. "This is where you ended up."

"Precisely. One woman will never do it on her own. It needs to happen with official sanction. We need to convince people at the top of the food chain all this secrecy has to end."

He put his knife and fork down. "Hold on, when did this become 'we'?"

She filled her fork with bacon and held it in midair. His reluctance was no surprise, but bed privileges came with responsibilities. "You are with me, aren't you?"

"Well yes, of course," he said, knowing immediately what she was getting at. "But what exactly did you have in mind?"

"We go to the President. Or just me. He knows me already. I tell him everything. Lay it all out on the table."

"Can I just point out our little disaster in Rome will be common knowledge by now in the halls of the CIA and the State Department. You sure you want to take responsibility for all that? What if Ike just wants to shoot the messenger?"

"He won't do that if I'm a good enough source of information. I was thinking, you have a connection with Paolo Favaloro, don't you? Will he come when you call?"

Paulson stared at her for a moment, then closed his eyes. She watched in awe as he descended into a trance-like state. He looked beatific, like he was deep in meditation.

As the apparition of Paolo materialized behind him, the room somehow darkened, even as the morning sunlight continued to stream through the windows; he appeared in normal human size, rather than his full eleven feet. Paulson's eyes opened as he became aware of the ghostly presence.

"Incredible," said Edna. "How do you do that?"

"Light is energy — and energy is mere vibration. It can be shaped by thought," said Paolo. "A pleasure to see you again, Edna Drake. I take it you are not badly wounded?"

She shook her head. "I'll live. How about you? Are they treating you OK?"

"I am fine. For me, nothing changes. Nina visits me herself now. I told her it was me who took the life of her little slave. She isn't sure what to believe. She is not so generous with her favors, but I know she is curious."

Six thousand years old and the man was still thinking with his crotch.

"Does the Pope have any idea that Father Morello is a member of the Sicilian mafia?" Paulson asked.

This was what Morello had meant by well-connected, Edna realized.

"The Pope has no idea," said Paolo. "Nor is he likely to find out. The gendarmerie and Swiss Guard have closed ranks to cover up the woman's death. There will be no investigation. As far as they are concerned, it didn't happen."

"But we were making quite a racket," said Edna. "There must be people who know the truth."

Paolo smiled. "When in Rome, you believe what you are told to believe."

"How did the Russians know we were coming?" Edna asked.

"They didn't," said Paolo. "They were merely prepared for new arrivals. Nothing escapes their attention and, as you have seen, they react with ruthless efficiency, unencumbered by religious belief or fear of capture. Nina Onilova only answers to one higher authority — her commander in East Berlin."

"Colonel Danilov," Paulson realized. "I've seen him at work. She's a chip off the old block."

"The Russians and criminals thrive in Rome because they always keep the church happy. This way, everyone gets what they want."

"I'm sorry we failed you," said Edna.

Paolo stared at her with ruthless candor, eyes blazing with a fortitude that had held him together across a span of time she found impossible to fathom. "You are but the latest in a long line, Edna Drake. I live beyond hope. It is an indulgent emotion I cannot harbor."

NINETEEN

M onday August 3, 1953

Edna couldn't help noticing the President's Room had seen better days. While the walls and the ceiling were remarkable — for the detail and volume of portraiture and murals that covered them — close inspection revealed they were coated with grime. Presidents once used the ornate Capitol Building chamber to sign legislation into law at the end of every session of Congress. But it had effectively become redundant in 1933, when a constitutional amendment established different end dates for congressional and presidential terms. Consequently, it now sat idle, unless its doors were opened for special occasions like today. The neglect was visible. Its rococo decoration was stained with the tar of decades of cigar and cigarette smoke, and its plush leather chairs were falling apart at the seams.

Faded glory notwithstanding, the room seemed a fitting venue for a wake. It was now crammed with mourners, come to pay their respects to Senator Robert Taft. The Republican Senate majority leader had lost a short, sharp battle with pancreatic cancer, and had died on July 31st, just a few months after his health had begun to go downhill.

It had only been a year since Taft and Dwight Eisenhower had locked horns in a bitter tussle for the presidential nomination. But they'd overcome their enmity when Eisenhower had extended the hand of friendship, hoping they could work together effectively on

Capitol Hill. In April, Taft had been in pain after a morning on the golf course with the President. He was taken to the hospital for tests. Then, a month later, more tests and biopsies from nodules on his head and abdomen; those showed up as malignant.

Senator Taft's body lay in state for several days in the rotunda, directly below the Capitol dome, where his funeral had taken place earlier that day.

Edna had met the man on several occasions in her capacity as a researcher for Senator Irving Ives, at whose side she now stood dutifully. Everyone in Ives's office was well aware that Taft's death was an opportunity, not that anyone was saying it today. Ives was now the ranking Republican expert on labor management.

"Would you like a drink, Edna?" Ives asked her.

"I really would," she admitted. She felt like a fish out of water in a room full of sharks.

Ives nodded in understanding and headed for the bar, but he fell into a conversation with Vice President Nixon. Edna knew she would be waiting a long time.

"Good to see you again, Edna." She turned and smiled, recognizing the voice of Hoyt Vandenberg, but was shocked to see him looking so unwell.

"Hello, General. How are you?" she asked tentatively. Menzel had told her he was sick, but he had the gaunt pallor of someone staring death in the face.

"No comment," he said. "This is all a bit too close to home. I just wanted to pop my head in briefly to pay my respects. I wanted to tell you I was sorry about Rome. I can't help feeling responsible. We shouldn't have sent you in there."

"It's good of you to say," she told him quietly. "I do feel like the whole operation was doomed from the start."

Vandenberg nodded in solemn agreement, then silently shook her hand with a disturbing sense of finality. As Senator Ives reappeared with her champagne, she watched ruefully as Vandenberg beat a rapid retreat to avoid an awkward encounter with the President's entourage, which had been moving in Edna's direction for some time.

"Poor old Hoyt," said Ives. "He's next, from what I hear."

"Senator, good to see you."

Another all-too-familiar old man appeared before them. "General Donovan, how are you?" Ives inquired, shaking Donovan's hand. "Let me introduce you to my research assistant, Edna Drake."

"The General and I have actually met," said Edna. "Back when I was a newspaper reporter." But Ives wasn't listening; the President had caught his attention. The room had become so crammed with important people, it was hard to know where to look.

Donovan grabbed her by the elbow and leant in close to speak, so he wouldn't be overheard. "Just quickly, I have a name for you. Eloise Page. She's well-connected in the agency. Knows about MJ-12. I trust her with my life and I told her you're on the level. If you ever need help, every Sunday you can find her at the Christ Episcopal Church in Georgetown. Go to the nine o'clock service. She'll find you." He was gone a moment later. It was a remarkable disappearance, calculated to avoid presidential scrutiny. It was almost like he'd never been there at all.

Donovan still had impressive tradecraft; she'd had no idea he was still in the country. But there was no time to think about why he felt the need to deliver the message, because Eisenhower's chief White House assistant had caught her eye. He was slightly shorter than Ike, who himself wasn't particularly tall. But stood side by side, they could have been brothers. Adams's short grey hair was groomed impeccably, and his fine tailored suit added to his air of total confidence. A man who knew he could get things done. He held out his hand by way of introduction. "Sherman Adams," he said, like there was anyone in this room who didn't know that already. She offered him a firm grip. "And you are Edna Drake."

She nodded, impressed both by the handshake and the recognition. "A pleasure, Mr Adams. But you know, I've been trying to speak to you for some time."

"Yes," he said, nodding sagely, "I do know. Needless to say, we've been busy. I am an admirer of your boss."

For a moment, she thought he meant Menzel. "Ah yes... Senator Ives is a progressive employer."

"And a man of his word. A rare thing in Washington these days, I find."

"Indeed."

"I won't keep you. I just wanted to let you know that I am aware of your situation."

"Well sir, that's the thing. I'm not entirely certain you are fully aware..."

Adams nodded somewhat impatiently, like he already knew what she was about to say. "We'll talk soon. I promise."

Nobody could get near President Eisenhower without going through Sherman Adams. He'd been described in the press as Ike's "Abominable No Man". She dearly wanted to take this opportunity to nail him down to a time and a place, but she'd already lost his attention; Adams was speaking to three other people at once.

She noticed Eisenhower was listening in. It was almost like Adams was the man in charge.

TWENTY

Monday August 3, 1953

Edna realized Benjamin Franklin was staring at her over the top of his bifocals, rather like he was wanting her to say something. His portrait gazed knowingly out across the President's Room, and she wondered what incredible moments this figure had witnessed over the years. How would this most revered of the Founding Fathers view the world in which they now found themselves? She found it hard to believe any man so dedicated to the pursuit of truth and knowledge would condone the secrets now kept from the world in the name of peace and national security.

An arm hooked through hers and spun Edna around by the elbow. She found herself facing a young woman with pale cheeks and light brown hair, lips painted deep red and sparkling eyes that demanded attention. "Edna darling, I've been looking for you everywhere."

Edna was wracking her brain trying to remember who this woman was, but she didn't look at all familiar. There was a vague hint of a European accent hiding beneath her Long Island lockjaw. She could have been Katherine Hepburn and Marlene Dietrich rolled into one. She leant in close, "Polina. That's my name. You haven't forgotten it darling, don't worry. We don't know one another. At least, not yet."

Edna decided to play along, but alarm bells were already ringing. "Hello, Paulina."

"No darling. Po-lina. It's Polish."

Her nationality was her calling card; Sister Josephine had said she was Polish.

"I heard about Rome," Polina said, leaving Edna in no doubt.

Edna pulled her arm free. "I don't think we have anything to say to one another."

Polina took hold of her elbow and subtly but forcefully pulled her close. "Don't be too hasty, darling. We've only just met."

"What do you want?" Edna hissed.

"To talk. About your quest for the truth." Which Edna took to mean the Verus Foundation. "Sometimes it's good to talk to somebody who understands," Polina said.

"Is that right?"

"I know you feel the same way. It can be so lonely, but we have much in common you and I. A sympathetic ear is hard to come by. I'll be at Shulman's Market, tomorrow afternoon at three."

Polina ambled away without looking back. It was an odd gait, favoring one leg like she was trying to hide a limp.

TWENTY ONE

Tuesday August 4, 1953

Edna couldn't work out how Polina had made it into the room. Secret Service agents were on the door — she'd recognized Agent Elmer Deckard from their first meeting in the bowels of the White House. And even though he knew her, he had still insisted upon seeing her identification. Surely Russian diplomats would not have been invited to Taft's wake. The funeral, maybe, but not the wake. Which meant Polina had fake American credentials. That would explain the Long Island accent, and her brazen approach.

Shulman's Market was a corner store in a predominantly black area of Southwest D.C. — it had also become popular with the Russian immigrant community. Edna made her way cautiously along an alley known locally as Union Street, past broken-down tenements and crumbling brick row houses. Small boys played ball in the street, and men sat on wooden crates smoking and watching for something to distract them from their terminal boredom. Many people felt unsafe wandering these streets, but this was Edna's old neighborhood, and she felt right at home. It was actually one of the safest places in D.C.; here people didn't even bother locking their doors — most of them owned nothing worth stealing.

But that vibe was changing fast; many of the houses looked empty now. Families were being forced to move ahead of the wrecking crews, coming soon to begin the so-called "urban renewal." There was a feeling of despair in the air, and she was starting to wonder if it had been a good idea coming here today without letting anyone know. She'd considered calling Menzel, but wasn't sure he would want to discuss the matter over an open telephone line. And he'd made it clear he didn't want to see her back at Verus HQ. She'd gone it alone, hoping to show him she didn't require his approval at every turn.

Edna reached Shulman's Market and stepped past a black teenager bouncing a ball on the front stoop, to glimpse a woman vanishing behind the counter and into a backroom. She figured it had to be Polina.

The teenager, who had followed her inside the storefront, tapped her on the shoulder. "Follow me." He led her through to the backroom, behind the counter and away from the gaze of other shoppers. Polina was sitting at a small table alongside a balding man Edna assumed was the store owner.

"My name is Dimitri," he told Edna. "Would you like coffee? Or a vodka perhaps?"

"Coffee is fine," she said.

Dimitri glanced at Polina, who nodded to indicate she would have the same.

"You came," Polina said. "I wasn't sure you would."

Edna waited for Dimitri to leave the room. "Color me curious." She tried to glance casually around the room, looking for something to use as a weapon if the need arose.

"You are safe here," Polina assured her. "I have eyes on the streets outside. I assume you know you're being followed."

"No," said Edna, caught off guard. "By who? Your people?"

"No darling, by yours. My people don't know I'm here."

Edna scoffed. "Come on, let's not kid one another."

"I didn't come here to tell you lies, Edna Drake. On this you have my word." Polina held her gaze a long time, then reached out and touched her warmly on the hand. "We have something in common. I was in Berlin at the end of the war, like you,"

"You and a million other Russians," said Edna.

"I think you were gone by the time I arrived. What a hellhole. I've never seen such destruction. And the people —as ruined as the city itself. No safe place for a woman."

"Were you ever... attacked?" Edna asked her.

"No. Our soldiers protected Russian women. They took out their frustrations on the Germans. I must confess that for a long time, I had no sympathy for the frauleins. I saw them as worthy of punishment. Their men had slaughtered so many Russian soldiers, and they kept killing us for weeks even when they knew their situation was hopeless. But in the end, it was Russians who showed them what it means to never surrender."

"What your soldiers did to German women made me sick to my stomach," said Edna.

"Your soldiers were no better," said Polina.

Edna disagreed, but she hadn't come here to argue about the war.

"Berlin was a rotting corpse," said Polina. "The survivors were wild dogs fighting for their pound of dead flesh. To Russians, those women were already dead."

It was to be expected that Polina could forgive the crimes her own men committed. Nobody ever wanted to believe their own side was guilty of war crimes. Using rape for vengeance during the occupation had been an abomination, but it was also true that everyone was more cold-blooded back then. Edna had never been able to find the words to describe what it was like near the front lines in the months after D-Day. How surviving amid so much pain and death so profoundly altered one's perspective on life. How hatred for the Germans had developed into an all-consuming passion once the full extent of their atrocities had become clear in the aftermath. This was the first time since returning to America that Edna had come face-to-face with another woman who'd lived through it.

Dimitri returned with two strong black coffees and a pot of sugar. "Sweet is best," he said.

Edna took one sip and thought it was the strongest coffee she'd ever tasted. Two sugars took an edge off the bitterness. "How long were you there?" she asked Polina.

"Two years. Working in intelligence."

"Much longer than me. I don't know how you could stand it."

"I was alive and, for the most part, safe. I had food and a roof over my head. So many Russians had already lost these things."

"I try hard not to think about the brutality of it," Edna said. "Sometimes it feels like it all happened to someone else."

"We have this in common. We know things, but cannot talk of them."

"What do you want from me, Polina?"

"Just this — to talk. Is good, yes? To get these things off your chest, as Americans like to say."

"I have nothing I need to get off my chest," said Edna warily, guessing Polina planned to shift the topic of conversation from Berlin to Rome. "But if you're keen to talk, I'm all ears."

Polina smiled. "I can help you," she said. "You're all alone now. No one to trust. In the cold, is that the right expression? I came to you to offer a friendly ear. I'd like to think we could be friends."

Just like Sister Josephine. "That's never gonna happen," said Edna.

"You have your priest, yes? Your father confessor, though I'm not sure staying the night in a woman's room is proper behavior for a holy man." *They were watching her hotel.*

77 "Nina Onilova has told me things about the priests that would make your toes curl," said Polina. "But I could care less what you do. I want to tell you this, Edna Drake — your position at Verus is untenable. This will not end well for you."

Edna picked up her coffee, and couldn't stop her hand from shaking. "How would you know that?"

"I know everything about you. Your trip to Italy was unsanctioned. You will be blamed for its failure."

Edna tried to steady the cup with her other hand, her mind racing. "What makes you think my people are following me?"

"I have seen them myself. They are not the same men who follow me — mine are FBI. Yours, I think, are CIA."

She put the cup down, her guts churning. "And this is the part where you use it against me."

Polina shook her head. "No. You can walk away right now — I won't stop you."

Edna messily pushed her chair back and began to head for the door, feeling dizzy.

"Bartholdi Park, by the fountain," Polina called after her. "A week from now, if you want to talk more."

Edna didn't stop walking until she hit the street. The pavements were empty. Nobody watching that she could see, but she felt utterly exposed just the same. She'd made a terrible mistake coming here. If the CIA was on her tail, they knew about Polina now.

Only traitors held unsanctioned meetings with Russian agents.

She was in over her head. She'd come here because she actually liked the idea of having someone to talk to about it all. But Polina would never be her friend. In matters of politics, Russians were all the same; they acted without remorse and they most certainly never played fair.

TWENTY TWO

Wednesday August 5, 1953

The owners of Crisfield clearly had no interest in making the place pretty for diners: it was more café than restaurant. But the seafood was trucked in fresh daily from Chesapeake Bay, and virtually every dish on the menu was to die for.

It was rather inconveniently located at Silver Spring in Maryland, just outside the D.C. limits, but that was to their advantage in this instance. Edna found Donald Menzel perched on a stool at the bar. He rose to his feet and immediately led her to a table. "I'm starving," he explained, "let's order first and talk later."

He went for a dozen fresh oysters, with Lobster Norfolk to follow. She opted for clam chowder and a shrimp salad. The place was very noisy, which also suited them perfectly. Nobody else would hear what she had to say. Thankfully, out here they were just two more faces in the crowd. It had become abundantly clear that Menzel was embarrassed to be seen with Edna in public.

Aware embarrassment might soon escalate to enmity, Edna kept her tone firm and sure as she outlined her meeting with Polina. The food arrived halfway through her story. He quickly began shoveling oysters into his mouth. Finishing the full dozen, Menzel sighed in satisfaction and eyed her calmly. "You did well. Exactly what I would have suggested — if you'd thought to come to me beforehand, though I understand your reason for not doing so."

"She claims the CIA are on my tail."

"Makes sense," he said. "I had to pass it up the chain that your operation in Rome had failed."

That really pissed her off. "For God's sake — up the chain? It was your idea not to tell them in the first place, why tell them now?" He stared back at her unmoved. Her chowder arrived, but she had abruptly lost her appetite.

"Eat," he told her. "I understand that you're angry, but you can't let it put you off your food."

"Up the chain to who, Donald?"

"MJ-12 — to Wally Smith." The former CIA Director. "He passed it along to Dulles, his replacement."

This had been an unsanctioned spy operation, run illegally inside the Vatican. Shots had been fired. A Russian agent had been killed. This was the sort of information that could ruin anyone associated with it. Polina's prediction was starting to seem remarkably credible. If news of the failed operation reached the ears of anyone close to Senator Joe McCarthy, it would destroy her.

"Have you had any response from Dulles?" Edna asked.

"Roscoe is briefing him on MJ-12 and Verus this week. I'd think we'll hear back from that meeting soon enough."

"Does that briefing extend to FS-1?"

Menzel winced slightly at mention of the flying saucer program, then shook his head. "No. We've decided to quarantine that from CIA oversight."

"Quarantine... What does that mean?"

"We're going it alone."

"Meaning they won't be told what Clarence and I were actually doing in Rome."

"No," Menzel agreed. "As far as the agency is concerned, you were conducting research in the Vatican archives and the Russians tried to kill you. That's all there is to it."

"We're lying to the CIA? Let's hope that doesn't come back to bite us. Hell, what am I saying? It's not 'we', it's you. Yet strangely it's my head on the chopping block."

"This is what we do, Edna. I'd have thought you understood that by now."

She took a long, slow breath and sipped her chowder. It was good. She could taste three different types of seafood, the salt and tang balanced without either flavor overpowering. She knew there was no point arguing; the damage was done. And he hadn't completely thrown her in the deep end.

Not yet.

"So... the CIA is tailing me," Edna said. "Which is illegal. The agency isn't supposed to be working on US soil."

Menzel smiled. "You're dancing with the devil and it's breaking the law that worries you? That's rich, kid, even coming from you."

TWENTY
THREE

Tuesday August 11, 1953

Edna was getting to know Washington's public transit system intimately. She'd spent almost three hours catching trains and buses back and forth across the city, stopping off for lunch along the way, and taking long walks through parks, even a church yard and on one occasion. Slipping into a crowded schoolyard, Edna hurried past as children were piling out to meet their parents at the end of the school day. She went out a side gate and hailed a taxi that delivered her three blocks from her destination. She was confident nobody could still be on her tail.

Bartholdi Park was a tiny triangle of land that had been named after the French sculptor Frederic Auguste Bartholdi, designer of the Statue of Liberty. It had been added into the adjacent Botanic Gardens in 1932, but was not visited as often as the main gardens. It was just a short walk across Independence Avenue and past the grand glass conservatory to the Capitol Reflecting Pool, a place reputed to be one of Washington's more favored locations for clandestine meetings.

Edna was half an hour late for the meeting, and half expected to find that the Russian had already come and gone. But Polina was still there, waiting calmly on a shaded bench in the southeast quarter of the fountain precinct; a place where nobody could eavesdrop without being spotted.

"I was almost ready to give up on you," Polina said.

"I've been doing my best to ensure I could turn up alone."

"You're assuming Mr Menzel won't give you up."

"I didn't tell Donald where or when I was meeting you. But I take it you have people following me too."

"You, Menzel, Father Paulson. You are of great interest to the Russian government. You and your strange alien man hiding in the Vatican."

They seemed to know everything about her and Verus. It was, frankly, quite terrifying.

Polina stretched out her left leg and grimaced. She rose slowly to her feet and walked in a short circle. "I have arthritis in my hip. I cannot sit on hard seats for too long."

"What happened to you?"

"I was shot. In Berlin. Not a serious wound, or so I thought at the time."

"I'm sorry to hear that."

"Is no matter," said Polina, sitting down again. "But I wanted to tell you more about myself," she said, perhaps sensing Edna's concern about the imbalance in their acquaintanceship. "My name is Polina Ilyin. I was born in Moscow, but began my career in Berlin with the Russian occupying forces. In 1947, I returned to Moscow and spent three years as an executioner of dissidents. Two years ago, I was forced to put a bullet in the head of the man I loved. He was accused of committing an act of treason. I knew he was innocent. I shot him anyway. He begged me to do it, knowing if I tried to spare him someone else would pull the trigger and the next bullet would be for me."

Edna's mouth was hanging open. She swallowed hard as Polina continued.

"Having proved myself to be a loyal Soviet citizen, I was stationed at the Russian embassy in America. My father and mother are both officers of the Russian secret police, which you call the MVD. They are loyal and above reproach. They raised me to respect and obey authority above all else. But they also taught me to think for myself, and to know the difference between right and wrong. The Soviet history they teach in our schools is a lie. Everybody knows this. But my family was in a position to know the truths behind the lies. They know I did what I had to do to stay alive. But every day I feel shame and know my parents feel the same, though they would never admit this to my face.

"It is why I am here today, Edna Drake. We are alike. We value the truth more than the people for whom we work."

"Are you telling me you want to defect?"

Polina let loose a hearty laugh. "No. This is not what I am telling you. I am offering hand of friendship. You have nobody you can talk to, correct?"

Edna shrugged. She wasn't in much of a giving mood.

"You don't need to trust me. Just understand that I know everything about you and your work. There is nothing you can tell me I don't already know. For you, this is good thing. You can speak without fear of betraying your country. And because you have no particular interest or skill in turning me into an American asset, I too can speak freely. It is a unique situation we find ourselves in."

"For what purpose?" Edna asked her. "Why would we do this?"

"Because secrecy serves no one," said Polina. "I know you believe this. I am risking my career, perhaps also my life, by talking to you. But I know this risk is worth taking."

Edna saw pain and fear in the woman's eyes, but also strength. "Maybe you could start by telling me about your time in Berlin," she suggested.

As Polina gave more and more of herself, tears now rolling down her cheeks, Edna wondered dimly if she might actually be the greatest Russian actress never to take the stage. Yet as Polina talked, Edna also knew they shared an experience of war, atrocity, and loss that would inevitably draw them closer together. Edna couldn't help liking her. She wanted to believe Polina's story was genuine. She couldn't bring herself to imagine this openhearted woman could be so brutally cruel as to tell these stories, if they were not substantially true.

Yet Rome had made Edna wary. There was a still part of her that reserved judgment.

TWENTY FOUR

Wednesday August 12, 1953

At a dirty lowdown little dive called Tony's on the edge of Chinatown, the smell of stale beer and quiet desperation permeated the carpet around the bar where Edna had parked herself to sip on a martini, the bartender's specialty. It wasn't terrible either.

Two seats away, a government worker in a cheap plaid suit was strip-mining the bar-top nut bowl for sustenance. He had already been stripped of his weekly earnings by the hooker who given him the blowjob of his life in the alley outside, then picked his pocket for good measure. He'd been complaining loudly about it for ten minutes, and was showing no signs of letting up. The half dozen patrons with nowhere better to be had lost interest nine minutes ago. Edna didn't mind so much — his complaints offered her some cover.

The phone rang behind the bar and, upon prior arrangement, the barman lifted it onto the counter, answered it to confirm the caller, then handed Edna the receiver.

"How much for the night?" Menzel asked her. He was trying to be funny, but it just came off as sleazy.

"I'm gonna pretend you didn't say that."

"OK, fine. Sorry. How's your Russian doll?"

"Talkative. She wants to be friends."

"She's fishing," he said.

"I like her."

"That's great Edna, you being such a fine judge of character."

"I've been sitting in a seedy bar and fending off indecent proposals to wait for your call. Why do I feel like there's a barstool here with your name on it, old man?"

"I take it your friend knows Sister Josephine?"

"Yes. And also claims to know everything about us."

"Yes, well, I'm afraid that's probably true."

"They're watching my hotel. You told me they were in disarray. I might not have done everything to your satisfaction, but that Roman holiday of ours was never going to work and you only have yourself to blame."

She waited for Menzel's response as the barman finally escorted the broke barfly out to the street. "You are totally compromised, Edna. I'm sorry it's come to this."

It was as close as he would come to an admission of fault. "What do we do?" Edna asked.

"Damned if I know. But you need to step away. Right away."

"What does that mean? You can't fire me, you know that, right?"

He snorted. "I can do whatever I goddamn want, young woman. Your ongoing freedom is entirely at my discretion."

Menzel wasn't admitting to a damn thing.

TWENTY FIVE

F riday August 14, 1953

      Clarence had offered to go with her to New York. It was sweet of him, but there would be no way of explaining their relationship to her mother. Edna wasn't even sure she could explain it to herself, apart from acknowledging he was yet another impossibility in her life.

She hopped off the bus to hear the all-too-familiar crash and grind of the Rockaways' Playland rollercoaster on the other side of the road. It was the best welcome home she could have asked for. How many times had she stood here — beach and boardwalk on one side, Playland on the other. Now it was almost like she was seeing it for the first time. The sea air was both fond and familiar, and all the years of absence simply melted away.

Alice Drake was waiting for her on the stoop of the bungalow that had been the only home Edna had ever known. Both were a welcome sight. She hugged her ma with a force that left the poor woman quite taken aback. "Goodness darling, how strong you are."

"Great to see you mum. Ooh, something smells good!" The aroma of roast beef filled the living room, where she threw herself down on the couch with adolescent abandon.

"Dinner is in half an hour," Alice said. "I'm out tonight, but your father will keep you company."

"Where are you going?"

"Friday is canasta night. A group of us take turns at hosting. It's my turn next Friday, if you're here that long."

Unlikely. "I'm not sure yet ma, we'll see."

There was the same awkwardness between them, but it had been there for so long that neither thought twice about it. A product of their views on life and death being so wildly divergent, together with the fact that Edna had always been daddy's girl. Her mother had long since come to terms with this, along with what she once disdainfully regarded as her husband's lack of ambition. Alice knew Edna would instinctively take her father's side in every argument. Edna knew her ma loved her to the best of her ability and it was this she craved now, more than ever. It broke Edna's heart to think she couldn't tell her family about the tumultuous events of recent months.

"You're looking thin, dear." This, in her mother's eyes, was not a good thing.

"The senator keeps me on the hop," said Edna. "But I've been learning a lot and making new friends."

Mostly Russian, of late.

"Plenty of eligible bachelors on Capitol Hill," her mother said.

Edna laughed and gave her mum another hug. "I think I'd rather marry a carny like you did. Politicians are awful creatures."

Alice slapped her daughter's arm. "Don't call your father that. He's a mechanical engineer."

"Which is a fancy term for grease monkey," Paddy Drake yelled, throwing his arms open to greet his girl.

"Dad!"

The familiar scent of engine oil filled her with joy. It was the smell of her father's pride and joy — the Atom Smasher, the greatest roller-coaster ever built and still the best thrill twenty-five cents could buy. Paddy Drake designed the coaster himself and kept it rolling with the precision of a master craftsman.

At the end of a delicious but somewhat hurried evening meal, they lost Alice to the call of the cards. Paddy and Edna cleaned the kitchen and took a stroll along the boardwalk as the setting sun turned from lilac to purple, and the last of the day's beachgoers made their way off the sand to consider the night ahead.

Paddy could barely walk ten feet without someone yelling his name, or giving him a friendly tap on the shoulder. He knew everyone by name. "This is the part your mother never understood," he told her. "It's what I love, being out here in the world with everything and everyone familiar to me. She thinks it's boring to see the same faces all the time. I couldn't live without it."

Edna threw her arm across his shoulders. "But you're still together. You've found peace with one another."

"They say familiarity breeds contempt. But if you wait around long enough, you slide right on into comfort, and at our age that ain't bad," he said.

"But here's something mum would never tell you: There's no way you two would still be together if you'd done what she wanted and gone into banking or real estate. If you'd done that, contempt would have turned to loathing. Honestly pa, I don't know how anybody stays together as long as you two. It's a genuine mystery to me."

The lights flickered on along the boardwalk like a chain of Christmas lights stretching into infinity. Paddy Drake laughed. "I never get sick of seeing that." He sighed, throwing his daughter a furtive look. "You telling me there's no one special in your life?"

"Special? Too soon to say. But I know ma won't approve."

"Is he poor? No prospects?"

"Worse. He's a priest."

Her father laughed in surprise. "Holy cow, Edna. You kiddin' me? What kinda priest?"

"The Catholic kind," she said. "But he's not active. He's sort of retired."

"Retired? How old is this guy?"

"Early forties. I think."

"Is it serious?"

"Don't think I know what that feels like," she said, catching herself by surprise as tears began to roll down her cheeks.

Paddy pulled her close and gave her a hug. "What's goin' on kid? Something's not right. Is he treating you bad, this priest? So help me, I'll come down there and wrap his rosary round his throat."

"Nothing like that. I've got a lot going on. Senator Ives keeps me on the hop and politics is a minefield. I'm making a lot of mistakes."

"Is that right," he said quietly.

She'd heard that tone before. "What dad? What is it?"

"I tried to call you the other day."

"When?"

"Got through to the senator's office. The nice young gal who answered the phone said you weren't there. I asked when you'd be back. She said she didn't know. I told her I was your dad and that it'd been a while since we'd spoken and I'd been trying to find you. I might have laid it on a bit thick, but I could tell she was holding back on me. Finally, she said, 'I'm not supposed to do this, but give this other phone number a try.' She wouldn't tell me nothin' more than that.

"So, I call the number, cos now I'm fascinated and a little bit scared. I had a feeling something strange was goin' on. When I call this other number, a guy answers. I can hear office noises in the background, but all he says is 'hello'. No business name, no nothin'. I give my name and say I want to speak to my daughter, Edna. And I can tell right away he knows your name. But he says nothin' to me. He just hangs up the phone. When I try to call back, no answer."

Edna wanted so much to open up to him. Could she take the risk? He'd keep her secret if she made him swear to it. But it was too much to ask, especially when so much was already coming apart at the seams. Except now the floodgates were open. The tears began slowly at first, then came in torrents. She ran down the nearest stairs and onto the beach, not wanting anyone to hear and paranoid the CIA were still following her.

Paddy followed her to the water's edge. "Tell me honey. What is it?"

"I can't, dad. I'm not allowed."

His mouth fell open in shock. But he saw the pain in his daughter's eyes. "You can talk to me. I won't tell no one."

She cried out in exasperation. "I know, dad. But I can't. If I do, I'd be putting you in danger."

"You're scaring me, Edna."

"I know. I'm sorry. I shouldn't have come."

"Don't be silly. We're always here for you. Always."

She hugged him again. "Buy me a beer. Put me on that crazy coaster, daddy."

They crossed the road to Rockaways' Playland. The crunch of metal on wood and the screams of laughter and exhilaration were a tonic that filled the silence left by all the words she couldn't say.

But by morning, the silence in Rockaway was deafening. Edna wanted to stay longer, but her head could barely take the pounding from so many thoughts crashing into one another. She woke before dawn and knew it was time to go.

TWENTY SIX

Saturday August 15, 1953

Clarence was knocking on the door to her hotel room within an hour of her arriving back in Washington. Edna let him in, but she was exhausted and made it clear he couldn't stay. He looked like a slapped puppy and she apologized, blaming it on stress.

"How did you know I was here?" she asked, tapping the bed and urging him to sit down next to her.

He sat, looking very sheepish. Hackles raised, Edna demanded he tell her what was up.

"It's Paolo," he said. "He pops in from time to time to look in on you. That's how I knew you were back."

"Jesus. Really? That's creepy."

"I'll tell him to stop. But he does it because he knows I'm worried about you."

"Yeah, well, my problem is I have people watching everything I do." Edna leapt to her feet. "All right, that's it. I'm getting out of here."

"What do you mean?"

"I'm changing hotels. For all I know, this room is bugged. I know for certain it's being watched by the Russians. The CIA too, most likely. They're probably out there giving each other a wave as the shift changes."

"Where will you go?"

"Not telling," she said, taking a perverse pleasure in the cruelty of denying him the knowledge. "But you tell our little friend I'll be calling and he'll need to pay for wherever I end up."

Two hours later, she had a suite at the Carlton. She called Menzel at home and cut him off mid-bluster, telling him bluntly to call her back at the hotel bar in half an hour. Which he did, though he was decidedly unhappy about it.

"What happened to leaving town?" he demanded.

"Turns out my dad has been calling me and having people hang up on him," she returned. "He wants to know what I'm really doing because the bright young thing answering the senator's phone is handing out your phone number."

"I'll sort that out," he said.

"Were you going to tell me he called, or is this just another secret I'm supposed to nut out on my own?"

"I'm not paying for a suite at the Carlton, Edna. It's a waste of resources."

"Don't think I'm worth it?"

"That's not what I said. Sheraton just bought the place. They've put the rates up."

"Either Verus pays," she said, "or I start reconsidering my future in journalism."

She could have cut the silence on the line with a butter knife. "Don't be a fool."

"Just pay the goddamn bill." Edna hung up without giving him a chance to answer, then calmly retrieved the key to her new abode from the night manager.

Her new home had a grand piano and a large red couch, upon which one could lie down and go to sleep if one was too drunk to make it all the way to the bedroom. She considered calling Clarence, then figured she might as well wait to see if he turned up uninvited.

She stayed inside the hotel suite for two days, room service all the way — five-star dining and French champagne. Paulson found her late on the second day, by which time her lunchtime bubbles buzz had metamorphized into a woozy torpor.

He knocked for several minutes before she got around to answering. From the look of apprehension on his face, Edna guessed she must look a fright.

"Come on in. I take it ghost boy told you where to find me."

"Donald, actually."

"Well, seeing as you're here now, you might as well take me to bed," she told him, taking him by the hand and leading the way into her large and elaborate boudoir. She fell face first down on the bedspread and woke to find herself stripped to her underwear and tucked in with the lights out.

She got up, wondering where he'd gone. He was asleep on her red couch.

"What are you doing out here?" she asked, seeing she'd woken him. "Am I that disgusting?"

"I thought you needed your space," he said. "But I also thought it might not be such a great idea to leave you alone."

"Jesus, Clarence, I'm not going to do myself a mischief if that's what you're worried about."

"Go to bed," he told her. "Get some sleep."

She stayed in bed until noon, by which time he was gone. She'd no doubt scared the life out of him. Needy and unhappy women probably weren't his forte. Her two-day bender had shaken something loose. It dawned on her a life of luxury might not be all it seemed. To put it plainly, Edna was sick to death of all of it.

TWENTY SEVEN

Wednesday August 19, 1953

It felt good to be back in her old neighborhood, but it felt like folks had become a whole lot angrier along M Street since the last time she'd visited Southwest D.C. Several people stared back at her with obvious disdain as they passed by.

In shop windows and all along the pavement, placards spelt out the reason for their anger. The posters decried the Redevelopment Land Agency's compulsory acquisition of property in the area, and called on neighborhood residents and business operators to write their local congressman to voice their opposition.

Fat lot of good it would do them.

A similar sign welcomed every customer at the entrance to Mamma Rey's café. A young man behind the counter gave her the evil eye when she approached. "OK if I just pick a booth?" she asked, sensing this might not be the day to take anything for granted. He stared at Edna like he wanted to tell her to take her business elsewhere.

"Edna!" Mamma Rey emerged from the kitchen and opened her arms to offer her old neighbor a hug. In another life, Edna had lived next door above the tailor shop. She'd been one of Mamma's best customers.

"Good to see you, Mamma," said Edna, relieved.

Mama Rey slapped the boy responsible on the arm. "What you frowning at, Moses? Ain't never seen a white girl up close? She won't bite."

"At least, not on the first date," said Edna.

Mamma roared with laughter. "Sit yourself down girl. Coffee coming right up. Where you been, anyway?"

The tables were as neat and tidy as ever, but there was a layer of dust over everything. Edna had never seen that here before. It was as if the staff had already decided the place was destined to become rubble.

Helen Barber walked in as Mamma arrived with the coffee pot. Helen slid into the booth and offered a thin smile at the proprietor. "I'd love a cup too, please." The last time they'd met here, Barber had been less than civil to Mamma. Seemed both of them still remembered that day. Mamma huffed and poured, and left without saying another word.

"Been a while, Helen. How are you?"

"Somebody just spat at me on the street," Barber said.

"This demolition thing is getting ugly," said Edna, pulling out a pack of Lucky Strikes and tapping the bottom to pull out a cigarette. She offered the pack to Helen. "Want one?"

Barber shook her head. "I'm trying to quit."

"Wow," said Edna. "Good luck with that." She put the cigarette in her mouth and lit it.

Mamma was wiping a table nearby and overheard their initial exchange. "They gonna bulldoze our whole neighborhood," she said. "Folks mad they got no say in it."

"Surely the Government will pay a fair price," said Barber.

Mamma scoffed. "What country you livin' in? They call this area a black ghetto and they payin' ghetto rates. But people gotta live. We still gotta move someplace else."

"Where are you gonna go, Mamma?" Edna asked.

"I'm moving to Barry Farm." This was on the other side of the Anacostia River, where the land was cheaper. The black community had been growing there for some time. "My sister got a house over there. I'm gonna buy another one close by."

Edna nodded. "And you'll reopen the café over there?"

"You know it, sugar."

"I'll be there on the opening day. Meantime, I've been dying for a plate of your fried chicken. It might be my last time for a while."

"Comin' right up, sugar."

Barber stuck with black coffee. She waited for Mamma to hit the kitchen before leaning in across the table, "I can't believe you dragged me out here. Again. I feel like a trespasser in my own city."

"That's how everyone feels around here," said Edna.

The previous year, Barber had fed Edna a story on UFOs. They'd met here to talk about it. But it was fair to say black civil rights were not big on Barber's political agenda.

"How's work?" Edna asked.

Barber eyed her suspiciously. "Same as always. How about you? Senator Irving treating you right?"

"That's sort of what I wanted to speak to you about. My work has brought me into contact with some sensitive information."

"I thought you were finished with journalism?"

"I'm talking remarkable information, Helen. Very like what we were talking about last year."

Barber was managing editor of the Air Intelligence Digest. She was a useful source of credible information, and well-connected.

"You mean flying saucers," Barber realized.

"Exactly."

"How exactly is Senator Ives is tied up in this?" Barber asked skeptically. Ives wasn't on any Senate intelligence committees.

"It's a long and complicated story," Edna began, "but Irving Ives is not the main game. Look, you helped me last year with getting sensitive information out to the public. You didn't have to do that, but you did it anyway and I've always admired you for that."

Barber smiled. "I'm waiting for the punchline here."

"I'm on the inside, Helen. Right on the inside. At the coal face. I can't say more than that. Not yet. But I want to know — if I was to tell you things, maybe even show you things — would you be willing to pass it on to the press?"

"You want to use me for cover."

"I suppose that's fair, yes."

"Meaning if the shit hits the fan, I'm the one who gets sucked into the propeller blades," Barber concluded. "I'm thrilled, Edna."

Edna sighed. "No, that's not what I meant at all."

Helen Barber finished off her coffee, wiped her mouth with a napkin, and then calmly pushed the cup across the table towards Edna. "You, my girl, can go straight to hell." She moved to stand up.

"Not so fast," Edna pleaded. "Look, I'd make it worth your while."

Barber frowned. "How?"

"Everybody needs something. What do you need, Helen?"

Barber rose slowly to her feet. "Nothing from you. For all I know, you're trying to entrap me into committing an act of treason."

"Don't be ridiculous."

"McCarthy's got people everywhere. My life is in a good place right now, not that you care. I'm seeing a man. Work is going well. Not great, but not so bad. I'm moving into a nice apartment in a better part of town. If you think I'm going to toss it all out the window, you've got rocks in your head. Have a nice life, Edna."

Edna opened her mouth to object, but no words came out. She just watched as Barber walked out the door.

When she thought about it afterwards, Edna really wished she'd said something — anything at all.

TWENTY
EIGHT

Wednesday August 19, 1953

Mamma's fried chicken was so good it was hard to feel too disappointed about Barber's refusal. It had really only ever been a long shot. But the act of approaching Helen Barber also underlined the risk Edna was taking in trying to peddle state secrets, under the watchful gaze of people who most certainly didn't have her best interests at heart.

Returning to Southwest D.C. had been her attempt at holding the surveillance at bay. The CIA wasn't in the business of hiring black people — they barely acknowledged the women in their ranks. She likewise figured it wouldn't be easy for the Russians to do so on short notice. City authorities had been steering clear of M Street for weeks, because right now a white face in this neighborhood was not a welcome sight. Given the simmering hostility, that might have been prudent circumspection on the part of police. It was more likely the cops had just washed their hands of the area until something happened that was too big for them to ignore.

Unfortunately, this meant she would have to find her way back to her hotel through several blocks of angry people who saw her lily-white face as the embodiment of things to come, and were quite happy to let her know about it.

Mamma must have sensed her concern as Edna paid up. "You gonna be all right, sugar? Why don't I get Moses to give you a lift down-town?"

Edna thought about the kid dropping her off at one of the city's most exclusive hotels. That didn't sit right. "I'll be fine, Mamma. I'm sure there are still people out there who know me."

Mamma raised an eyebrow. "You sure?"

"Tell you what," Edna said, "if I'm back in five minutes, you know I've changed my mind."

She was half a block from the café when she first noticed the tail. She stopped in front of a shop window to check the reflection, and in the corner of her eye caught him stopping to check his shoelaces at exactly the same moment. A black man. The face wasn't familiar, but he was well dressed. He didn't look like someone aiming to pick a fight; he looked like he'd been told to follow her and wasn't very good at it.

Edna took a left turn up Third Street, still weathering angry faces and the occasional cuss thrown in her direction. It was alarming and off-putting, but it didn't feel dangerous. Not compared to having a Russian gun pointed in her face. She took a right turn into L Street and hid in a doorway to wait for her tail to pass.

As he came into view, she calmly asked him, "Why are you following me?"

The man leapt in the air like she'd lobbed a brick at him. "You scared the heck out of me," he told her indignantly. "I ain't followin' you."

"Like hell." She stepped out and grabbed him by the collar of his brown jacket. "Who sent you?"

Two old men walked past, one whispering to the other and point-ing. They thought she was just a honky, wailing on her sugar daddy. "Get your damn hands off me," he complained, flicking her hands away and trying to leave.

"Take one more step and I'll yell rape," she said. "Black man, white woman — who do you think the cops are gonna believe?"

He stopped. Edna knew then he was an amateur. Anyone half smart would have kept moving. The cops weren't getting here any time soon, but he was terrified just because she'd invoked the law. "Who sent you?" she asked again.

He turned around, looking nervous. "It was Mr Menzel, OK?"

"What's your name?"

"I ain't gonna tell you that."

Not completely stupid then. "OK fine, so just tell me how this works. Do you report back hourly, daily... What?"

"Look, all I know is he pay me to watch you and say if you go back to your old neighborhood. He says I should get you out of trouble if you need it. That's it."

Edna sighed. As if she didn't already have enough to worry about. Menzel had outdone himself this time; setting a man on her tail with no apparent skill in surveillance, but assuming he'd blend in because he was black.

But Donald Menzel didn't mix widely in the black community — how had he found this man? Maybe someone from Lee Tavon's catering company? Tavon hired black staff exclusively. Tavon might have even agreed to it, if he thought it would help Edna. But this guy was like a flashing beacon over her head, alerting everyone to her approach. The professionals didn't need to follow her – they could follow him instead.

"You got a car?" she asked the guy.

"Yeah."

"You know where I'm staying?"

He didn't want to answer, but eventually nodded.

"OK," she said. "You're giving me a lift back there. Then you're done."

TWENTY NINE

Friday August 21, 1953

The police found Helen Barber's body just before dawn.

A neighbor had called, saying he heard gunshots. But it could only have been one shot, because it looked very much like Barber had blown her own brains out with the pistol found on the floor beside her. Officers had to force their way inside her bungalow. They were greeted with the disturbing sight of a corpse with a cat on it, hissing and howling at them like a creature possessed.

It looked like a clear case of suicide. No signs of forced entry, no indication of a struggle. Just a half-empty whiskey bottle on her kitchen bench, and a crystal tumbler sitting on the arm of her couch. As far as the officers at the scene were concerned, there was no point digging any deeper. Case closed.

But homicide detective Vincent Kaplan wasn't about to let such a blithe presumption dictate his approach to a potential crime scene. One look at the Pentagon ID in Barber's purse told him there could be more to this than any first impressions dictated. He insisted on doing things by the book. Which meant door-knocking all the neighbors, starting with the man who had called the police in the first place.

Everyone said pretty much the same thing: Barber had been a loner, a quiet neighbor who kept to herself. One or two mentioned there had been a man on the scene, not for long — a couple of months tops. That was enough to pique Kaplan's interest.

It might have taken the detective days to penetrate the Pentagon's outer defenses in order to speak to the folks who knew Barber best, if not for the fact that Kaplan knew Jack Peterborough, the US Special Police captain in charge of Pentagon security. Peterborough was a former murder cop, and intimately aware of the many ways politics could play havoc with police work. Two hours after their initial phone conversation, Peterborough met Kaplan personally at the Pentagon's river entrance to escort Kaplan through a labyrinth of corridors and divisions, to the tiny windowless office of the Air Intelligence Digest.

Peterborough sat in as backup, while Kaplan interviewed the three staffers who had worked closely with Barber and knew her best. They were all shocked and deeply troubled to hear of the violent death of their boss. But none of them could shed light on whether she might be motivated to pull the trigger herself. The first two were unaware — they were in fact, surprised — that she'd had a man in her life. That seemed to shock them almost as much as the news of her death.

But Kaplan got lucky with interview number three. Jean Williams was officially Barber's secretary, but in fact had long been helping Barber with anything and everything to get the monthly publication to print. They'd worked closely with one another for more than five years. Williams knew of Barber's boyfriend.

"I'd like to speak to him and break the news gently," Kaplan explained.

Jean said his name was Havermeyer. "Lieutenant Toby Havermeyer. He works for the Air Force chief of staff, General Twining."

If news was already travelling fast through the Pentagon corridors, it hadn't reached Havermeyer's desk by the time they arrived. He didn't see it coming. He was a bookish, slightly overweight man in his late forties, with a soft handshake. Didn't look like much of a military man. When Kaplan told him of his girlfriend's demise, Havermeyer fell to pieces.

Grief and shock could be faked to a point, but Havermeyer crumbled; he wasn't holding anything back. Kaplan read his response as genuine. Nevertheless, with no small degree of regret, Kaplan threw salt in the wound, telling the lieutenant it appeared she had committed suicide by shooting herself in the head. He watched the man closely for any signs of guilt.. But Havermeyer surprised him by saying suicide made no sense at all. Kaplan made a mental note to circle back to that. He asked how long they'd been seeing one another.

"Not long," Havermeyer said. "A couple of months."

"I see you're wearing a wedding band," said Kaplan.

Havermeyer sighed. "I keep meaning to take that off. Old habits." He explained how a year earlier his wife had run off with the husband of a close friend. Divorce papers were pending. He'd known Barber for several years, and for most of that time only considered her a colleague and a friend. Romance had blossomed after Barber offered to take him out one night to cheer him up, knowing what his wife had done.

All details that were both plausible and easy enough to double check, Kaplan figured. "You said before it made no sense. What did you mean by that?"

"I don't believe Helen was suicidal," Havermeyer said. "And whiskey? Forget about it. She barely drank at all and she particularly hated whiskey. That was her father's poison, and she loathed the man. The other thing is, she didn't own a gun."

"You sure about that? Isn't it possible she had a pistol and never told you about it?

Havermeyer shook his head emphatically. Explained how Barber had laid bare her family's sordid history. Her father had drunk himself to death — Helen had somewhat shamefully admitted to being glad of it. The man had terrorized his family for years. "Helen was scared of guns. Her father had a revolver. Her mother would hide the bullets."

An interesting story. And convenient. "How exactly did this come up in conversation?" Kaplan wondered casually.

"I'd offered to buy her a pistol for her own protection," said Havermeyer. "She wouldn't hear of it. I asked her why, and she told me."

"What sort of pistol would you have bought her?" Kaplan asked.

"A Beretta," he said. "They're lightweight, easy to conceal. Not particularly accurate over long distances but fine for..." Havermeyer stopped and a look of panic crossed his face. "Is that what she used? A Beretta?"

Kaplan kept him sweating. "I'm afraid I'm not at liberty to divulge that information."

It had been a thirty-eight special. More powerful than a Beretta, and far more damaging to the human skull at point-blank range.

"Lieutenant Havermeyer, when was the last time you saw Helen?"

"Wednesday night. I remember because she was angry."

Kaplan raised an eyebrow. "Go on."

"She'd had coffee that day with a woman. I forget her name, but she used to be a reporter for the *Times-Herald*. Now works as a senatorial researcher."

"Which senator?"

"Ives," Havermeyer remembered. "Irving Ives. Helen and this woman had history."

Kaplan knew a woman who used to be a *Times-Herald* reporter. She'd helped him track down a killer. "What sort of history?"

Havermeyer grimaced and shook his head to indicate he wasn't sure. "Helen said it was better I didn't know. I'm trying to remember the woman's name. Something to do with ducks."

"Do you mean Drake, by any chance?" Kaplan suggested.

"Yeah — Drake, that's it. First name started with an E — maybe Emily or Edie..."

"Edna," said Kaplan.

Havermeyer nodded. "Yeah. Edna Drake. That's her name."

THIRTY

Saturday August 22, 1953

Donald Menzel showed up at Edna's door with a look on his face like the harbinger of doom. She ushered him quickly inside. He wasted no time in telling her about Helen Barber's death. The news came as a terrible blow — she immediately felt responsible. But shock quickly turned to anger. "Mind telling me why you're the one breaking this news to me?" Edna asked.

Menzel looked like he'd been expecting the question. "The police are looking for you. They know you met with her on Wednesday, and that Miss Barber came away from the meeting angry. Edna, I want to help you, but I really need to know what's going on here."

Edna almost laughed. "I'd have thought your man told you all about it after dropping me home."

Menzel stared at her blankly. "What are you talking about?"

"Oh, come on. Don't go coy on me, Donald. You were having me tailed. I spotted your man and confronted him." Menzel just stared at her and she could almost see the wheels turning in his head. Edna walked to the window and stared out at the street. "Was it you? Did you have her killed?"

"For God's sake," he cried, "you think me capable of that?"

"I didn't tell her anything, although I admit I wanted to. But she didn't want to hear it."

"Jesus Christ, Edna. Do you really think I'm that cold-blooded?"

Edna turned to face him. "I do. I think you'd do it to show me what can happen if I don't toe the line."

"You need to leave town," he said. "Today. I'm here to make that happen. Under no circumstances are you to talk to the police, do you hear me?"

"Why not?"

"Because I know how your mind works. More to the point, you're not a very convincing liar. If this Detective Kaplan asks you why you were meeting Helen, he'll know if you don't tell him the truth."

"Kaplan? I know him."

"Even more reason to avoid him," said Menzel.

"To cover your tracks."

"I told you, I didn't do this," he said.

"No. Of course not. I believe you."

"Like I said, you're not a convincing liar."

"I'd like you to leave, Donald."

"I've booked you a plane ticket to Los Angeles." He reached into his jacket pocket and pulled out the ticket. "It's under the name Daisy Compton. Your flight leaves in three hours." He held it out. She made no move to take it from him, so he placed it on her bed.

"How much does Kaplan know?" Edna asked.

"He has your name. He knows you work for Senator Ives. Thankfully they stuck to protocol and gave him the address of your former apartment on M Street. That's a dead end."

"Yes, but it's also right next door to the café where Helen and I met the other day. This just gets better and better. Are you trying to make me look guilty?"

"I'm trying to keep you out of jail."

"I didn't do anything."

"Would you rather I had them send him over here?" Edna shook her head. "Look, all we've done is buy you some time. Kaplan's a good cop, he's going to find you eventually if you stay here." Menzel let that sink in for a moment. "As for prison, for all I know you've already broken your security oath by talking to this woman. That's a life sentence. Maybe it's lucky for you she's dead."

"Lucky?" Edna said in disgust. "I told her nothing. Mamma Rey will back me on that. Our meeting was over in a few minutes. Not a lot of time to divulge our secrets. They need some explaining."

"I'll send someone to talk to Kaplan and feed him a version of the truth, but I need time to work out what that is and how to make it sound convincing." Donald Menzel had shame written all over him.

Edna was scared now; she needed to get as far away from him as possible. "All right, fine," she said. "I'll go to California. But only for a few days."

Menzel looked relieved. "Good. I'm glad. I'll go down now and pay your hotel bill. You should leave as quickly as you can." He touched her on the arm in an effort to be empathetic. "It's the right move, Edna, believe me."

He made her flesh crawl; Edna didn't believe him for a second. "Tell me this, Donald: if you didn't kill her, who did?"

"No idea," he said. "I've got Clarence and MJ-12 working on that as we speak."

THIRTY ONE

Saturday August 22, 1953

She threw the dead bolt across her door the moment Menzel left, then opened a window and stuck her head out, making sure she was clearly visible from the street. Another warm day ahead. She watched as Menzel left the hotel, then pulled her head back inside and began packing her bags. She was in the hotel foyer less than fifteen minutes later.

Edna was relieved to discover he had already paid the bill, although she had no intention of taking up his offer on the plane ticket. Whatever was going on here, she wasn't about to place her life in his hands. If he did mean her harm, sending her to Los Angeles was a great way to get the job done. That city was a den of vice and corruption. She only had one place left to go. Two places actually, but one final destination.

In Washington's best hotels, there were many things money could buy. One of them was having errands run no questions asked. She left her suitcase at the front desk, slipped the concierge a five dollar bill and asked him to wait half an hour before taking the bag to Union Station and depositing it in a locker. She said she'd be back to pick up the locker key. He nodded and smiled like the request was nothing out of the ordinary. She thanked him, then walked to a pay phone and asked the operator to put her through to Detective Vincent Kaplan at city homicide. It was a Saturday, but she knew he'd be at work.

"You're playing hard to get, Edna," he told her.

"I didn't know you were looking for me until about half an hour ago."

"But you know why."

"That was news to me too, detective. I honestly don't know what to say. I feel…"

"Responsible?" he suggested.

"Yes," she said, "though probably not in the way you think."

"You were one of the last people to see her alive. You and her boyfriend. But I don't think he's got a clue what's going on."

"I had no reason to want her dead. But I think she was killed because someone knew about our meeting and didn't like it."

"What did you tell her?"

"Nothing."

"Yet here we are. Why would she be killed just for talking to you?"

"I'm not at liberty to say," Edna told him.

"Where are you? Are you in trouble?"

"It's looking likely, yes."

"Let me come pick you up."

"No. Listen, Vincent," Edna said, lowering her voice, "I work for an intelligence organization. I can't believe I'm hearing myself say that, but it's true. Somebody thought I was feeding secrets to Helen Barber. I didn't. Maybe I wanted to, but I didn't. These secrets — they're a big deal."

"I can get a subpoena to order Senator Ives to talk to us."

"Ives has nothing to do with it. My work for him is just a cover for what I'm really doing."

"You're not helping either of us here."

"I don't know who killed Helen. Not for certain." Though she certainly had her suspicions. "But I mean to find out. When I do, you'll be the first to know."

Kaplan didn't like that idea one little bit. "If I don't see you by first thing Monday morning and I have to come looking, I'm going to charge you with obstruction of justice and being an accessory after the fact."

"Two days it is," she said and hung up.

Edna caught a taxi to Chinatown and walked around for a while, jumping in and out of shops, then caught another taxi to Union Station. She was headed for the ticket queue, when a man tapped her on the arm. "You want a taxi miss?"

He didn't look like a taxi driver.

"Sure," she said, following him out to a parking bay at the northern end of the station. He took her to one of three identical cars parked alongside one another. There were drivers in two of them. He opened the back door to the third and ushered her in, then all three cars headed south along First Street at the same time. They turned sharply into G Street, then south again on North Capitol Street, before splitting three ways at Massachusetts Avenue.

Her driver went straight ahead for two blocks, turned right into E Street, then quickly right again into McCollough Court. A gang of workmen stepped onto the road as they passed, placing a road-closure barrier that prevented any more traffic from following. Her driver pulled into the rear parking lot of a restaurant; they were no longer visible to the street.

"The rear entrance is just across the way," he told her, pointing. "Here, put these on." He handed her a black scarf and a pair of sunglasses. She wrapped the scarf around her head and put on the glasses. "She is waiting in room 603," he said.

Thirty seconds later, Edna was back inside the foyer of the Commodore Hotel. This time, she took the elevator.

Involving the Russians was a risk, but it was the quickest way to lose the Americans on her tail. Now she only had one tail to worry about.

Given the resources employed to bring her here, it was abundantly clear that Polina had been lying when she'd said she was acting alone.

The Russian agent answered the door smiling. "Come in." The room was identical to the one Edna had stayed in several floors below. She wondered how long Polina had been here, and why she'd stayed after Edna had moved to the Carlton. They had known where Edna was all along — opening the window of her suite and popping her head out was the pre-arranged signal for a meeting.

"I shouldn't be here," Edna decided.

"Nonsense," said Polina. "No such thing as shouldn't. We drink, we talk. You say what you want, I respond."

"The police are after me. A friend of mine was killed. I think it was because she met with me."

The Russian nodded. "I know," she said. "Everybody knows this." Polina opened a bottle of vodka and poured two shots.

"Killing doesn't bother you much, does it?" Edna asked her.

"You really need to ask?" She downed her shot in one go.

Edna followed suit. It burnt, but it felt good. She pulled out a cigarette and lit it.

"Careful," Polina warned, "vodka and cigarette can be lethal combination." She smiled. Gallows humor.

Maybe it was her imagination, but Edna couldn't help feeling the Russian agent's accent was becoming more obvious. The Long Island lockjaw was long gone. Was Polina letting her guard down? Edna sat down on the lounge chair beside the bed, and Polina poured them both another drink.

"Stalin had millions of Russians killed," Polina said. "He had a system. Sometimes there were quotas we had to meet. We killed for no reason other than to control. He was worse than Hitler in the treatment of his own people. He was irrational. Insane. Hated criticism of any sort. He terrified even his closest comrades because he played them off against one another. Yet today, all across Russia, he is beloved.

Hailed as our greatest leader of all time. Why is that, I wonder?" She downed another shot and poured again, holding out her hand for Edna's glass.

"Because people prefer the legend," said Edna.

"Yes. Also, because he got away with it," said Polina. "You Americans did nothing. Britain did nothing. You let it happen. In our world of secrets, death is always by your side. You must not let it stop you doing your work."

There was something broken in this woman. It kept Edna on her guard. They talked some more about cold war politics. Polina said her country might have its faults, but did at least treat men and women as equals. "Your men do not treat you well," Polina concluded.

Feeling this was a path in the conversation best avoided, Edna changed the subject. "What does Russia know about UFOs?"

"We know the Roswell crash was real, that you have saucer wreckage and bodies. We know, of course, you still have the saucer stolen from Lebanon by Bill Donovan and your lover.

"You mean they stole it before you could."

"Exactly," Polina said, offering a semi-soporific grin.

"Have you retrieved any craft of your own?" Edna asked.

"Come work with us and you'll see."

"You mean like Kim Philby works for you?"

The name appeared to catch Polina off guard for a moment. "British intelligence found Philby innocent of this."

"Yes, but what do you say about it?" Edna persisted.

Polina looked away. "If I was running MI6, I'd put a bullet in his head." Her eyes were cold as ice. "You can never be too careful."

A confirmation of sorts. "I don't think I'm ready to put myself in that position," said Edna.

"Don't take too long to decide. You came to me, remember?" Polina pulled open the curtains to reveal the top of the Capitol Building dome in the distance, and stood staring out the window. "You and I know the real world is not what we see out this window. Communist, capitalist — none of this matters."

"Try saying that to your boss and see how far it gets you," said Edna. Polina turned around and almost lost her balance. If this was an act, it was a bad one. "Did you tail Helen Barber after we met for coffee?" Edna asked.

Polina nodded.

"What did you see?"

"It was an American who killed her. A contract killer."

Edna stared at her in horror. "Who would do that?"

"CIA. Verus. Take your pick," said Polina.

"Are you sure?"

"They saw you talking. They send you message. No more talk."

"Why should I believe you?"

The Russian sat down roughly on her bed. "I want you to trust me, Edna. I help you, one day you help me. Look into my eyes." They were bloodshot, pupils dilated; it was hard to get a good read on her. "I am telling the truth. In our business, you must know truth when you see it."

But Polina was so drunk the only truth Edna could see was self-loathing. Edna poured two more drinks and handed one to her. "Drink up," she urged, holding the glass to her lips. When the Russian was distracted, Edna emptied her shot glass on the carpet.

"Why did you come to me today?" Polina demanded.

"Because I needed your help to get away," said Edna truthfully.

"Is not enough," the Russian agent told her. "We go to much trouble to bring you here. This is not how friendship works. You must give me more." The booze was a truth serum; it was undermining Polina's cool demeanor.

Edna poured one more time. She thrust the glass at the Russian, then threw back her own shot theatrically before staggering toward the bathroom. She closed the door, spat the vodka in the sink and waited a while. When she emerged two minutes later, Polina was still sitting on the bed, looking very much under the weather.

Edna sat down beside her in the armchair. "I'm tired. That vodka has gone to my head. I need to rest." She slumped back and closed her eyes, making like she was ready to take a nap. But she didn't close them all the way and saw it had the desired effect on Polina, who lay down on the bed.

Polina mumbled in Russian, like she was having a conversation with someone else and trying to make up her mind about something. There had to be someone else listening in. Eventually, Polina's breath evened out and Edna knew she was asleep.

Edna rose slowly from her chair, trying desperately to remain silent so as not to wake the Russian. But the room door posed a problem. She didn't want to close it behind her because the noise would alert them, but she was afraid to leave it open in case a draft forced it to slam, which would be worse. She grabbed one of Polina's shoes and shoved it under the door like a wedge, leaving it open just enough to squeeze out.

She only needed to be a couple of minutes ahead of them.

She took the stairs to the first floor, anxious not to run into one of Polina's henchmen and unsure of what they would do if she did. There was a restaurant on this level; a service elevator went from here down to the loading dock.

The hotel was just across the road from Union Station. Hidden behind her Russian scarf and sunglasses, her heart pounding in her ribcage like it was ready to burst out, Edna crossed the road and entered via the station's main doors. Ignoring the ticket booths, she headed straight out again to the line of taxis waiting outside. She took a taxi across town to Garfinckel's department store, right by the White House, and spent as long as she dared perusing high-end fashion. Purchasing a black scarf and a hat, she donned both before jumping another cab towards her final destination.

Clarence Paulson looked both pleased and mortified to find her on his doorstep. "I have nowhere else to go," she told him apologetically.

He ushered her in without a word and closed the door. "Does anyone know you're here?"

"The Russians, maybe. I tried my best to lose them, but I can't be certain. I set up a meeting with Polina because it was the only way I could think of to shake the CIA."

"Meaning the CIA now thinks you're working for the Soviets."

"Don't forget the police," she reminded him. "They think I'm responsible for Helen Barber's murder."

Paulson shook his head. "Well, I hope Donald will set them straight on that."

"Not if he's the one who had her killed."

Paulson shook his head a second time. "He wouldn't do that."

"I'm not so sure," she said. "Don't forget, he's still covering his own tracks. He doesn't want anyone to know the Roman debacle was his idea."

Paulson rubbed his chin pensively. "All right then, what's the next move?"

The room darkened before she could open her mouth to respond, confirming her suspicion that Paolo Favaloro had been listening in. He appeared before them human-sized. Edna smiled. Paolo might be terrifying, but she also knew he was the smartest person in the room.

She could tell from the look in his eyes he already knew what she required.

THIRTY TWO

S unday August 23, 1953

Sherman Adams awoke early to a shock. Standing at the foot of his bed was the tallest man he had ever seen. For quite some time, Adams was convinced he must be dreaming.

"Good morning Mr Adams. My name is Paolo Favaloro."

Adams had no idea what this giant intruder could want, and he figured it could be nothing good. Yet Adams was a man who hung his hat on his powers of persuasion; diplomacy might be the thing. "Good morning, Mr Favaloro. Would you mind telling me what you're doing in my bedroom?"

"First of all, and most importantly," said Favaloro, "you should know I am not really here."

This gave Adams pause. "You're not?"

"No." Favaloro took a step closer.

Adams sat bolt upright in bed. "That's close enough, please."

But Favaloro didn't stop. He sat upon the edge of the bed, close enough to touch. "Please, reach out your hand," he demanded, holding out his own.

Adams moved slowly toward a handshake, suspecting this was a precursor to violence, but knowing he was trapped. To his shock and astonishment, he found only thin air where Paolo Favaloro's hand should be. He began to wave his hand about more freely and found it moved through him like...he wasn't really there. It was at that point Adams realized there was no indent on the bed where Favaloro's backside touched the sheets.

"What the hell?" Adams cried out, scared he was seeing a ghost.

"I wish you no harm, sir," Favaloro assured him. "In fact, as you might surmise, I am incapable of inflicting physical injury."

"How...?" Adams began, his question derailing after the first syllable.

"While there are many secrets in this world to which you and your president are privy," said Paolo, "there is much you do not know. First of all, I am not dead. I am very much alive."

Adams wished his wife Rachel was here to see this, instead of back home in New Hampshire. He found himself flummoxed; she would know what to make of it.

"I come to you," Favaloro continued, "on behalf of the Verus Foundation's representative, Edna Drake. She wishes to meet with you in her office, but circumstances currently prevent her from arranging the meeting in person."

Adams blinked hard. He knew exactly why Drake was indisposed — the latest CIA report was still in his briefcase. She was the last person he wanted inside the West Wing. "Who are you, Mr Favaloro, and what do you have to do with any of this?"

"I am a man of old. In the Bible, my kind were called the Nephilim. We were the sons and daughters of Anu, the children of the Ryl who lay with human women to produce hybrid offspring. I have been alive on Earth for six thousand years."

Adams rubbed his hand through his hair, realizing with some degree of annoyance he was not looking his best. Nobody ever saw him this way. "Steady on now, this is all a lot to take in. And none of what you just said went close to answering my question."

"There is no easy way to do so," Favaloro replied. "I am alive. Not just in spirit, but in flesh and blood. In your mind this is impossible, yet here I am before you as proof. In spirit, I am free to roam the world. In flesh, I remain locked inside Archivum Apostolicum Vaticanum, the vaults kept hidden by the Papists in Rome. Edna Drake was sent to Rome by Verus to secure my liberation. Alas, the Russians were waiting."

Adams felt a chill of rising suspicion. "When you say sent by Verus, you mean Donald Menzel. He knows who — and what — you are?"

Favaloro nodded slowly.

"Yet he never thought to mention as much to the President," said Adams.

"This is the very topic of conversation that Edna Drake had in mind for your meeting."

Adams thought about it. "She's been implicated in a murder."

"Only by association. She had no hand in the killing."

"That may be," said Adams, "but she's radioactive right now. I'm not about to let her walk into the White House — the press would have a field day. And right now, I'm struggling to think of a way Washington's most wanted woman could have a secret meeting with the world's most conspicuous man."

"Miss Drake has thought of a way. But it will require the cooperation of your Secret Service."

THIRTY
THREE

S unday August 23, 1953

The alleyway was empty as Lee Tavon slipped through the rear gate of Verus Foundation headquarters. It was still early in the morning and a light sprinkle of rain had started to fall, which was a stroke of luck for someone trying very hard to remain unnoticed. Lee knew the ways to get inside people's heads, make them forget they'd ever seen him, but these memories could never be completely erased — merely hidden from view. It was always better not to be seen at all.

Donald Menzel was waiting at the staff rear entrance. His face was glowing red with the raging fury he was struggling to contain. Tavon merely nodded and made his way up the stairs towards Menzel's study.

"I assume the Russians are watching you too," said Menzel, who viewed Edna Drake's dealings with the Soviets as another sign she was in over her head. Her incompetence and naivety had betrayed them all.

Tavon said he had seen no sign of the Russians. "She has been careful to avoid me since returning from Rome. Which is why she felt safe in sending me here today."

But Menzel was in no mood to forgive. "I've got the CIA and the White House ordering me to turn her over. Meanwhile, she's AWOL. I tried to get her on a flight to California, but I'm told she never showed up at the airport."

"She's having a hard time knowing who to trust right now," said Tavon.

"Is that coming from Edna's friend, or from the lead representative of the Outherian people on Earth?"

"I am here as both."

"Meaning she thinks I had Helen Barber killed to teach her a lesson." Menzel shook his head in disgust. "Maybe I should have. But goddamn it, Lee, I had no idea those two were meeting."

Tavon nodded. He was skilled in the art of telepathy, could literally see the difference between truth and lie; it was why Edna had asked him to be here. Tavon saw that Menzel believed what he was saying; there was no hint of deception in his voice. To the contrary, he was livid at being wrongly accused of a murder conspiracy, by a woman who'd been actively seeking to break her own vow of secrecy.

"Who do you think killed Helen Barber?" Tavon asked.

"The way I see it," said Menzel, "there are three possibilities. Four if you include suicide, but the police don't believe she shot herself and neither do I. Which leaves the CIA, the Russians, or a crime of passion."

"But you're not talking about Barber's new man," Tavon realized.

"No. I'm wondering about Clarence Paulson."

"Why would Clarence want to harm her?"

"Passion can do strange things to normal men. But Paulson is a country mile from normal. He's fallen in love with Edna and doesn't want anyone coming between them. More to the point, he won't like the idea of his lover going to jail for an act of misbegotten journalistic zeal."

"Edna thinks you were having her followed."

Menzel bristled. "I told you," he said, "I didn't know she met with Helen Barber."

He was being cagey now.

"A black man was following her," said Tavon. "When she confronted him, he mentioned you by name."

Menzel laughed. "Edna spotted this man tailing her? If that's the case, he wanted to be seen. Her street skills aren't that good."

Tavon had to admit he had a point. "Allow himself to be caught — then claim to be working for you."

Menzel nodded. "The only other point I would make here is that the CIA has done about as much recruiting in the black community as the Ku Klux Klan."

"Which cuts your list of possibilities down to two," said Tavon.

THIRTY FOUR

Sunday August 23, 1953

Well aware of how disturbing it could be for humans to witness a man materialize from thin air, Lee Tavon had warned Edna Drake and Clarence Paulson that he would return to them at midday precisely. He did so on time, as promised. They heard the crackling echo of what sounded like distant footsteps immediately preceding his arrival.

This was different to the manifestation of Paolo Favaloro. The air in the room vibrated with a static electric charge — a by-product of the dimensional window opening in a confined space. It acted as a sort of early warning system, for those who knew what to expect.

By prior arrangement, Lee Tavon had established the connection for his portal in Clarence Paulson's own living room. This meant nobody watching the apartment would see him arrive. More importantly, anybody who had tailed Lee to Verus Foundation HQ would be unaware he'd left.

Lee Tavon noted how accepting Edna and Clarence had become of the alien presence. He wanted to take it as a sign of hope. He reached into his pocket and pulled out a small device with a red button, which made a noise like a child's party clicker when he pressed it. "The portal is closed," he told them.

Edna ushered Tavon toward Paulson's dining table, and they talked through his meeting with Menzel. "In short," Tavon finished, "I don't believe Donald is responsible for the murder of Helen Barber. He thinks it is most likely either the CIA, or the Russians."

This gave Edna pause. She'd known all along it was a possibility that Polina Ilyin had been lying, but she had very much hoped otherwise. Not because she held any illusion about the Russians' intentions, but because she liked the woman and thought they had made a genuine connection.

Tavon deliberately avoided mentioning Menzel's third option. He wanted time to get inside Clarence Paulson's head — the priest was staring at Edna, waiting for her to speak.

"I don't think it's the CIA," she said.

"No," Tavon agreed, "it would seem extremely heavy-handed on their part – and unnecessary, given neither of you had yet committed an act of treason."

"But why would the Russians do it?" she asked.

"To drive a wedge between you and your own people," said Tavon. "Do you agree, Clarence?"

Paulson thought about it and nodded. "We saw in Rome what they're capable of. Edna, you said Polina admitted she was one of Stalin's murder squad. Human life is cheap to them."

Tavon touched Edna gently on the arm. "Did you have a clear idea of what you would do if Helen Barber accepted your offer to feed her sensitive information?" He was aware that Edna already blamed herself, but Tavon hoped to elicit a more emotional response from Paulson.

"Not really," she admitted. "I've just had enough of the lies and secrecy. I thought I might be able to force their hand. It was stupid, really."

"Clarence," Tavon asked, "did you try to talk her out of it?"

Paulson sat back in his chair as Paolo Favaloro's warning came to him: *Tavon thinks it might be you.*

Tavon heard it too, though Favaloro's words were only intended for Paulson. Tavon decided to go full frontal. "Paolo is not quite right," he said, "but he's close." He noted the shock on Paulson's face, but saw no sign of guilt. "Donald Menzel told me he thinks there's a chance it was you who murdered Helen," Tavon admitted.

"Is Paolo here?" Edna asked. "Why can't I see him?"

"Because he doesn't wish to be seen," said Tavon.

Edna looked searchingly at Clarence Paulson. "Menzel's wrong, isn't he? Why would you want to hurt Helen?"

"To protect you," Tavon explained. "To stop you going to prison."

Paulson was staring at his hands; they were clasped tightly on top of the table, like he was saying a prayer in anger. "I get so tired of having you all inside my head, I really do. Can't a man have his privacy?" Father Paulson pushed his chair back and stormed off toward the kitchen. "I need a drink."

Edna stared at Lee Tavon in silent alarm. She felt a sharp pain in her chest. Was it possible? Could he really have killed Helen? If he did, she couldn't stay here.

Yet she had nowhere else to go.

Paulson returned with two glasses and a bottle of whiskey, pouring himself a double before sitting down again. He downed it in one go. "Anyone else?" he asked.

Edna and Tavon both said no.

"I didn't touch a hair on that woman's head," Paulson assured them with cast-iron conviction.

Tavon nodded. He looked Edna in the eyes. "Clarence is no killer."

"Which only leaves the Russians," said Paulson.

THIRTY FIVE

M onday August 24, 1953

It was half past three in the morning. Hardly morning at all, more the middle of the night. Presidential Mess Officer Lieutenant Commander Leo Roberts tapped his fingers nervously on the steering wheel. He had his truck parked in the District Grocery Store loading dock at Park View. The store was dark. Normal deliveries wouldn't start for another two hours. This was a one-off.

He didn't normally run deliveries personally, but Roberts couldn't entrust this one to anyone else. The request had come from Elmer Deckard. A request from Deckard could not be refused without a good reason, because it was actually a request from the President himself.

Roberts was trying not to think too hard about how many laws they were breaking. The "package" was about the size of a side of beef and wrapped in hessian. Deckard, dressed for the part in navy grey overalls, had this slung across his shoulder. Only the most astute observer would have noticed a human foot as it appeared briefly from under the hessian during loading. Deckard and the goods were on board a moment later.

The city's hardest workers were the only people on the streets before dawn; Roberts was able to make good time on the journey down town. Charlie Friedman was guarding the Pennsylvania Avenue gate and recognized both Roberts and the delivery truck immediately. He glanced at the navy man's ID briefly and nodded. "Don't usually see you out and about this early, sir."

"Special delivery," said Roberts. "Required the personal touch."

"You sure you're in the right place? Mess deliveries usually go up West Executive Avenue to the basement entrance there."

A jolt of panic up shot Roberts' spine. "You're right, Charlie, but I want to get this inside on the Q-T. We're arranging a lunch that is all hush-hush. I've got a bit to move in, and the front door access is going to be easiest."

Friedman's eyes widened in concern. "You allowed to do that? Mr Adams had my guts for garters last time I let someone in when they weren't supposed to be let in."

Roberts smiled. At least he hoped it was a smile; his guts were churning. "It's all good, Charlie. I've got a letter from Mr Adams saying it's OK. You want to see it?"

"If you don't mind sir."

Roberts tapped his pocket. "I've got it here somewhere."

Charlie Friedman waited. He only had his radio and crossword to go back to; he had all the time in the world.

Roberts looked around the truck cabin, feeling the rising grip of panic. He checked the seat, the floor. He was winging it – there was no letter. "Damn it. I must have left it on my desk. Will you take it on faith? I'm surprised that letter hasn't made it down to you already, to be honest."

Charlie shook his head. "They don't tell us nothin' down here."

Roberts was itching to get moving. He moved to throw the truck into gear. Finally, Friedman gave him a nod. But then he threw up a hand at the last minute. Roberts fought the urge to ignore him and hit the gas. "What's up?"

"Seeing as we're bending rules here, any chance you could get me and the wife into the Mess for lunch some time? It's our twentieth anniversary in a couple of weeks."

Roberts almost said no purely out of habit, but stopped himself just in time. "You bet, Charlie. Pick a day and I'll make it happen."

"You're a peach, sir. Thanks a bunch." Friedman grinned like he'd just won the lottery. In a way, he had. Dining in the White House Mess was by invitation only. Building staff were mostly too far down the pecking order to make the cut.

Roberts made a mental note to explain the deal to Sherman Adams, so he could smooth out any ruffled feathers on that score. Roberts got going before Charlie decided to push his luck any further. He pulled up the truck outside the West Wing lobby entrance under the portico, where the view from the street was limited, and jumped quickly around to the rear to pull open the doors. Agent Deckard and Edna Drake hopped out.

"The President thanks you for your cooperation," said Deckard, patting Roberts on the back. Deckard led Edna through the entrance and around to the right, along a corridor and down a set of stairs to the basement lobby. From here, Edna recalled the path to the secret tunnel leading to the PEOC.

After being lumped around in a hessian sack, she felt in no fit state to meet the President or his top advisor, but thankfully she had time to tidy herself up. This time, Deckard followed her into the PEOC. It looked exactly the same as the last time they'd been here. There was a thin film of dust on the conference table, and the air had was warm and stale. She doubted anybody had bothered to turn on the ventilation system. There was a mirror in one of the rooms off the main conference chamber and she took several minutes to straighten herself out for what promised to be an important meeting. When Sherman Adams arrived about twenty minutes later, she felt vaguely presentable. She'd deliberately sat at the far end of the long conference table to watch him enter, but rose to her feet when he finally did arrive.

Adams lumped a heavy-looking folder onto the table as he pulled out a chair beside her. There was no warmth in his expression, and he looked like he was here against his own better judgment. "A fugitive hiding out in the White House. Wouldn't the Founding Fathers be thrilled?" Adams said.

Edna Drake ignored the sleight on her good character and held out her hand, as he had done for her the last time they'd met. Adams shook it almost reluctantly, like it was an act of cooperation he might soon be forced to rescind. "I appreciate you going to all this trouble for me," she said, "and I promise you won't regret it when you hear what I have to say."

"Does Donald Menzel know you're here?"

She hesitated, wondering if perhaps Adams thought she was talking out of turn. "No, sir."

"Good," he said. "I think that's best." Edna smiled, feeling reassured. "This Paolo Favaloro fellow had me questioning my sanity. He appeared at my bedside and then simply vanished. Astonishing. I still haven't told the President about that — I didn't want to sound like a crackpot."

"I've seen the same thing," she said. "I've also met him in the flesh. In Rome."

"What's he doing there? And what does any of this have to do with the Verus Foundation?"

Edna explained how Paolo had entrusted Bill Donovan and Clarence Paulson with the knowledge that led them to unearth an ancient flying saucer beneath Sumerian ruins in the Lebanese town of Baalbek. How they had flown the ship back to America under Russian fire, and how Donovan had personally struck up an agreement to placate Joseph Stalin that had kept Paolo Favaloro trapped in Rome.

"And you thought you could get him out from under the Russians' noses?" Sherman Adams asked. He clearly thought they were fools to even make the attempt.

"Dr Menzel believed the instability at the Kremlin offered a window to extract Paolo Favaloro and bring him back to America. He thought the Russians would be distracted. He was wrong."

Adams tapped the folder in front of him. It was an inch thick. "This, Miss Drake, is only half of the intelligence the CIA has gathered on you since your Roman holiday. It turns out the Israelis also had people at the Vatican when you were there."

He pulled out a photograph from the top of the file, taken by a Mossad agent. It showed Sister Josephine — Nina Onilova — ushering them into a black sedan outside the Vatican archives. "This looks very much like you two cooperating with a known Russian operative and a member of the Sicilian Mafia."

Edna sighed. "The CIA has no idea why we were there."

"Nobody knows why you were there!" he screamed at her in exasperation.

Edna flinched. "I did tell Dr Menzel it was a mistake to do this without CIA involvement, but he insisted there was no time to get the operation sanctioned."

Adams stared up at the ceiling as if to silently call for divine assistance. "No, of course not. Why bother with the rule of law or longstanding international agreements?"

Edna knew now was the time to lay it all on the table. She'd had about enough of being Menzel's human shield. "Majestic-12 had decided not to inform President Eisenhower about the FS-1 project. That wasn't my doing and, to be honest, Mr Adams, I'm sick of being the patsy. I agree with you. What they did was illegal, corrupt, dangerous and just plain wrong. But they have me by the throat. I've never been in a position to refuse them. And you'd still be in the dark now, if not for me."

He nodded. "What about this friend of yours who was murdered? What do you know about that?"

"We believe it was either the CIA or the Russians."

"You're saying the CIA is capable of murdering an innocent American? That's a powerful accusation."

She chose her words carefully, saying somebody was out to frame her. Then Edna explained why it might be the Russians.

Adams shifted in his seat. "All right then, let me ask you a different question. Have you been meeting with a KGB officer stationed at the Russian embassy?"

She nodded. "Polina Ilyin, yes."

"What is the US government to make of that?" Adams asked her.

Edna looked up at him nervously, knowing she was still a long way from earning his trust. "You're asking if I'm spying for the Russians?"

Adams stared back at her stone-faced. "I'm asking you to convince me you're not."

Edna tried to look offended. "Meaning I'm guilty until proven innocent?"

Sherman Adams scoffed at her reaction. "I'm afraid that's very much the case in this instance, yes."

"I have no time at all for the Soviets, sir. But you won't like the reason I wanted to meet with her. Maybe you won't even believe it."

He frowned. "Try me."

"I met with Polina because I wanted to talk to someone. That doesn't mean I was ever going to give her what she wants. She was a sympathetic ear, that's all. I know she's a spy for a country we now call 'the enemy,' but I found comfort in her presence. I have no one to talk to about any of this. Polina knows more about the activities of the Verus Foundation than almost anyone in the US Government — you and the President included. I've given away no sensitive information, nor do I intend to. This was two soldiers from opposing sides striking up a conversation in no-man's-land. If that's enough for you to condemn me as a spy, I guess I can't defend myself."

"It's possible, perhaps, you were thinking of recruiting her as an asset?"

Adams was throwing her a lifeline. But she couldn't help wondering if someone else might try to strangle her with it. Edna sighed and shook her head. "Not really. I mean it crossed my mind once we started talking, but I knew I lacked the finesse to pull it off."

"I see. Well, I guess I appreciate your honesty."

"I knew meeting with her was a mistake," Edna said, "but I did it anyway. Haven't you ever done that, Mr Adams? Acted against your own better instincts? I'm not hiding anything. I just wanted someone to talk to. I'm surrounded by crusty old men. Sometimes dancing with the devil has a certain allure. That's what spies do, right? Talk to other spies?"

Adams nodded. Edna had a good feeling about this man. She wanted to trust him, and wanted more than anything for him to trust her back.

Adams turned toward the door. "Agent Deckard?" he called out. "Go wake up the President for me."

THIRTY SIX

M onday August 24, 1953

Eisenhower had gone purple. Unlike his chief advisor, the President wasn't directing his anger at Edna, but she felt the brunt of it just the same.

"I must admit," said Edna, "I'm surprised General Donovan didn't tell you any of this. I know you're close."

Ike shook his head. "I know he felt divided in his loyalties between me and Harry Truman, but I assumed once I'd taken office, he'd bring me up to speed with everything."

"To be fair — and I can't believe I'm defending the man now — he was probably in the same position as me in being beholden to the members of MJ-12 and sworn to uphold the decisions of the collective."

"Even if that means lying to the Commander in Chief," said Eisenhower.

"The reason he was so hell-bent on stopping me from reporting on FS-1 when I worked at the *Times-Herald* is he believed the Russians would start dropping nuclear bombs on us if they thought we were anywhere close to unravelling the saucer's secrets. Bill Donovan took all of that pressure on his shoulders. I think it just about destroyed him."

"We have suspected for some time there were projects out there operating without proper oversight," the President told her.

"It's why the CIA have been so hot on my tail," she realized. "General Smith never briefed Allen Dulles about FS-1 when he handed over the agency. Truman wanted as little oversight as possible. MJ-12 took that to heart."

Eisenhower nodded. "During the war, when we were planning the Normandy invasion, we had a very short list of people in the know. We called it the 'Bigot' list. This FS-1 project is every bit as sensitive. If it's in the hands of Lockheed, it's in their interests to keep that bigot list as short as possible."

"In the interests of full disclosure," said Edna, "I guess I should also tell you about the Outherians."

"The who?" said Eisenhower.

"They're human; that is, they inhabit human bodies, but they are most certainly not of this world. Verus has been working closely with them — in particular, a man named Lee Tavon who came to everyone's attention last year."

She told them about Tavon's farm and his research, and how not even Lockheed was aware of it. How the Outherians had been responsible for the saucer flap over the Capitol the previous year. By the time she'd finished, both Adams and the President were shaking their heads in disbelief.

"We need to shut Verus down," said Adams.

Ike nodded, but said nothing.

"With respect, Mr Adams, I disagree," Edna protested. "Verus is an amazing resource. It might have gone off the rails, but I think President Truman had the right idea in setting up an independent archive of the nation's secrets."

Adams didn't look pleased to have his judgment second-guessed in front of the President. "You have dragged this administration into murky and treacherous waters, Miss Drake," he said. "From here on, knowing who to trust will be critical. Tell me this: why should the President trust you?"

She took some time to consider how best to respond. "I guess you're asking me whether I'm a communist sympathizer," she said, taking care to look them both in the eyes. "I hang out in jazz bars, I spend time with the sorts of people the CIA and the FBI call dissidents, or fellow travelers. People who believe Marx and Trotsky had the right ideas about using the power of the collective to create a better world.

"But I've seen with my own eyes how the Soviets corrupted those ideals. As far as I'm concerned, communists and fascists are different sides on the same coin. They're extremists who've sacrificed personal liberty to force their views upon their people. Stalin stymied dissent and killed anybody who didn't toe the line. Hitler did the same. What do they have in common? Secrecy. Official and institutional lies presented as truth to gullible people, who wanted to believe their governments were acting in their best interests.

"Mr President, with everything I've witnessed these past twelve months, I'm worried America could end up going down the same road. Now, I'll be the first to admit the way I've lived my life has been far from perfect, but telling the truth is one thing I've always valued above all else. Either you see that in my eyes and hear it in my voice, or you don't. But that's about all I have to say on the matter."

Eisenhower and Adams appeared to make their minds up without speaking. It was an odd sort of empathy they shared. Their own form of telepathy. "Where do we go from here, Miss Drake?" Adams asked. "What do you want?"

"I want to use my role at the Verus Foundation to get inside Edwards Air Base. I want to gather as much information as possible on FS-1 and everything else they're hiding in there."

"If Lockheed is running FS-1, it won't be at Edwards," Adams revealed. "The Air Force has given Lockheed the contract to develop a commercial aviation research hub just south of Edwards. That'll be where they're hiding this flying saucer."

"All right then," the President decided, "from now on, Edna, you work for me. You're my spy on the inside."

She felt relieved and enormously privileged to have the Commander in Chief in her corner, but also knew it put her under a lot of pressure. From now on, Edna Drake could trust almost no one.

"Know this too," warned Adams, "the CIA's head of special operations, James Angleton, has you marked as a commie sympathizer. I will do my best to talk him down, but I doubt it'll make a whole lot of difference — he's like a dog with a bone."

"What about Bill Donovan, won't he vouch for me?"

"Bill's persona non grata in the agency," the President said. "And frankly, I'm not sure I trust him either."

"You can," Edna assured the President. "He's a loyal soldier. Always has been."

When did she become Bill Donovan's defender? These people turned on their own far too quickly.

"Forget about Bill," said Adams. "Angleton worked under him in the OSS, but regards him as yesterday's man. More to the point, Angleton has a personal interest in seeing you go down. He's become as paranoid as Hoover about traitors in the ranks."

"And God help you if Angleton throws you to the FBI," said Eisenhower.

"I thought you got on well with Mr Hoover," said Edna.

"One must walk a fine line with J. Edgar," said Ike. "We get along because our interests run parallel. But if your actions put me on a collision course with the FBI and I'm forced to choose, I'll cut you loose, Miss Drake."

"If it comes to that," said Adams, "we won't be in a position to do anything to save you."

Edna's eyes widened in surprise. "Well, I suppose I appreciate *your* honesty."

"There's one other thing Angleton could do," said Adams. "He could make you disappear. He has a black site in Maryland. He could lock you up indefinitely. If he does that, he will have already decided you're guilty. Then he won't stop working on you until you confess to being the KGB's greatest asset."

"Even if it's a lie?" Edna asked.

"Angleton is good friends with Kim Philby," said Adams.

Philby had been head of British intelligence in Washington, but was tarred with suspicion after his colleagues Donald Maclean and Guy Burgess defected to Moscow.

"I thought Philby was forced to quit in disgrace," said Edna.

"No," said Adams. "MI6 didn't want to lose him. They recalled him to London because of the pressure being applied by the Truman administration, but he's still working for them. The Brits don't believe he's done anything wrong. Angleton still supports him, though I suspect he's backing the wrong horse there."

Edna nodded in agreement.

"Meanwhile," said Adams, "he's seeing spies everywhere. It's like he's overcompensating."

"What Sherm is trying to say," added the President, "is for God's sake stay away from the Russians."

"Bill Donovan gave me a name. Someone in the CIA he trusts. Eloise Page."

"Ah yes," said Eisenhower, recalling the name. "Very capable woman."

"She works in the DOP," said Adams, "the Directorate of Plans. They control all clandestine operations. If they're still watching you, she'll know."

"I could pay her a visit," Edna suggested. "See what she'll tell me."

"Worth a shot, I suppose," said Adams.

Edna was starting to have her doubts about the CIA being responsible for Helen's murder, but they might still be happy to help pin it
on her.

THIRTY

SEVEN

Monday August 24, 1953

Edna walked out of the West Wing side entrance on West Executive Avenue like any normal person, dressed in a grey men's suit, her hair pinned up inside a trilby. She had donned a pair of thick-rimmed black spectacles that gave her the appearance of a bookish, if somewhat effeminate, young man on the presidential staff.

She had expected Tavon to be waiting outside, but as she reached the pavement, she saw no sign of him. A tall woman in a striking red dress, her short auburn hair swept back, waved at Edna lovingly. Edna was certain they'd never met.

The woman bounded up to her. "Hello darling, are you surprised?"

"Very," said Edna.

"I thought I'd pick you up." The woman's eyes told Edna that Tavon had sent her. She gave Edna a joyous smack on the lips and whispered in her ear, "call me Deborah," then stepped back and tossed a set of car keys into the air. "How about you drive us home?"

Thus, with no small degree of trepidation, Edna found herself behind the wheel of the baby blue Buick Roadmaster. It was a beast of a thing, but to her great relief it was a Dynaflow automatic. Deborah immediately turned on the radio. Perry Como was mid-croon on *No Other Love*, his hit version of the Rodgers and Hammerstein show tune. It was pure American soda schmaltz, the kind of music Edna hated.

"Watch the gas pedal," Deborah warned. "This thing gets away from you in a heartbeat."

"You're one of Lee's harem, I take it," said Edna.

Deborah ignored the insult. "He didn't think it was a good idea for him to come in person."

In his place, he'd sent the perfect American housewife. "You look like that woman from the Tide commercial," said Edna.

"Important to live the part," said Deborah, taking the observation as a compliment.

Edna cautiously edged the car into the afternoon traffic, glancing over at her pretend wife. "OK *honey*, where are we going?"

"Lee has a house over in Arlington Forest. It's a short trip to the airport from there."

"Wait a minute, that wasn't the plan," Edna told her. "I'm supposed to be meeting Clarence at his place."

"Lee says the CIA are watching the priest's apartment."

"I'm curious — do you share the beds of women as well as men?" she asked Deborah. "Sorry if that sounds like a rude question, I'm just curious."

"No offense taken," Deborah said. "There are those of us who do enjoy such pleasures. Only when we're sure it will not be noticed. Our primary focus is to remain in the human world unseen. To do that, we must appear wholesome and completely normal."

"Wholesome. There's a term I've never had much time for. Listen, I need a phone."

"You can call Detective Kaplan from the house. It is safe."

"I don't think I'll ever get used to you people reading my mind."

Deborah smiled. "Lee had already told me about him...honey. Relax, I'm not reading your mind."

The house in Arlington Forest was an ordinary brown brick two-story cottage, with white shutters on the windows and a modest wooden portico over the front door. Edna parked the Buick in front of a lockup garage at the back, and Deborah led her up the back stairs and into the kitchen. Everything inside was spotless. Another designer living room leading to a large eat-in kitchen, with a red metal and formica breakfast table surrounded by four cheerful red and white vinyl chairs. All the appliances gleamed like new.

Edna parked herself at the table. "Any chance of a coffee, hon?" She'd only been a man for an hour, but already it was starting to rub off.

While Deborah warmed the coffee pot, Edna put a call in to Vincent Kaplan. He didn't sound happy to hear from her. "I was hoping I'd see you in person," he said.

"Sorry detective, that's not possible."

"You aren't doing a lot to allay my suspicions, Miss Drake."

"You know I didn't do this. I can tell you who did, but you're not going to like it."

She was right about that.

"I have no jurisdiction in the Russian Embassy," said Kaplan. "That's FBI territory — and they're going to need more than your say-so before they go knocking on the door. And definitely not before you come down here to give us a formal deposition."

Edna considered mentioning she had the CIA already on her tail, but figured that would only make matters worse. "Like I said, not possible right now."

"This organization you're working for, what's it called?" he asked.

"I'm not working for them anymore."

Kaplan sighed. "Just a part-time thing, was it? A bit of espionage and capital crime on the side? You do understand murder is a mandatory death sentence, right? Because I'm not hearing a lot of cooperation from your end. Are you going to give me the name of your organization or not?"

"I can't, Vincent, all right? Look, you need to believe me — Polina Ilyin is the one you want. Think about it. The killer managed to get in and out of Helen's house without being noticed. But somebody must have seen her. They just haven't mentioned it because nobody, least of all the police, regard a lone woman as dangerous."

"What was the motive?"

"She tried to pin the killing on my boss. She was out to recruit me. Wanted me to think I couldn't trust my own people. That's all I can give you, I'm sorry."

Edna hung up the telephone before Detective Kaplan had time to object.

THIRTY EIGHT

A ugust 25-28, 1953

Detective Kaplan, clearly unhappy with her allegation the Russians were involved, released Edna's name to the press on Tuesday. By that night, her face had been splashed across newspapers and, more alarmingly, on television screens across the nation. She'd become the lead item on Douglas Edwards' Tuesday night CBS news bulletin: a wanted woman. Edna wasn't being directly accused of murder, but hers was the only face associated with the crime. Which meant being damned by association, in a murder case vaguely but ominously described as being "linked to defense intelligence." From that moment on, Edna knew she was destined to remain with the Outherians indefinitely.

But after several days of hiding inside Lee Tavon's version of the American idyll, Edna was almost ready to surrender herself to Kaplan just to spice things up a bit.

The first two days had been a welcome break from the growing turmoil of recent weeks. She had relished the chance to put it all out of her mind and live something resembling a normal life, even if it was all pretend. During the day — when America's menfolk went off to work — Deborah played guard, but left Edna alone to read or watch television. She was not allowed to leave the house, which at first felt heavy-handed but turned out to be a wise precaution.

Deborah offered to buy Edna whatever she desired, from cigarettes to ice-cream and chocolate and whatever other tasty edibles her heart desired, but rather annoyingly drew the line at alcohol. She told Edna bluntly that heavy drinking had played a part in all of her worst decisions. In saying this, it wasn't as if Deborah was passing judgment — Tavon, after all, owned a bar. But this, in a way, made it worse because it had come as more of a clinical assessment. Deborah had an infuriating and impenetrable manner, like a mother who knew she was right, and whose pronouncements were never open to debate.

Edna was surprised to learn Deborah's house was one of six on that street owned and occupied by the Outherians. There were three others on the opposite side of the road, as well as the neighboring properties on either side of Deborah's house. A tunnel network connected all of them to an underground facility much like that beneath Tavon's farm, although this one was smaller. The Outherians used this to freely interact with one another and maintain their collective relationships, without anyone else in the street having the slightest idea about what was going on. This minimized the risk of prying eyes seeing something untoward, because they had cleverly acquired properties at the apex of the curve on their hill; they could see into one another's houses, but nobody else outside the group of six houses had a clear line of sight on them.

One of the seven Lee Tavons lived here permanently. Edna had been right in assuming Deborah was his current lover. That first night, the three of them discussed the situation and formed a plan of action. The Outherians were adamant Edna should cool her heels for a week to let her trail run cold. Tavon, himself no stranger to being pursued by authorities, said the important thing now was to remain one step ahead, and that this required careful consideration.

While she was far from a prude when it came to sex and relationships, Edna found herself anxiously wondering whether they would ask her to join their love circle. Part of her was curious, but another part struggled with it. This collective arrangement of theirs included shared custody of children. It sounded far too complicated and a long way from a stable family environment.

Tavon, as usual, was way ahead of her. "You can relax, Edna, I'm not going to lure you into bed. You're not my type."

"Or mine," said Deborah. Was that a smile curling up the edge of her mouth?

"All right. Fine. Good." Why did she feel disappointed?

"The way we live is only possible because of who we are," said Deborah. "You are not like us."

"You can say that again."

"We're not making any of our choices lightly," said Tavon. "We foresee the consequences of our actions. Can you truly say the same?"

Edna was the first to admit that had never been one of her strengths. "Sometimes I wish I could see the future. But then doesn't that take some of the fun out of it?"

"Nothing is set in stone," said Deborah. "We can predict your actions with great accuracy over the next few hours. Yet if we tell you this in advance, you remain free to make different choices and change the outcome."

"I'm working on a way to do this in a more systematic fashion," said Tavon. "I'll explain it to you one day."

Edna nodded. But she wasn't at all sure she wanted confirmation of the fears already gripping her about her own immediate future, given how events were now well and truly beyond her control. She felt certain her time as a Verus operative was at an end. It would no longer be possible to trade in the nation's secrets while hiding behind her work for Senator Ives. Even if there was a way to put all this behind her, she doubted Donald Menzel would consider it. This meant she was of limited value as the President's woman on the inside, and had likely been labeled a political liability.

She needed to prove them wrong.

Despite the increased public focus on Edna, Tavon insisted they proceed as planned. By early Friday morning, the arrangements were in place. He'd approached Garrick Stamford with a request to take Edna to view the flying saucer up close.

"Garrick did remind me you're wanted by authorities. I don't think he was of a mind to cooperate until I told him I'd be coming along for the trip to keep an eye on you."

"Did you get a read on him?"

"It's much harder over the phone," Tavon said. "It'll be harder in person too, because he's on his guard now and trying his best to confuse. He's scared of me." Tavon had at one time been Stamford's chief financial advisor. Tavon had made him a very wealthy man, perhaps so wealthy that he'd made himself redundant as an advisor. But the estrangement between them had begun when Stamford found out the true nature of Tavon's brilliance. "I also invoked the name of Sherman Adams," Tavon said. "He told me the Eisenhower administration knew nothing about FS-1. He wasn't at all happy to hear the cat was out of the suitcase."

"I think you mean out of the bag," said Edna. "How do we get there?"

"Garrick is lending us his plane. He'll arrange it so we can drive straight onto the airport concourse and into the Lockheed hangar. That way we keep you out of sight."

"You'll dress as a man again," said Deborah. "Keep your mouth shut and you'll do fine."

Edna recalled that Stamford had booze on board that plane.

"I can make you a Tom Collins — without the gin," said Tavon. "How about that?"

"What's the point of that?" she replied, sighing. Damn mind readers. "I don't trust Garrick Stamford. How do you know he won't have the FBI waiting for me in that hangar?"

"It's a possibility," Tavon admitted. "But if they arrest you, they'll probably arrest me too. Stamford won't risk that."

"You're the reason he's playing along," Edna realized.

"He's dying to find out if I can fly that thing."

THIRTY NINE

Sunday August 30, 1953

Deborah stopped the Buick outside the Christ Episcopal Church in Georgetown. "You sure about this? It feels like a mistake."

"I'm gratified you're leaving it up to me," said Edna, "and you might be right. But there's no reason to think I'm expected here. I don't think she'll duke it out on hallowed ground."

"I'll be waiting," Deborah said.

The service had already begun; this had been part of the plan. It was almost a full house, but Edna was happy to take a seat in the back row. Sunbeams streamed through windows high above, bathing the congregation in light like the visible embodiment of God's love. This left the distant altar shrouded in shadow, but the elaborate flower arrangements were still obvious. Donovan had said they were a point of pride for Eloise Page, who insisted on doing them herself. Tall stalks of pink foxglove on either side of the pulpit leant the service a cheerful air. A well-spoken white priest spoke of God sending his only son Jesus to forgive our sins and give the world proof of life everlasting. Edna found it unendingly curious to hear what passed as proof for Christian believers. In her mind, it boiled down to real estate. It was hard to argue with bricks and mortar. This church was beautiful. Stately, elegant, dripping in wealth. Who wouldn't want to believe this was the home of their god?

Edna spent the remainder of the service scanning the heads in front of her, trying to decide if any of them might be working for the CIA or the Russians. But every face she saw looked either devout or bored, and nobody paid her the slightest mind.

After the service, she remained in her seat to look as many people as possible in the eyes, as parishioners filed past in a placid and orderly procession. Many smiled at her and offered their blessing. She returned the sentiment politely once or twice, but that made her feel like a hypocrite, so after that she simply smiled. She was still watching the last of them leave the church when she realized there was a woman sitting beside her.

"Your flowers are beautiful," Edna said.

"Thank you very much, Miss Drake." Eloise Page was staring up at the altar. "I assume Bill sent you. I'm afraid you're wasting your time."

Edna bent down and fiddled with her shoe lace. "Is it because people are watching?"

Miss Page laughed like the comment was overly naïve. "Everybody is watching. You, my girl, are a hot potato. I don't want to get my fingers burnt."

"I need someone to tell James Angleton I'm not a spy. That Polina Ilyin killed Helen Barber."

"Nobody tells Angleton anything, my dear, least of all a woman," she said bitterly.

"Surely he'll hear you out. General Donovan…"

"Is no good to you now," said Miss Page. "He's leaving the country on stage one of his retirement plan. This is not the God you're looking for. Walk out of here now and I won't tell anyone you came. If you come back, the consequences will be dire for both of us."

Edna wanted to object, to insist she was no friend of the Russians, but Miss Page's manner told her it was pointless.

FORTY

Sunday August 30, 1953

"Move over," Edna demanded, "I'm driving." For once, Deborah didn't try to argue.

Donovan's mansion was only a few minutes away from the church. Edna thought she might have one last chance to confront him before he left for Thailand.

She pulled into the driveway of the Donovans' house a little fast. The tires of the big car skidded on the gravel as she braked hard and brought it to a shuddering halt. Edna wanted to give the man a piece of her mind, hoping this might go some way to alleviating her rising sense of panic. She also thought he might have some idea of how she could pull herself from this whole flaming car crash.

Throwing open the driver's door, Edna ran to the portico, pounding on the front door with both fists, knowing in her heart her efforts were pointless. She could hear the sound of her blows reverberating through the marble hallway inside like it was an echo chamber. She ran into the garden and peered into the parlor windows, only to find a large dusty room, devoid of furniture.

The Donovans were long gone.

FORTY ONE

Sunday August 30, 1953

The Jewel Box was busy, but the place didn't have its usual happy ambiance. Edna sent Clarence to find them a booth while she stood at the bar, trying to catch Beverley King's eye. She was certain the barman had seen her, but he took his sweet time in approaching. He flipped his eyes sharply to the right to let her know somebody was watching.

Edna nodded. She knew someone was watching. That was the whole idea.

"What'll it be?" King asked, showing no obvious sign of recognition. Smart man.

"A whiskey neat and a Tom Collins," she said. Deborah could go to hell.

When he returned with the drinks, she handed him a five-dollar note. "Same again in a few minutes, if you would. We're over in the corner," she said, pointing at the booth Clarence had claimed. King nodded.

Paulson downed his first shot like water, which gave her pause. She wondered what Deborah would say about his alcohol consumption. He leant across the table. "You sure I can't tempt you back to my place later?"

Edna smiled. "What I want and what I need are mutually exclusive right now."

Lee Tavon had clearly not been giving the bar his attention of late. The piano player was so bad that Edna thought they'd be better off with a juke box, while the patrons were just a bunch of lowlifes. Perhaps better musicians played later in the week? But somehow, she doubted it. The place had lost its buzz. Lee's commitment to jazz had apparently been short-lived.

She downed the last of her cocktail with a gulp as Beverley King delivered their second round. "Eyes everywhere, best watch out," he told her quietly. She had already spotted the Russian "taxi driver" who had delivered her to the Commodore Hotel. He was sitting with his back to the door, which gave him a clear eyeline on everyone who walked in. It meant Polina was close.

They sipped their drinks. She reached out and touched Clarence on the hand. "You ever heard of Bonnie and Clyde?" she asked.

"Of course. The famous bank robbers."

"Actually, they rarely robbed banks together. It was usually grocery stores. That's how they got caught and sent to jail."

"I thought they were killed by the police?" he said.

"That was later, when Clyde started killing policemen 'cos he didn't want to go back to prison. But I bet you didn't know this: he chopped two of his own toes off in jail to avoid the work detail. Then six days later, his mother got him paroled.

"A year or so later, they were on the run again. By then they were both hobbling around like cripples. Clyde always drove too fast on country roads. He crashed into a ditch one time and wrecked their car. Bonnie had battery acid sprayed all over her leg."

"You're saying thieves aren't too bright?"

She leaned in to whisper in his ear. "I'm saying there's only one way to avoid trouble: don't get caught."

When Polina Ilyin slid into the booth beside Clarence, she looked both familiar and different. She'd dyed her hair and was dressed in a pinstripe suit, gangster-style — though she definitely wasn't posing as a man. A white silk blouse under her jacket was unbuttoned just far enough to reveal an alluring lacy camisole. She was sex on legs, but her expression held a ruthlessness Edna had never seen before. This was the killer revealed. Polina pulled open the jacket to show she was carrying a gun, "Whatever this is, you have exactly one minute to tell me before we throw you to the FBI."

"I don't need anywhere near that long," said Edna.

All at once, ten men leapt to their feet. Edna yelled, "She's armed!"

On cue, Polina reached for her pistol. Clarence slapped it out of her hand before she'd managed to get a good grip on it. It was the bravest thing Edna had ever seen; Polina would have shot him first if his timing had been even a little off.

Moments later, Kaplan's men had the Russian on the floor in handcuffs. Polina's minder, who had remained seated during the whole thing, simply rose to his feet and abandoned her.

"You cannot arrest me!" she screamed. "I have diplomatic immunity."

Polina Ilyin was still screaming as two men in black suits entered the bar to join the fray, obviously alerted by the commotion. One of them flashed a badge. "Agent Price Wilkins, FBI. No need to worry comrade, we're not charging you — we're deporting you."

Polina didn't like the sound of that at all. This was, of course, all part of the plan. Oddly, the pianist continued playing through the entire incident. It was almost like this sort of thing happened all the time, and he wanted to reassure patrons it was business as usual.

Kaplan figured their best hope of getting Polina Ilyin to talk was by offering her the chance to defect. Edna was pretty sure she'd refuse — Polina wouldn't want to compromise her parents in Moscow. But it was also difficult to know how the Kremlin's new management would react to Polina being deported as a spy. They could view it as an embarrassing failure and simply throw her in prison on some jumped up political charge. A possibility Kaplan and the FBI would do their best to sell as the most likely outcome.

They had come up with the sting after Edna had heard about Kaplan's breakthrough. He'd personally recanvassed all of Helen Barber's neighbors. Sure enough, no one had seen any suspicious men in the area on the night concerned. But two remembered seeing a woman out walking early that morning. Both said they'd mentioned it initially, but the cops had immediately discounted her as a suspect. It never got passed up the chain.

Placing a woman at the scene around the time of the murder might have incriminated Edna, but for one thing — both witnesses had mentioned without prompting that the woman had a limp.

With the help of the FBI, Kaplan obtained a photo of Polina Ilyin. He mixed it in with those of five other women of similar age and appearance. One of the neighbors immediately identified Polina.

It was Deborah who had urged Edna to call Kaplan back. An Outherian sixth sense, maybe? Either way, Deborah was not surprised to hear there had been a breakthrough.

Luring the Russians into a trap had been a simple matter of delivering a message to Dimitri at Shulman's Market. In a hastily handwritten note, Edna had claimed she was desperate and she needed permanent protection, naming the Jewel Box as a safe place to meet. She figured Polina wouldn't believe her, but knew the plea would be too good to resist.

Edna spotted the recognition dawning on the face of Agent Wilkins as they got outside and into the light. She almost laughed at the dirty look he threw Kaplan. "You didn't tell us Drake was part of this," he said.

"You didn't need to know," said Kaplan.

"Am I under arrest?" Edna asked them.

"Yes," said Wilkins.

"No," said Kaplan, overriding him. "But I'll need formal statements from you both."

The homicide interview room stank of sweat, fear, and stale cigarette smoke. Kaplan kept her waiting for about half an hour before sitting down to speak with her. He clearly had a lot on his plate.

Edna explained in broad terms that she worked for a quasi-government organization with a high security clearance that prevented her from naming the organization or anybody else who worked for it. She told him it was a storage house for highly sensitive material, and that they operated under direct presidential sanction.

"But if you asked the President about it, he'd probably deny it."

"Convenient," said Kaplan.

"Actually no," she said, "it's distinctly inconvenient. I'd love to tell you more, but if I do that, I'll be violating the Official Secrets Act and they can throw me in jail for the rest of my life."

He nodded his understanding. "How might you meeting Helen Barber for coffee have played a role in her murder?"

Edna pulled out a pack of cigarettes and placed one in her mouth. Kaplan leant across the table and offered her a light. "I wanted to talk to her about what I'm doing. It was wrong and we both knew it. In fact, Helen wouldn't even discuss it. She left after a few minutes. But the Russians have been watching me closely and trying to recruit me. Polina Ilyin killed Helen and then made me think my boss had done it. She hoped it would drive me toward her. She and I had started a friendship of sorts. Not the good sort, as it turns out."

"Tell me the nature of your relationship with Father Clarence Paulson."

This took her by surprise. "What do you mean?"

"Is it business or personal? Or both?"

"Probably fair to say it's both," she said.

"You're having an affair with a man of the cloth."

"I'm not sure he still regards himself as a man of the cloth, but officially I suppose, yes. I'm sleeping with a Catholic priest. Is that what you wanted to hear?"

Kaplan stifled a smile but avoided her gaze. "Do you and he work for the same secret organization?"

"We do, as a matter of fact."

"Because the FBI is questioning his immigration status. We think he's overstayed his visa."

"I understand Father Paulson is in America as a papal envoy, a personal representative of the Vatican who should thus be granted diplomatic status."

"That may be," said Kaplan, "but Father Paulson doesn't have the paperwork to back up such a claim. As such, we need to keep him in custody. He'll be handed over to the Immigration and Naturalization Service."

Her heart sank. It hadn't even occurred to her she was putting Clarence at risk. "Jesus, Vincent, is that really necessary? He helped you catch a murderer."

"It's out of my hands, Edna. You need to get your boss to provide the INS with the proper paperwork. Otherwise, Father Paulson will be deported. You might as well tell me the name of your boss. We can't let you go until someone vouches for everything you've just told me."

She thought about that a moment. Giving him Menzel's name would compromise Verus. And she wasn't confident he still considered her an active member of the organization. "Sherman Adams," she said.

Kaplan was taken aback. "*The* Sherman Adams?"

"The President's chief White House assistant. That Sherman Adams, yes."

FORTY TWO

Sunday August 30, 1953

Edna Drake remained locked in that fetid detention room for more than an hour before Kaplan returned to speak to her. In that time, they had offered her coffee and donuts and escorted her to the bathroom, but at no point did she catch a glimpse of Clarence.

She was worried about him. Paulson had come to America aboard a flying saucer. Obviously neither he nor Bill Donovan had bothered to fill in paperwork, and whatever arrangement he had with the Vatican probably amounted to a verbal agreement with the Pope. It was possible this could be put in place formally, but maybe not before he was sent back to England. Edna couldn't remember whether Paulson's name had ever come up in her discussions with Adams and the President.

She was on her last cigarette in the pack by the time Kaplan finally returned. "There's good news and bad news," he said. "I found Sherman Adams. He's vouched for you, so we can let you leave."

"That's great," she said, sighing in relief. "What's the bad news?"

"I'm afraid Mr Adams has no knowledge of Clarence Paulson. He told me he's not fully briefed on all the names of the personnel in your little cabal, but that I should take you at your word."

"Then, do you?" she asked.

"I do," Kaplan said. "Unfortunately, it's not up to me. Hoover's boys will reluctantly bow to the wishes of the White House in your case, but they won't let Father Paulson loose without something in writing. He's not an American."

It was her fault. Clarence had been at the bar with her because he was afraid to go alone. She had never stopped to think what that might mean for him. "How long before they deport him?"

"It won't be quick. They'll allow some wiggle room for negotiation behind the scenes. You should have time to do something."

"Will you let me see him before I go?" she asked.

Kaplan was about to refuse, but he saw the concern on her face and nodded his assent. "Two minutes. Best I can do."

They had him behind bars in a holding cell. Kaplan opened the door to let her inside. Paulson was surprised by the force of the hug she gave him as he rose to his feet to meet her. "Wow, you reek of cigarettes," he said.

She laughed, but swallowed it quickly as she fought back tears. "I'm so sorry, Clarence. Are you all right?"

"I'm fine. They're treating me well."

She threw him a dubious look. The cell was bare and smelled like a cattle pen. No mattress, no blanket. There was a toilet in the corner without a seat. "I'm not sure you and I have the same definition of well. You realize they want to deport you?"

Paulson nodded. She still had her arms around him and leant close to whisper in his ear. "What about mentioning Bill's name? He's out of the loop now, it wouldn't compromise Verus."

Paulson shook his head. "Wouldn't work. They'd still demand to see paperwork. I would too in their position."

She had one more idea. It was radical, but the more she thought about it, the more it appealed to her. Edna whispered it to him.

Paulson pulled away to look her in the eyes. "No, you don't mean that."

"Actually," she said, "I rather think I might."

"Time's up," Kaplan told them. Edna pulled away and stepped out of the detention room.

"Think about it," she told Paulson as a uniformed officer closed the door between them.

"You are free to go, Miss Drake," Kaplan told her.

"How are you coming along with Polina?"

Kaplan shrugged. "The FBI are taking the lead on that. I don't think she's saying much. Listen, thanks again for your help." He held out a set of keys. "Clarence said to give you these. For his apartment." She smiled in appreciation. "Do me a favor," said Kaplan, "don't leave town."

She smiled wearily. "I wouldn't dream of it."

FORTY THREE

Tuesday September 1, 1953

Her previous trip on this airplane had not ended well. Edna had higher hopes for this journey, but she was also determined to remain on her guard.

By the calendar it was the first day of fall, even though in reality it was the autumnal equinox on September 23 that marked the change of seasons. Lately she'd been amusing herself spotting the myriad ways modern humanity had rounded off so many of life's rough edges to keep the world contained. In this instance, it was literally a case of the Earth turning one way and human beings another. Edna knew from bitter experience those rough edges wouldn't stay smooth forever.

Looking west over the tarmac, she saw no clouds in the sky and hoped that meant smooth flying. The Super Constellation had a cruising speed of three hundred miles per hour. It would take a little over seven hours to fly more than twenty-two hundred miles across the continent. They would arrive just after three in the afternoon, local time.

Two momentous events in her life had occurred on September the first. The first was the resignation of New York mayor Jimmy Walker in 1932 after months of investigations, court cases, and finger pointing over his links to murder and police corruption. Though Edna Drake had only been nine years old at the time, the blanket press coverage over the months leading up to that day was what first awakened her to the reality that men in charge could be criminals. Walker's fall was largely due to pressure placed on him by crusading New York Governor Franklin Roosevelt; it was no coincidence that two short months later FDR had defeated Herbert Hoover in a presidential election landslide.

September the first was also the day Hitler's Germany invaded Poland, plunging Europe into the bitter war that had consumed the greater part of her youthful ardor, rendering Edna Drake bitter and cynical beyond her years.

She drew neither comfort nor pleasure from the luxuriously appointed cabin of Garrick Stamford's private plane, though she was more than willing to partake in its temptations. Ignoring Tavon's admonitions, she called for her first gin and tonic at midday shortly after takeoff, then readily agreed to a plate of filet mignon in red wine sauce with baked vegetables. She did this because she could, though the opulence was all but lost on her. Edna appreciated the flavor and the intoxication, but could not say she derived any actual joy from the thought of how much it might have cost. Pleasure of any sort had become lost to her amid the dull, existential dread that gripped her upon waking each morning.

"It's called Plant 42," Tavon said.

She had no idea what he was talking about.

"Lockheed's hangar in California," he explained. "The site itself is owned by the Air Force, but Lockheed have the place to themselves. It's south of Edwards Air Base — what used to be called the Palmdale Army Airfield. It has its own runway."

"Door-to-door service. How convenient," she said.

Tavon crossed the cabin and sat down beside her on the plush three-seater lounge. "I must tell you this will not go well for either of us," he told her in hushed tones. "Stamford isn't exactly welcoming us with open arms."

"I thought you said he was keen to get you inside that saucer? You could open the project up for them — tell them something they'd take decades to work out on their own."

"Garrick thinks I betrayed him," said Tavon.

"But he knows who you are."

"Yes, that's true. But he's also been told he will be charged with illegal share trading if he doesn't do as he's told and, of course, I am definitely to blame for that. But whatever happens Edna, I will have your back."

"Thanks Lee. I know you will. And I'll have yours."

He shrugged. "Good of you to say, but I won't hold you to it."

"What do you mean?"

"You might find yourself faced with a choice — to help me or save yourself." He knew something. But Tavon wouldn't tell her what it was. Since last year, he'd come to the conclusion human beings didn't deal well with knowledge of their future. He placed his hand on his heart. "Promise me when we reach that moment you will save yourself."

FORTY FOUR

Tuesday September 1, 1953

The Skunkworks hangar was set back a short distance from the runway. As they taxied closer, Edna got a clearer idea of exactly how massive it was. The cartoon image of a skunk was painted above the main hangar door. It was an odd touch for the exterior of a Top Secret facility.

The Constellation came to a halt about a quarter of a mile from the hangar, where a mobile stairway vehicle was waiting for them. It touched up against the hull of the plane a moment later. By the time they reached the tarmac, Garrick Stamford's limousine was waiting. The driver opened the back door.

Stamford, the man in charge, was waiting for them inside the car. In a moment of acerbic brilliance, Lockheed test pilot Tony LeVier had dubbed him "Skunkford" and the nickname had stuck, though nobody said it to his face. He acknowledged them with a wry smile. Edna opted for the rear-facing bench and watched as Stamford shook Tavon's hand like he was afraid whatever had happened to Tavon was catching.

"I didn't realize your plant was so big," Edna said, hoping to break the ice. "Quick work. Didn't you only win the Air Force contract here a few months ago?"

"We started construction here in July last year," Stamford told them.

"Before you got the contract," she pointed out.

Stamford smiled. "You haven't been in this business for long. The contract was just a formality. This hangar sits over our underground bunker, built to keep FS-1 under wraps. Not an easy thing to manage in secret, even on a site controlled by the Air Force. Compared to that, stacking a tender process is a piece of cake." He turned to Tavon. "By the way, Lee, that's a joke. I don't want you telling tales out of school. Which brings me to another point. I can't let you both in here without the proper clearance."

Skunkford had just played his wildcard. One last effort to keep them out. "I thought you might say something like that," said Edna, reaching into her attaché case. She pulled out a document and handed it to Stamford. "Written approval from the Commander in Chief."

THE WHITE HOUSEWASHINGTON

August 31, 1953

Personal and Confidential

I authorize and deputize Lee Tavon and Edna Drake as presidential envoys reporting personally to me on the matter of the Top Secret Lockheed Skunkworks research project known as FS-1.

Please extend them both all courtesies, privileges, and access to all areas of the operation. No door should remain closed.

I am expecting a detailed report and will review future funding and operational status based upon the information received.

Sincerely,Dwight Eisenhower

Skunkford offered the letter back to Edna. She almost suggested he keep it as a souvenir, but decided it was better in her possession. No paper trail that way.

"Curious thing," said Stamford, "but I'd been assured Mr Eisenhower wasn't in the loop on this project. Nobody has advised me otherwise."

"I disagree, sir," she said. "You've just been advised by the President himself."

Stamford wasn't amused. "Quite."

The giant hangar doors slowly swung open as the limousine approached. They drove into a vast open space as high as it was wide. It contained four planes, but with enough floor space for three times as many. Around each of the aircraft, groups of technicians in grey overalls continued about their work without bothering to cast a glance in their direction. No doubt they had become highly skilled at turning a blind eye to all matters that weren't their immediate business.

The hangar roof was at least a hundred feet above their heads. Crane gantries crisscrossed the rafters. Multi-story viewing platforms had been built into each of the furthest corners. With so much to take in, the elevator in the hangar wall was the last thing Edna noticed. Here Stamford placed a key in a lock and turned it, activating the elevator button, which he pushed.

She couldn't help but compare the facility to Tavon's barn in Virginia. Lockheed's version was a pale comparison, but impressive nonetheless. The elevator took them to the lowest of the facility's three subterranean levels. Here the ceiling height was much lower, though still at least thirty feet from floor to ceiling. Paolo Favaloro's gleaming silver saucer hovered in the middle of the room as if suspended on invisible wires.

"Oh my God," Edna heard herself gasp. "It's incredible."

It was about twenty feet in diameter, the outer shell made of a single sheet of metallic alloy. It showed no seams nor rivets, gleaming like a mirror. Realizing she could see right underneath it, Edna bent down to see how that was possible.

"What's holding it up?" she asked.

"The craft's mass is counterbalanced by its internal antigravitational propulsion system," Stamford explained. "This basically renders it weightless."

"How do you fly it out of here?"

"We don't. Not anymore. Flight is no longer the priority. It's chewed through too many of our test pilots. Does something to their heads. Our focus is on understanding how it operates, with a view to replicating it one day."

"How's that coming along?" she asked.

"Slowly."

"You're not getting anywhere, are you Garrick?" Tavon decided.

Skunkford said nothing.

"Mind if I get up close and personal?" Edna asked.

"Knock yourself out," said Stamford, signaling to someone behind glass on the far side of the chamber. Lights behind the saucer switched on and Edna watched in amazement as the skin of the craft completely changed color.

"It reacts to bright light," said Stamford. "We think it's some sort of cloaking device."

She touched the hull and found it remarkably warm. "It almost feels alive."

"It is," said Tavon, who placed his hand next to hers. There was a click; something under the surface rippled like water as a hatch opened, and stairs lowered to the ground.

Stamford's mouth fell open.

Edna turned to Tavon. "Did you do that?"

Tavon smiled. "Want to go inside?"

They ascended the short staircase to a sparse cabin, containing two white seats that rose from the floor as if they had grown from it. Everything was pure white and again, no seams were visible anywhere. But it was darker on the inside, and it took her eyes a few moments to adjust. There was just enough room for them to stand, but Edna felt an almost irresistible urge to sit.

As she did so, she noticed a plain white panel in front of them begin to glow when Tavon touched it. Edna did likewise and felt a gentle hum pass through her like a tiny electric shock. The cabin itself became brighter. She pulled her hands away then, suddenly remembering what Skunkford had said about the ship messing with test pilots' heads.

But Tavon did not hold back. He placed his hands in various places across the panel, like he was feeling his way through its operating systems.

"Do you understand it?" she asked.

"I think so, yes." A square porthole opened right in front of them, revealing the walls of the underground hangar. Which was when Edna realized they were moving. They bounced off the wall of the chamber like a ping pong ball, and started to pick up speed. Curiously, Edna noticed at this point the portal instantly reverted to the leading edge of the craft, so they could always see where they were going. It had to be some sort of TV screen, though the picture was so clear it was impossible to distinguish from a window.

Technicians were waving their hands at them in a desperate call for Tavon to slow down, but were eventually forced to dive out of the way when he didn't.

"Don't hurt anyone," she pleaded in alarm.

"Not possible," he said. "The ship can't do that. Its anti-grav system makes it bounce off all exterior objects. Brilliant design."

He kept them moving around the chamber, demonstrating skill and dexterity in maneuvering and control of the ship. All the while, people outside kept waving in desperation and refusing to clear the way. It was the oddest thing to watch; the viewing screen jumped about so much she often had to look away to avoid getting dizzy, but at the same time felt no sense of movement inside the cabin.

"They're not going to be happy with you," she said.

"I'm just having fun. Showing them it's not as hard as they think it is."

"Tell me how you're doing it," she urged.

Tavon had an oddly distant expression on his face. It was a look of detached concentration, almost like he was in a light trance. "The ship is talking to me. Explaining itself. You try," he urged.

"Oh, I'm not sure that's a good idea. I don't want to become a basket case like Bill Donovan."

"You won't," he insisted. "I've recalibrated the system. It's now modulating at a vibrational frequency within human tolerance. The problem was it had been set to match Ryl physiology."

Edna put her hands on the control panel and felt a surge of power beneath her palms. Immediately, myriad options appeared in the air before her. She sensed she could move through these options by focusing her thoughts, and a moment later Edna understood exactly what she was looking at. It was like the ship's brain and hers were plugged in to one another. She could detect navigation, propulsion and elevation controls, and even spotted sleeping quarters hidden right below them. There were maps of the Moon and the surface of Mars, along with detailed routes along trenches deep in the Atlantic and Pacific oceans. She literally had the galaxy at her fingertips.

"Garrick won't let me leave now," Tavon said. "He thinks he's one step ahead of me, but he forgets I know how his tiny mind works."

"He wouldn't dare — we're here on behalf of the President."

"These men are a law unto themselves, Edna. But don't worry, you'll be fine."

Edna frowned, "It's you I'm worried about."

FORTY FIVE

Tuesday September 1, 1953

When they finally emerged from the saucer, they found themselves surrounded by men with machine guns. Stamford stood safely behind them. "Take them to separate rooms," he ordered.

The last she saw of Tavon was him being led away with two barrels in his back. She was mad, but also scared. Two of the men nudged her forward. She turned around to glare at Stamford. The gunmen looked like they would happily open fire on command. Tavon was right; Stamford's word was law here.

"I'll remind you we're here on the President's authority," she said, trying her best to sound incensed rather than terrified.

"Relax," Stamford told her, "I'm not going to hurt you. I'm just regaining control of my hangar space. That was quite a show you two put on."

"That was Lee. You better not hurt him either."

"Are you kidding? Lee's never steered me wrong. I wouldn't harm a hair on that man's head. But we haven't seen one another for quite some time, you see. We need time to catch up, that's all. You, on the other hand... What am I to do with you, Miss Drake?"

"How about some food?" she suggested blithely. "I'm starved." Edna was bluffing; food was the last thing on her mind. She just hoped he didn't notice she was so scared her whole body was shaking.

"Good idea," Stamford decided. "Let's get you some dinner."

His office suite took up the entire top floor of a much smaller two-level building a short distance from the main hangar. Stamford drove her there in a three-wheel golf cart with an armed guard sitting where the golf clubs should be. Somebody had phoned ahead. By the time they reached his rooms, waiters were laying out a generous spread on a conference table. It was a utilitarian room, no doubt used more for engineering and planning purposes than executive gatherings. But the chairs were comfortable, and might double as a weapon if the occasion arose.

Every seat at the table had a clear view across the tarmac to the runway, as well as the hangar building a few hundred yards away. Arranged neatly on food platters was a baked ham, roast chicken, oysters, lobster, coleslaw, and green salad, along with a choice of red wine or champagne. Far more than the two of them could eat.

"Help yourself," he told her. "It's all fresh. I know it feels like we're in the middle of nowhere, but Los Angeles is only sixty miles to the south of us. I have food brought out three times a week."

Edna grabbed a plate, knowing from previous experience food should never be refused in captivity — there was no way to know how long it might be before the next meal turned up. There was, of course, a risk the food was drugged. Perhaps anticipating her reluctance, Stamford filled a plate for himself. She did likewise, then poured herself a half glass of red wine. She knew if she started on champagne, she wouldn't stop; she needed to keep her wits about her.

"You've come a long way since your days as a reporter," Stamford observed. "Right to the heart of the action."

"Believe it or not, today is not the strangest experience I've had in recent months," she said.

"Are you truly this indifferent or just trying to impress me?"

"No, I wouldn't say indifferent. Overwhelmed might be a better way of putting it. I've heard so much about this saucer of yours, and seen all the films of your test flights."

"Then you should know how big a deal it is that you and Lee just made my entire research operation look like a bunch of fools." She sipped her red wine and ate her lobster, waiting for him to fill the silence. Like most men of power, Stamford loved the sound of his own voice. "I was sorry your trip to Rome was a failure, but I rather think you've delivered me something even better. I suspect Paolo Favaloro is no pushover. I hear he looks down his nose at us mere mortals. But Lee is one of us — you know what I mean."

"He's given you what you want. You need to let us go."

"What I want?" Stamford stared at her with a look of admonition. "None of this is what I want. I'm working in the service of my country."

"Without any sort of legal or governmental oversight. Or so you thought."

"Ike will play ball once we show him what we've got. Oh, and by the way, I'm not detaining you. The scary man with the gun has gone. Leave any time you like, I won't stop you. But I'm afraid Lee isn't going anywhere. He's one of us now. I must say, I've kinda missed him. He's always been my lucky charm."

"What if I told you I won't leave without him?"

"Then I will have someone deliver you to the nearest motel," Stamford replied. "As I say, I'm not going to hold you against your will. Please don't try to tell the President any different. My advice? Jump on that plane and fly back to Washington. Safest place for you, sweetheart."

Stamford's meaning was clear: this was no place for a woman. Edna resisted the urge to throw the dregs of her red wine in his face. "I'm going to Edwards Air Force Base. I plan to see the Roswell crash wreckage."

Stamford nodded, apparently unsurprised. "I wish you the very best of luck with that. I haven't been able to get anywhere near the place." Judging by his tone, he obviously thought if Edwards was closed to him then Edna had no hope, even with a presidential letter of entry. "Then again, who knows?" Stamford said, shrugging. "Maybe a pretty face will open doors. Tell you what, there are still a few hours of daylight left, take one of my cars. It won't do you any harm to arrive in a Lockheed vehicle."

Stamford's magnanimity was hard to pin down. She knew he had something up his sleeve, and she didn't want to leave Tavon. Lee had warned her it would come to this. And she did need a car.

"Fine," she said. "As long as it's an automatic."

FORTY SIX

Tuesday September 1, 1953

Skunkford made good with his promise, providing her with a white Ford Meteor with Lockheed printed clearly on the driver door. The friendly airman on the front gate gave her clear directions and said it should take her a little over half an hour to get to Edwards, which was about thirty miles north.

For the second time in two days, Edna Drake had been forced to abandon a friend to an unknown fate as she continued about her business. But this might be her only opportunity to access the Roswell wreckage. Here at least, she felt certain her letter from the President would hold sway, despite Garrick Stamford's initial skepticism.

It was six o'clock by the time she hit the open road. Edna noted every side road and landmark along the way, knowing she would be driving home in the dark, with little or no street lighting to show the way. She cut through the eastern outskirts of Lancaster. It was a small town, but she saw several people out walking their dogs. A sharp turn to the east took her past a few lonely houses dotted along the road in a locality known as Redman. What was it that brought people out here? It couldn't have been the natural beauty.

Just past Redman, the road turned north again. With the day fading fast, she was the only car on the road, until a fleet of cars approached her from two directions at once.

The car approaching from the north slowed down and pulled across both sides of the road, blocking her way. She slowed to a halt some distance away, wary about getting too close. Two men in suits hopped out of the car and pointed revolvers at her. Edna hurriedly stuck the Ford in reverse, but backed into another car that had pulled up behind her. This driver got out too and likewise brandished a gun.

They yanked open her door and grabbed her by the arms.

"What the hell do you think you're doing?" she screamed at them.

"This is as far as you go, Miss Drake," one of them told her.

"Who are you?"

"We won't hurt you unless you try to get away. I'd suggest you don't do that."

One of them threw a hood over her head. They bustled her into the back of their car. "What about my car?" she complained.

"We'll take care of it."

They drove her south — away from Edwards. By her estimation, they had made it about as far as Redman before the car turned in the opposite direction and headed into the middle of nowhere. About fifteen minutes later, they came to a dusty halt. She was marched inside an old wooden cottage that, from the smell of it, was not being well maintained.

One of the men pulled off her hood. "Take a seat," he urged.

Edna looked around. There were empty wine and beer bottles scattered around the threadbare carpet. Wallpaper hung from the walls. A dirty old two-seater lounge was the only place to sit. It looked like someone had been using it as a bed.

"I think I'll stand," she said. "What am I doing here?"

"Waiting." Same guy again, the biggest and most imposing of the three. Tough guy and designated speaker.

"Waiting for who?"

"For the boss," he said.

She wasn't buying the hard man routine. "You're CIA, right?"

Tough Guy slapped her across the mouth. "Enough talking." She tasted metal and felt the cut on her lip. Bastard. She spat blood on the floor; it splashed across his black Florsheim bluchers. He looked at her in disgust. "Commie whore spat on my shoes!" he yelled in outrage, like this was an offence against God.

Definitely CIA. With some degree of vindication, she quickly took a seat on the lounge lest he raise his hand a second time. She told herself they didn't mean to do her serious harm, just to scare her. It was starting to work.

Edna sat in stony silence until the boss made his entrance twenty minutes later. He was pale and gaunt, of average height with a slight stoop, dressed like a funeral director in a dark suit and homburg hat. The other three men turned attentively toward him. He acknowledged them each in turn without saying a word, then set his eyes on Edna. He looked pleased. Like they had her bang to rights.

"I take it you're James Jesus Angleton," she said.

"You're smart, I'll give you that," he said. "But not smart enough. You think you can just waltz into Edwards Air Force Base without me knowing?"

She glanced in Tough Guy's direction, half expecting him to be snickering. He remained expressionless, his shoe trauma forgotten. They were measured, these men. When they did something, they did it for a reason. That was good. It meant they still had a code, even if it wasn't the law.

"How would I have any idea what you know? And why would I care?" she asked. "You really don't know who you're dealing with, do you?"

"I've had eyes on you for some time, Miss Drake. Since Rome, in fact. How ironic you chose the very home of Christianity as the place to betray your country to godless heathens."

She shook her head, laughing. "Mossad led you up the garden path and now you're seeing fairies. We were lucky to get out of the Vatican with our lives. I'd been shot in the arm by the woman you're suggesting recruited me as a Soviet spy."

"I only have your word on that. For all I know, you could have shot yourself to fool everyone. You're good at fooling people, aren't you?"

"I'm part of an operation that functions above your clearance level and well above your pay grade, Mr Angleton. You're the one making a fool of himself. I don't think the President will be at all happy when he finds out about it."

Angleton threw her a look of pity. "It was Sherman Adams who alerted me to your trip to California in the first place. He doesn't trust you either. Told me to keep an eye on you."

That caught her off guard. Would Adams really do that? She trusted Eisenhower, but could his chief advisor actually be in bed with the CIA? "Did he tell you who I've been working for this whole time?"

Angleton was staring through a window at the darkening desert. "The Verus Foundation, you mean? Yes, I know all about your job with Verus...collecting secrets."

"Then you'll know why we were in Rome."

"Nobody knows why you were in Rome!" he shouted at her. "That's the problem. You were there without permission. Senator Ives certainly didn't send you. The President didn't know. Neither did the State Department, the CIA, defense intelligence — nobody. I've even spoken to Dr Menzel. He says you weren't there for Verus either."

It genuinely shocked her to hear that. If that was true, Menzel had told a bald-faced lie and hung her out to dry. But then she realized Angleton had overreached. It defied the law of probability that both Adams and Menzel were working against her.

"What business do you have at Edwards?" Angleton asked.

"The President's business. I have a letter of entry written on White House letterhead and signed by Dwight Eisenhower himself. Would you care to see it?"

"Let me rephrase the question then," said Angleton. "What does the President want you to see in Edwards?"

She saw no reason to lie. "I want to examine the Roswell saucer crash wreckage."

"There was no flying saucer crash at Roswell," said Angleton. "It was a weather balloon."

"Yes, same old cover story. Very good. Except I have a lot of documented evidence that tells me otherwise."

"How exactly does this work? Do you inform Mr Adams immediately — or only after you've reported to Nina Onilova?"

For a moment, Edna thought he'd gotten his names mixed up. "Meaning Nina's in Washington now."

"Like you didn't already know," said Angleton.

"I just helped the police and the FBI arrest Polina Ilyin. Why would I do that if I was a Russian mole?"

"An ingenious way to cover your tracks. I might have even believed it if they hadn't rushed in Sister Josephine to take her place. Who better to handle you than the woman who recruited you?"

Edna took a breath to calm herself down. "Do you have any idea how paranoid you sound right now?" But there was no point haranguing the man; her only hope was to play him at his own game. "Look, I do understand. You see Rome as hallowed turf. It's where you and Kim Philby became good friends, is it not?"

Angleton bristled at the mention of Philby.

"We made a mistake going into the Vatican without agency sanction," Edna admitted. "But it wasn't my decision. Ask yourself how I got there, for starters. We took the same plane that's sitting out there on the runway at Plant 42. Garrick Stamford's plane. Are you saying he's a Russian spy too?"

Angleton appeared to consider this a moment. "Stamford is a fool. The man's not a good judge of character. He'd be in jail already if he wasn't so well-connected. Lee Tavon is the man who interests me —

he's even harder than you to pin down. Whenever I think I have him cornered, he pops up somewhere else."

He was changing the subject to keep her off-balance. "Nina Onilova didn't try to recruit me," she said. "But Polina Ilyin most certainly did. I might have even led her to believe I was considering it." She had his undivided attention now. "For a Russian, she doesn't hold her vodka too well. It makes her chatty. She told me something very interesting. For one, she confirmed your friend Philby is working for them. Something you might want to pass on to his masters in London. Unless you'd rather protect an actual Russian spy."

It was a terrible risk throwing Philby under the bus, particularly if it wasn't true. Polina hadn't confirmed it directly but, in her gut, Edna believed it. Donovan had told her to trust her gut. And she knew it would give Angleton pause.

"You're not getting into Edwards," Angleton told her. "I've given orders you be arrested on site if you turn up at the gate."

"I might just have to call your bluff on that," she said. "You don't have the authority to have me arrested, otherwise I'd already be in jail. That's a bit of a problem for you, I'd say, Mr Angleton."

"How so?"

"You're operating outside the law. You can't tell the FBI what you're up to, because that means admitting you're spying on American citizens. Maybe I'm the one who should go to the FBI. Tell them about you. I've become quite friendly with Agent Price Wilkins. How would that go down, do you think?"

"You're forgetting one thing," he said. "I could tell my men here to put a bullet in your head and bury you in the desert. Maybe then all my problems would be solved."

Edna glanced at Tough Guy. Suddenly, he wasn't so sure of himself. Killing a woman in cold blood probably wasn't on his list of things to do today.

"The Stalinist approach. How ironic," she said.

It touched a nerve. Angleton turned his back on her. "Go on," he said, "get the hell out of here. But make sure to stay away from Edwards. That road is now closed to civilian traffic."

FORTY SEVEN

Tuesday September 1, 1953

The CIA men hung on her tail all the way into Lancaster, making sure she stayed away from Edwards. They were quite brazen about it, though out here there was no traffic to hide in.

Lancaster began life as a stop on the rail line from Los Angeles to San Francisco. It had grown steadily since the 1930s with the construction of Muroc Air Force Base (renamed Edwards in 1949). Most folks in town had connections of some sort with the Air Force.

It was after eight at night when Edna pulled up on the main street. There was a chill in the air; the temperature dropped sharply out here when the sun went down. She was only wearing a short sleeve shirt with light trousers and felt goosebumps rising on her arms, a reminder that she was a long way from home.

She was relieved to see other people out and about. The Rendezvous Café was right next to the liquor store, in a line of shops that ran down Lancaster Boulevard. She resisted the urge to buy booze, and instead made her way to a pay phone at the back of the café. While she waited for a cup of coffee, she made a call. Sherman Adams had given her his direct line. He picked up on the second ring.

She explained everything that had gone down, including the fact that Stamford was holding Lee Tavon against his will, and that Angleton had said Sherman Adams was the man who had double-crossed her.

Adams groaned. "I take it you didn't believe him."

"Do you think I'd be calling you if I did?"

"What now?"

"I need to get back inside Plant 42 and see if I can help Lee."

"That sounds like a really bad idea."

"It's why I'm telling you in advance."

"Wouldn't it be safer if you just sit tight until I can get someone out there to help?" Adams suggested.

"There's no time," she said. "Stamford expects me to go back. If I don't, he'll know I'm up to something. It's safer this way." She wasn't walking away this time.

"I'd tell you not to do anything stupid, but I think that ship has sailed," he said.

"Mr Adams, you need to hear me now: you and the President have a problem. There's too much secrecy. Too many people operating outside the law. If you let this continue, the US government will no longer be in control of this country."

"You just get yourself back here safely," Adams said. "Write it up for me and we'll talk some more."

FORTY EIGHT

Tuesday September 1, 1953

If the Air Force guards at Edwards had been ordered to arrest her, the man at Plant 42 didn't get the memo.

"About time," he complained. "I expected you back hours ago."

She'd expected trouble — not relief. "Sorry to keep you waiting."

He opened the boom to let her in. "We don't normally man the gate at night. Mr Stamford said I had to stay here until you came back. I was starting to have my doubts. Can you give me a lift back to the hangar?"

"Tell you what," she said, "why don't you drive?"

He padlocked the gate shut, then jumped behind the wheel. As he drove into the hangar, she saw Stamford's plane was still parked on the tarmac outside, gleaming in the flood lights that now illuminated the concourse. She stepped inside the main hangar, keen to get out of the evening chill, but it was pitch black in there and more than a little creepy, so she remained outside where she could see what was happening.

By the time Stamford appeared, she was shivering from the cold breeze blowing across the desert runway. He ushered her back inside the hangar. It was still pitch-black inside. A light near the elevator was the only illumination. It was positively ominous.

"Did you have any success?" he asked, pushing the button that opened the elevator doors. She wondered if he already knew.

"I was run off the road by CIA goons. They said they'd have me locked up if I tried to go to Edwards."

"How rude," said Stamford. "Pity. I'd hoped you might actually pull it off."

The elevator doors opened on the lowest level. The flying saucer was once more in the center of the chamber, locked into position by scaffolding on three sides. Like they were guarding against the possibility Lee Tavon would try to fly it away.

"Where is he?" she asked Stamford.

"You tell me, Miss Drake. That man is slippery as a sack of eels."

"You mean he's gone?"

Stamford reached into his pocket and pulled out a metal disc a little bigger than a quarter, holding it up for her to see. "I left him in a locked room this afternoon while you and I had lunch. He was still here when I returned. We spoke for some time. He told me he'd reconfigured the saucer's operating system. I'm most grateful for that. But then I turned my back just for a moment, and he vanished. No sign of him anywhere. This little disc was all he left behind. Any thoughts on what it might be?"

Edna suspected her freedom hung upon answering him truthfully. "It's a device that opens a portal between two separate points in space. If he used it, he's long gone."

"A portal. Any idea how it works?"

"No," she said. "You're on your own there."

"Pity." Stamford flipped the disc in the air like a coin. "We think this thing was single use. It's no good to us now. All burnt out on the inside."

"I know that feeling," she said. "So, I guess we're done here. Any chance of a lift back to Washington?"

"You know, Dr Menzel is not at all happy you told the President about us," said Stamford.

"Dr Menzel needs to stop blaming other people for his own bad decisions. I might also point out Sherman Adams will have the FBI on your doorstep by early tomorrow if I'm still here."

Stamford sighed in resignation. "I have a pilot on standby. You'll be in Washington before dawn. Tell the President I am at his disposal."

FORTY NINE

Wednesday September 2, 1953

It was only a fifteen-minute taxi ride from the airport to Clarence Paulson's apartment in Columbia Heights. It wasn't yet seven in the morning as she struggled wearily to get the key in the front door. The voice behind her came as a shock.

"Miss Edna Drake?"

It was a woman's voice. Edna restrained herself from cursing as she turned around. "Who's asking?"

"I represent the Congressional Committee on Government Operations. Are you Edna Drake?" Edna tried to turn the key, but it wasn't properly engaged in the lock; she couldn't get away. The woman persisted. "Edna Drake I am serving you with a subpoena to appear before the Committee on Government Operations tomorrow morning at ten o'clock in the morning." She held the notice out in front of her.

"What if I refuse?" Edna asked her.

"Senator McCarthy wouldn't be too happy about that," the woman said.

Edna took the subpoena. The woman turned tail and fled. Edna reinserted the key and the door opened on the first go. Of course. As soon as she was inside, she tore open the envelope. The notice declared that, pursuant to lawful authority, she was ordered to appear before the Permanent Subcommittee on Investigations at the Senate

Office Building in committee room 357, to deliver verbal testimony in relation to Communist infiltration among employees of the State Department and their links to staff and operations in the US Senate.

Until a moment ago, she had been ready to collapse from weariness after the sleepless red-eye flight from California. But there would be no sleeping now. She needed to speak to Sherman Adams. She walked to the pay phone outside the corner store and dialed his office number, but Adams' secretary said he wasn't in. She left a message, gave the pay phone number, and demanded a return call as soon as possible.

She bought herself a fresh pack of Lucky Strikes and began smoking and pacing the pavement as she waited for the call. The ground was littered with butts when the phone finally rang an hour later.

"I'm happy you're back safe from California," Adams told her.

"I was too until an hour ago," she said.

"I've been trying to find out what they know," he said. "McCarthy's investigator Roy Cohn has the photos of you and Clarence in Rome. Looks like Angleton has cherry-picked the CIA's intelligence and fed the worst of it to the investigation's subcommittee."

"Don't you mean the CIA's illegally gathered intelligence?"

"Yes, but they don't need to reveal the source of their information. It's enough for them to know you were conducting business in Rome without the knowledge of Senator Ives, your employer."

"Employer in name only."

"You can't tell them that," Adams said in exasperation. "You can't tell these bastards anything. Remember, you have the Official Secrets Act to hide behind."

"Christ Sherm, that'll make it worse. The press would have a field day. Senate spy ring in bed with Russian agents. The whole thing is already a circus."

"This is an executive session, which means the hearing won't be public — thank God."

"That could be worse. They can tell the press their version of events afterwards, and they'll still parade me past the cameras like a lamb to the slaughter."

"I know you place a high value on the truth," said Adams, "but that's the last thing you can give them. It won't go down well. I doubt they'd believe you anyway. And you need a lawyer with you."

"Who's going to pay for that?" she asked.

There was silence on the line.

"Right, so not you."

"We can't, Edna. How would that look?"

"Well, you can bet Donald Menzel won't stump up the money. But come on, Sherm, you could shut this down, you know you could."

"You weren't in Rome on behalf of the President, Edna. We didn't even know about it until you told us last month. We won't lie for you. And we especially won't lie for a foreign national."

"Clarence is implicated?"

"We have to assume so, yes."

Meaning deportation was a virtual certainty. "You guys tell lies all the time when it suits you."

"That's not fair, Edna."

She took a breath. "No, you're right, it's not. But you don't have to take responsibility. Just say we were on a classified operation working against the Russians — not with them."

"Without CIA or State Department sanction? I'd be throwing the President under a bus. I'm afraid I won't do that," Sherman Adams said flatly.

He was throwing Edna under the bus instead.

FIFTY

Wednesday September 2, 1953

Donald Menzel waited for Edna in Crisfield at his usual place. Upon catching sight of her, he picked up his martini from the bar and headed for their table.

"I've already ordered," he said. "For me, not for you. You want something, you pay for it yourself."

She'd expected as much. "I'm not hungry."

"They must be jostling for parking outside with so many people on your tail," he said.

"Your name has been kept well clear of this," she assured him. "If anyone asks, I'm just having lunch with an old family friend."

"Friend, is it?" Menzel observed wryly.

"I came to plead with you to do something about Clarence. They want to deport him."

Menzel's expression darkened. "Another ruinous decision on your part, taking Clarence to the Jewel Box."

She grimaced. "You're right. By all means, blame me for that one. I certainly blame myself. But you need to help him, Donald. Pull strings. Talk to the Twelve. You need him."

Menzel put his drink down on the table like he'd just lost the taste for it. "Impossible. The damage is already done. I can't intervene without alerting the FBI to our existence."

Edna felt her face grow hot. She leant across the table to whisper, even though she felt like yelling. "You might want to bear in mind that Clarence and I travelled to Rome on your order, despite the misgivings I expressed to you quite clearly at the time. It remains within my means to casually drop your name into the middle of this communist feeding frenzy."

Menzel stared back at her with contempt. "I made a mistake trusting you to get it done in Rome."

Edna almost laughed; the man was incapable of admitting culpability. "It was a mistake to send anyone there. Donovan himself couldn't have gotten it done. They were ready and waiting."

At this, Menzel merely smiled condescendingly. "Bill would have seen it coming. But it wasn't Bill, was it? It was you. Your problem is you keep expecting somebody else to take responsibility for your actions."

"Jesus Christ, are you serious? How about you try looking in the mirror when you say that?" He'd made her so angry that it took all her willpower not to slap him across the face. "You could at least pay for a lawyer to help him. Please, Donald. He's your money man. You need him."

The man should be offering her a lawyer, but she was only willing to beg for Clarence. Menzel shook his head, like the idea wasn't even worthy of consideration. "It's too dangerous. Paulson can fend for himself. It's you I'm worried about. You cannot tell that committee what you were doing at the Vatican."

"Christ on a bike. Will you listen to yourself? You want me to protect you, but you won't lift a finger to help me."

"You talk and you'll put the entire Verus operation in jeopardy."

"I'm well aware of that," she hissed.

"You have to take the hit, Edna. You'll survive. This isn't Moscow. Nobody's throwing you in prison, they don't have enough evidence for that."

"No, they'll just tar me with their innuendos and throw me to the press hyenas."

"You used to be one of those hyenas not so long ago."

Edna thought about that. "You're right. I'd write this story with relish if I was in their shoes. Because when I stand up there tomorrow and plead the fifth, I'll sound guilty because of all the things I can't say."

"Hear me now," said Menzel, his tone measured and devastatingly clinical. "If you talk, the gloves will come off. We will bury you. In any event, you and I are done. I'm arranging six months' severance pay. It's more than you deserve, but I'll do it to ensure you never speak a word about your work to anyone. Ever."

Edna Drake stared at Menzel long and hard, before rising to her feet. "Try not to choke on your oysters."

FIFTY ONE

Thursday September 3, 1953

The taxi deposited her on the steps of the Senate Office Building, right into the middle of the melee. At least a dozen reporters and photographers gave her their undivided attention as she opened her door. She was the meal of the day.

"Edna, are you a Communist?" The voice was familiar, but she avoided the urge to look the questioner in the eyes.

Cameras snapped from every angle, but mostly in her face and blocking her way.

"Miss Drake, what will you be telling the committee today?"

"What does Senator Ives have to do with all of this?"

She said nothing and tried to keep her focus on the path ahead. Up the stairs and across the terrace to the building entrance. They weren't going to make it easy.

"Has Senator Ives fired you?" asked someone else.

"Why were you in Rome?"

McCarthy's subcommittee had already leaked then; it amazed her that there were any secrets at all in this city.

A Capitol Police officer directed her to wait in a chair outside the committee room. "Your name will be called when they're ready for you," he said.

Room 357 was much smaller than the Caucus Room, used for public hearings. There were seven senators on the investigations sub-committee — all of them Republican since three Democrats had re-signed in protest in July, an act against McCarthy hiring staff with-out consultation. Edna wasn't expecting a balanced discussion. Chief counsel Roy Cohn was, by all accounts, McCarthy's youthful and arrogant attack dog, with zero tolerance for socialist or communist sympathies of any description.

The woman ahead of her emerged from the subcommittee room ashen-faced and devastated. Her lawyer whispered urgently in her ear, trying to offer consolation. Edna was just starting to think coming here alone had been a terrible idea, when an arm pushed open the committee room door and her name was called.

Chairs lined the places around a U-shaped bench, but there were only three members of the subcommittee left — all Republican — and they sat bunched together on one side. It didn't exactly lend them an air of impartiality. A chandelier hung from the ornate committee room ceiling, its light reflecting in a mirror that hung directly behind Senator McCarthy, who was sat alone, godlike, facing her directly at the head of the room. The American Inquisition.

Roy Cohn was the only man on his feet; he stood alongside Mc-Carthy. "The next witness is Edna Drake, Mr Chairman," Cohn said. His dark and oily hair was plastered neatly across his head. He stared clinically as Edna was directed to a seat, his bulbous and hooked nose immediately giving her the impression he was a man with something to prove. She sat down behind a microphone that would record her testimony.

McCarthy said nothing. South Dakota Senator Karl Mundt was the first to address Edna directly. His fat, balding head and bow tie made him seem less threatening, but she didn't for a moment think any of these senators would give her an inch. "Miss Drake, do you solemnly swear the testimony you are about to give us is the truth, the whole truth, and nothing but the truth, so help you God?" Mundt asked her.

"I do, sir."

"Please be seated," said Cohn, doing so himself beside Senator Mc-Carthy like daddy's good boy. "You're appearing on your own today, without legal counsel, is that correct, Miss Drake?"

"Yes, that's correct."

Cohn nodded. "Please state your full name for the proceedings."

"Edna Jean Drake."

"What is your address?"

"It is currently apartment three, 1441 Girard Street in Columbia Heights."

"You say currently," said Cohn. "Are you in the process of moving?"

"It's not my permanent address. I am staying there, but I don't know for how long."

"You have no permanent address?" He made it sound suspicious; this was just a first attempt at getting her off-balance.

"That's right, Mr Cohn."

"Before we begin," said Senator McCarthy, "I want to advise you that if, at any time, you feel you need legal counsel, we will adjourn this hearing so you can do so." Edna nodded her understanding and McCarthy turned his attention to his chief counsel. "Please proceed, Mr Cohn."

They began by questioning her about the most tedious aspects of her work for Senator Ives, perhaps trying to catch her in a lie, but ultimately seeking to demonstrate their working theory that her role in Ives' office was no more than a front for her other activities. This much she knew, thanks to what Sherman Adams had been able to glean through friendly Senate sources.

But she had this covered. She'd made sure to perform an active role for Senator Ives in order to certify her cover; Edna had no trouble answering their questions. He asked if she had ever met anyone in the State Department who had expressed Communist sympathies. She told them she hadn't. Realizing this was going nowhere, Cohn changed tack. "Have you ever been a member of the Communist Party?"

She stared him straight in the eye. "No, I have not."

"Have you ever been involved in Communist activities of any description?"

"No sir, I have not. I have nursed and treated women in Germany who were raped by Russian soldiers, but I don't think that's what you're asking me."

McCarthy intervened now, shifting forward in his seat and moving papers about in front of him. "Miss Drake, we have positive evidence of your Communist activities," he said, pointing to the papers. "You're an intelligent girl. It would be a mistake for you to think you are going to fool this committee, because you can't."

Cohn rose to his feet and walked towards her. "I am going to show you a photograph now," he said, handing her a copy of the image. It was one of the photos fed to the CIA by Mossad.

"Yes, I'm aware of this photograph," she said.

"Please explain where this was taken and who you are with," Cohn demanded.

"This was in Rome. The Vatican, to be more specific. The man standing beside me is a Catholic priest, Father Clarence Paulson. The woman on my other side was known to us as Sister Josephine."

"What is the nature of your relationship with Sister Josephine?" Cohn asked, standing close to her now like he was moving in for the kill.

"I have no relationship with her."

"You're not being truthful with us," said Cohn.

"What I've just told you is the God's honest truth of the matter."

"Are you aware that this woman — who you've called Sister Josephine — is in fact Nina Onilova, an agent of the Russian secret intelligence service?"

"I would like to take my Fifth Amendment rights and decline to answer that question," she said.

Cohn began pacing in a circle. McCarthy sighed loudly, clearly frustrated by her refusal. "It's a simple question, Miss Drake," Cohn continued. "Did you know she was a Soviet agent when you chose to spend time with her in Rome?"

Phrased in that way, it would have been safe to tell him she'd had no idea who Josephine was, but she was afraid this would open her up to further questioning. "Again, I take the Fifth and decline to answer."

"Are we to infer from your response that the answer is yes, you did know she was a Russian agent and you are refusing to answer because in doing so you might incriminate yourself?" McCarthy asked.

"In taking the Fifth, I am neither confirming nor denying any such thing."

Cohn took a few more steps, still trying to find a way to get something out of her. "Very well," said Cohn, "let me ask you a different question. Are you working for a secret cabal of senior government and military men and are they, in fact, affiliated to the Communist Party?"

He meant Majestic-12. She was surprised he'd gotten so close, but Edna knew this committee would take any rumor with a grain of truth and twist it into something sinister. "I will decline to answer that question too."

"You're condemning yourself by your responses," said Cohn.

She pondered this a minute. He'd clearly gone too far, but in doing so she felt it gave her an opportunity to express a personal view without breaking security oaths or perjuring herself. "Let me say this: I am no friend of the Soviet Union or its corrupt system of government. I am a proud American and have no interest whatsoever in promoting either the Soviet Union or the Communist Party."

Michigan Senator Charles Potter interjected. Though he was losing his hair, he might have been the youngest of the men at the table. His tone was more measured; he spoke slowly and deliberately, "I've heard this group is called 'Magic' or some such. If what you say is true, why not tell us whether or not you've heard Communist sympathies being expressed?"

Edna could quote her security oaths to them, but that would be making an admission of an entirely different sort. The agreement she'd signed included a specific clause stipulating she must never acknowledge the existence of the Verus Foundation, or Majestic, to anyone lacking adequate clearance. "I will decline to answer on the grounds that it may tend to incriminate me."

Senator McCarthy shook his head in clear disappointment. "If you have no sympathy for communism, as you have just told us, you have a duty to answer our questions."

"With respect, Senator, I don't accept the self-appointed role of this committee as judge and executioner of lives and reputations. Freedom of expression and critical thought is the very thing that separates us from totalitarianism. I believe you have overstepped the mark, sir."

McCarthy bristled and his face turned red. For a moment, he looked like he was dying to slam the desk, to scream at her to shut her dirty little commie mouth. Edna could see the words on the tip of his tongue. But McCarthy held himself together. "I would remind you, Miss Drake, you can be indicted for perjury if you lie to this subcommittee. There is a jail penalty attached to that."

"I have claimed my Fifth Amendment rights and I stand by that."

"Were you interviewed by the FBI when they detained Father Clarence Paulson just a few days ago?" asked Cohn.

"No sir, I was not."

"I've literally just warned you about perjury, Miss Drake," McCarthy spat back.

"I spoke to the FBI informally," she said. "I did not consider that an interview, in the official sense of the word. I was, however, interviewed by homicide detective Vincent Kaplan."

"Because you were the prime suspect in a murder investigation," said Cohn.

She shook her head. "I assisted the police and the FBI in uncovering a killer."

"By using your personal relationship with a Russian agent who has been working on US soil," Cohn suggested. "By my count, that's two Russian spies you've been seen spending time with. Now I know you don't work for the CIA, so who do you work for, Miss Drake?"

"Once again, I take the Fifth, Mr Cohn."

"Isn't it the case that the FBI is so concerned about the activities of you and Father Paulson that they are having him deported to England as an undesirable alien?"

"It's not for me to say what concerns the FBI," Edna said.

"To your knowledge, is Father Clarence Paulson a member of the Communist Party?" Cohn asked her.

"No, I don't believe he is."

Cohn pressed the point. "You mean you can't be sure of it?"

"We have never discussed the matter," she said, "but to the best of my knowledge, he is not."

"Have your connections to Russian intelligence come about directly as a result of your work with Senator Irving Ives?" McCarthy asked.

"I reject the premise of the question and refuse to say any more under my Fifth Amendment rights."

"We understand completely that you would be reluctant, and perhaps even frightened, to speak to us about Senator Ives' role in all of this," said Cohn. "But do you understand that we are trying to protect government integrity?"

Edna stared at her shoes and breathed deeply. McCarthy hated Irving Ives because he'd been one of a handful of senators who had condemned McCarthy's overzealous pursuit of communists. They could attack her, but she drew the line at them poisoning Ives' reputation. She stared daggers at them, and gave them a response that would become the focal point of front-page headlines for days. "Senator Ives has no connections to communism, Mr Cohn. By even suggesting as much in this forum, it is you who commits an act of perjury and slander. I demand you withdraw the statement at once."

Cohn stared back at her like he had been physically struck across the face. She refused to back down.

"That's quite enough, Miss Drake," Senator Mundt declared.

"I agree entirely senator, and I would like Mr Cohn to withdraw the remark. He has not one shred of evidence to back it up."

"You are the evidence, Miss Drake," said Cohn. "You work for Senator Ives."

She sighed. This was it. Time to fall on her sword. "Senator Ives had no knowledge of my trip to Rome. I was not there on behalf of the government."

A flash of jubilation crossed Roy Cohn's face. "Very well, in that case I withdraw my remarks about Senator Ives. But will you please tell this hearing why you were in Rome?"

"Again, I take my Fifth Amendment right and decline to answer the question."

"On the grounds that your answer might incriminate you?" asked McCarthy.

"I assert my Fifth Amendment rights, senator."

"Answer me this, Miss Drake," said McCarthy, "if the Congress of the United States were to declare war against the Soviet Union and you considered that declaration to be unjust, would you accept money to be a spy for the Soviet Union?"

What sort of idiotic question was that? "I would not," she said.

"Would you act as a spy without payment?" Senator Potter asked.

The suggestion was so ludicrous Edna almost felt she shouldn't dignify it with a response. "No Senator, not under any circumstance would I act as a spy against my own country."

"Have you ever been engaged in espionage against the United States?" Cohn asked her.

"No."

"Yet on multiple occasions you have been observed in the company of a Washington-based Russian diplomat named Polina Ilyin," said McCarthy. "I know you're not as dumb as you're trying to make out, Miss Drake. What did you discuss in your meetings with Polina Ilyin?"

Here it was. The killer blow. Edna looked up at the ceiling and drew a long, slow breath. "I must refuse to answer that question on the same grounds as previously stated."

FIFTY TWO

September 3-4, 1953

It was a curious and terrible thing to see her own demise writ large in newspaper headlines. The pain of it was made more acute by the fact that, while it was all so shockingly wrong and slanderous, there wasn't a thing Edna could do to prevent it. Nor was anyone coming to save her.

The *Evening Star* had been first with the news, splashing her face across its front page late on Wednesday:

Ives senate staffer refuses to explain meetings with Russians

Edna wondered if the reporters who had been awaiting her arrival at the Senate Office Building on Wednesday morning had already been told Senator Ives was firing her. It had been one of the first questions thrown at her upon heading into McCarthy's inquisition. That she had been damned simply for facing McCarthy's inquisition was unsurprising. Nobody from Senator Ives' office had spoken to her before or after the hearing, yet all the papers quoted Ives directly in saying her employment had been terminated. It was some small comfort that the senator had seen fit to remain silent about the terms of her employment in his office — that the work she had performed was indeed designed to cover her work at Verus.

On the TV news that night, her refusal to answer questions both before and after the hearing was used to illustrate how little information she had provided the subcommittee.

"What was Edna Drake doing in Rome with a Russian agent and why did she later meet with a Russian diplomat in Washington who has since been arrested in connection with murder? Just some of the questions that remain unanswered tonight."

By late Wednesday evening, as the implications of it all began to sink in, Edna sat in the dark inside Clarence Paulson's apartment listening as the television said her name. She stared out the window and tried to make sense of it all.

She awoke in the same armchair at the break of dawn, gripped by an entirely new sense of dread: she would have to call her parents. She would have to go outside for that. Facing the world was the last thing she wanted to do, but she'd have to go out there eventually: the only thing vaguely edible in Paulson's ice box was beer and a moldy wedge of blue stilton that turned her stomach when she unwrapped it. What was it about Englishmen and stinky cheese? Edna would either have to survive on water and whiskey until the media pack lost interest, or risk going out to buy food and make a phone call. Now was probably as good a time as any; the press hadn't tracked her down yet, but it was only a matter of time.

With a scarf wrapped tightly around her head in an effort to mask her appearance, Edna made it to the grocery store. She bought fresh bread, butter, apples, milk, some delicious pastrami, and a jar of Nescafe. She also grabbed copies of the *Washington Post* and the *New York Times,* taking care to fold them over before going to the counter so the clerk wouldn't realize it was Edna's face splashed across the front pages. It didn't work; he'd seen the papers already. With her arms full — she hadn't thought to take a bag — she chickened out on the call home. She told herself it was a call better made on a full stomach. Edna made it back to the apartment without being spotted, made herself coffee and toast, and sat down to see how the respectable papers had chosen to shoot her down.

The *Post* headline summed it up:

Senator Ives 'unaware' staffer met with Russian spies

The story was the work of her old friend and former lover, Joe Eldridge. He must have been there in the press pack the previous day; she hadn't noticed. His story did, at least, go some way to offering Edna the benefit of the doubt, noting she had told the hearing, "I am no friend of the Soviet Union or its corrupt system of government."

But those words sounded hollow when set against all the other questions she'd refused to answer. Questions dutifully repeated by Cohn and Senator McCarthy to any reporter who bothered to ask. Seeing her own evidence in print made Edna seem remarkably un-cooperative. Like a criminal seeking to dodge the noose, but only succeeding in pulling it tighter.

Eldridge had also managed to find out Polina Ilyin was in FBI custody, and that Edna had been "instrumental" in aiding authorities in the Russian's arrest. He went on to quote Cohn, saying Edna's usefulness to authorities might not be enough to save her from accusations of selling information to America's enemy.

The *New York Times* noted her stern defense of Irving Ives and her claim of disinterest in communism that again jarred against all the things she had refused to say. Both papers also revealed the INS would deport Clarence Paulson to the United Kingdom, following his refusal to appear before the subcommittee.

She wondered if her parents had seen the news yet. There was no more putting it off; she had to speak to them. Adding sunglasses to the scarf, Edna headed back to the street corner telephone outside the grocery store. She called her dad.

He sympathized, but sounded so disappointed in her. It was almost too much to bear. Particularly given she couldn't answer any of his questions, even though they were perfectly reasonable. He wanted so hard to understand what she'd been doing that had gotten her into so much hot water. She reassured him she wasn't a Communist sympathizer, and suggested he say nothing to reporters should they call for comment.

There would be no trip home for consolation. It hadn't worked last time, and now the silence would be unbearable. There was nothing Edna could say to alleviate their fears, and she didn't want to drag them down into the mud with her.

Edna pulled another nickel from her pocket and asked the operator to put her through to Agent Price Wilkins at FBI Headquarters. She asked him to help her get in to see Clarence. He told her she didn't have a snowball's chance in hell, and didn't sound the least bit inclined to do anything to help.

Knowing by this point it was a fruitless exercise, she dialed Sherman Adams at the White House. He wouldn't take her call. His secretary said he was busy, but made it abundantly clear Edna should not attempt to call back.

There was one person left who would speak to her; Lee Tavon would take her under his wing. But she couldn't go near him now. It would risk bringing the Outherians to the media's attention.

Edna pulled open the pay phone cage door to find Joe Eldridge waiting for her.

He was clean-shaven, wearing a freshly ironed shirt with hair well cropped, and twenty pounds lighter than the last time she'd seen him. In short, he looked good. "Hello Edna."

"You found me," she said.

Joe grinned. "I wish I could say it was the brilliance of my investigative technique, but the truth is the grocery store owner put a call in to the paper when you made an appearance this morning."

"I'm glad they sent you, that was a smart move. But I really don't have anything to say, Joe."

She heard a camera snapping and recognized the snapper. "Hey, Carl."

Carl Ogden looked up from his viewfinder. "Hey Edna, how are you babe?"

"I've been better, I won't lie," she said.

"Come on, it's me," said Joe. "There must be something you can give me. Even off the record. I want to help you if I can. I know how much you hate the commies."

"Hate is a very strong word, Joe. Oversimple and overused of late, I find."

"What have you really been doing for Senator Ives? Does he have links to the CIA I don't know about?"

"Like I said, Irving Ives has nothing to do with any of this."

"Any of what?"

Joe's dogged persistence made her laugh; it was really quite admirable. "No comment."

"Somebody has hung you out to dry. Who is it? Who are you protecting?"

"I was trying to protect myself. And Senator Ives, of course." He was writing down every word that left her lips. All of it would be in the next day's paper. She had to tread carefully.

"If Irving Ives knows nothing about this, who are you really working for?" Eldridge asked.

She recalling having this conversation a year ago with Majestic-12 member Gordon Gray. Back then, she'd been a *Times-Herald* reporter, trying to break open a story on what the Truman administration knew about flying saucers. Edna had barely managed to scratch the surface before they silenced her. She offered Eldridge the benefit of the same response Gray had given her. "I'm bound by US government security oaths that prevent me from explaining any further," she said. "I believe it's in everyone's best interests that I make no further comment."

She knew Donald Menzel would say she had gone too far in saying this much. But Menzel had refused to come to her defense, so he could go to hell.

Joe Eldridge's mouth fell open. "Are you serious?"

"Do you need me to repeat it?"

"No", he mouthed silently, slowly shaking his head as he scribbled madly to get it down on paper. "Why didn't you say this in your own defense yesterday?"

"No comment," she said.

He got that down too and smiled at her in admiration. "I knew it. You're a goddamned spy."

"I didn't say that."

"This is gold," Joe said. "You're a gem. I could kiss you."

She held up a hand to hold him back. "Please don't. Go write your story, Joe. And never darken my door again. I won't be saying another word to anyone."

FIFTY THREE

Sunday September 6, 1953

For three days, Edna kept her head down and remained inside the apartment, which was made possible thanks to a bag of groceries that arrived at her door mysteriously on Thursday afternoon. Either the grocery store owner's way of saying sorry or, more likely, Joe Eldridge's way of saying thanks.

His piece in the *Post* on Friday might have gone some way toward ensuring her future wouldn't be spent in poverty or prison. Eldridge had intimated she was linked in some way to classified government work. He quoted Senator Symington in suggesting there was a secret alliance of senior men operating inside the Pentagon — for reasons unknown but deeply suspicious — and that they believed Edna Drake was working for them. It was deemed to be evidence of McCarthy's obsessional, but hitherto unproven, assertion of Communist infiltration of the State Department. Senator Ives denied all knowledge of such things, but let it slip that Edna Drake had only worked in his office part-time. Edna's quote, citing security oaths, painted her as a spy. Eldridge then made the point that not all spies were bad; some were working to advance American interests.

She felt vindicated to some extent, if still weighed down by a growing sense of desolation and abandonment. It was impossible to imagine what sort of life she might have in the wake of all this. Being bound by secrecy appeared to rule out any return to journalism, given she would never be able to adequately explain herself. The McCarthyist taint had destroyed bigger and more robust careers than hers. Edna was no communist and there was no evidence to suggest she ever had been, yet most prospective employers would view her as radioactive.

Right on ten o'clock, with church bells ringing somewhere in the surrounding neighborhood, there was a shimmer in the sunlight streaming through the window that alerted her to the imminent arrival of Paolo Favaloro. He snapped into focus like a cathode-ray tube that had just warmed up. It comforted her to think of him as a TV signal, rather than a ghost. "Salutations Miss Drake."

"Hello Paolo, how are you? Nice to know someone's still thinking of me."

"You're feeling lonely and misunderstood. Something we have in common, I believe."

"You're really brightening my day here, Paolo."

"I come to you as an emissary of Clarence Paulson. He wants me to tell you they are treating him well and that you should not worry."

Edna frowned. She should be happy to hear it — so why did the message have the opposite effect? "Will you tell him I'm sorry? It's my fault entirely and, well, I just feel terrible about it."

Paolo's image faltered for a moment, like he was having signal transmission problems. He froze and the light seemed to go out of his eyes. But after a few seconds he was back, and she realized what had been happening: he'd been talking to Clarence. "He would have insisted on being with you in that bar no matter what. He says to tell you that despite what you may think, he's not twisted around your finger. He is his own man."

Edna laughed in delight. "Tell him I will find a way to get to England."

"He thought you might say that. He forbids it."

She frowned. "Forbids? Who does he...?"

"Apologies," said Paolo. "My word, not his. Clarence says you must stay focused on your work."

She sighed. "I have no work."

Favaloro smiled knowingly at her. "You will."

Did he know something she didn't? "I don't know who you've been talking to."

"You will know soon enough," Paolo told her enigmatically.

She sensed he was getting ready to leave. "Do me a favor. Tell him..." Did she really mean to say it? "Tell him we'll see one another again. Tell him I love him."

Paolo Favaloro nodded in understanding and vanished like somebody had yanked his electrical plug from the socket.

She spent much of the day ruminating on all that might be, feeling a growing sense of optimism even as the logical part of her brain told her a little hope could be a dangerous thing.

Then, late in the afternoon, Lee Tavon and Sherman Adams showed up.

FIFTY FOUR

Sunday September 6, 1953

Edna heard a crackle like cellophane and looked up as two Lee Tavons appeared in Paulson's lounge room, one after the other. They smiled at her in carbon-copy expressions of delight. "Hello my dear," they said as one.

"Jesus Christ, are you trying to give a girl a heart attack? You're both mad to come here like this," she said, wondering for the umpteenth time whether it was better to address them as one person, or as separate entities.

"Mad, yes, most likely," they replied in unison. It was the strangest thing. Theirs was a single voice in stereo, coming from two mouths at once. The right-hand Lee flicked a small disc into the hallway, then took a step over it and, in doing so, vanished. Another portal device. The apartment was becoming a Swiss cheese of wormholes. The other Tavon clicked a button on a black box the size of a cigarette packet, then bent over to retrieve the disc from the carpet.

"Eyes and ears," Tavon explained. "We'll know immediately if something happens outside." He pulled another controller device from his pocket. "This one is for you."

"I'm not sure I want it," she said.

"Believe me, you do." He walked over and switched on the wireless atop the lounge room mantelpiece.

Edna had it tuned to WOOK-AM. Duke Ellington's orchestra filled the room, playing a new rendition of *The Mooche*. The track was twenty-five years old, but was re-recorded for Ellington's album, *Uptown*. It took Edna right back to her childhood in Rockaway. She remembered hearing those wistful and foreboding trumpets for the first time, blaring out over the boardwalk like a call from her future. She had always marveled at how Ellington extracted beauty and pleasure from passion and pain. Now the circle had finally closed; it filled her with a powerful feeling of déjà vu. Was this the moment she'd felt coming all those years ago?

It also meant Tavon knew somebody was listening. He pressed the disc into her hand and stepped in close. "This is your ticket to freedom," he told her quietly.

"Why do I need it?" she asked.

"The CIA has stopped tailing you, but I'm afraid the FBI have taken over."

This came as no great surprise. "You shouldn't have come here. I'm probably on Hoover's most wanted list." She pointed at the radio. "I take it that's for them?"

Tavon shook his head. "No. That's for the Russians. They have this place bugged."

A muted trumpet sounded its amusement behind them. She smiled ruefully, wondering how Lee Tavon could possibly know what the Russians had done. Lately, it felt like someone else was always having the last laugh.

"How are you doing, kid?" Tavon asked her.

Edna took a long, deep breath. As she let it out slowly, she pondered how best to put the depths of her emotions into words. "I feel like my existence has been obliterated. I'm completely alone and misunderstood with nowhere to turn." She felt tears welling up in her eyes and wiped them away angrily. "Sorry. You were probably hoping for a simple, 'I'm fine how are you?' right?"

"It's OK to be upset. Nothing to be ashamed about. You've had a torrid time of it."

"The worst part is nobody else understanding. I'm sure my father thinks I'm selling secrets to the Russians. I should just tell him everything and be done with it, except I'm terrified that would only put him in danger. There are so many people keeping secrets from one another. And now McCarthy has everyone paranoid."

Tavon pulled her into a hug, which let loose her tears in a torrent. They remained in that embrace for a long time, and it gave her enormous comfort. "I want you to know you'll be all right," he said. He showed her how to use the black box. "There is a disc we've embedded underneath the carpet in here. Nobody will ever find it. But it will allow you to come and go from here without being observed." The box had two buttons: one blue and one red. The red one was glowing. He pushed it and the light went off. "That's the activation button. When it's lit, the portal is open. The blue button sets your current location as the hub for your network. No matter where you go, you will always return to the hub. But from the hub, you travel to wherever the dial is set."

The dial was set above the buttons. It clicked through six different settings.

"What network?" she asked.

"We've built one for you," Tavon said. "Your first stop is a small clearing inside Meridian Hill Park. And because it's an outside location, this unit has a vibrational distortion field built in. Which means when you arrive outside, even if somebody is standing right beside you, they'll never know."

Edna held the box gingerly, like it was a deadly weapon. "Vibrational distortion — is that dangerous?"

He shook his head. "It throws all atomic particles within close vicinity of the device into a different vibrational phase. This renders you invisible for the moment of arrival, and allows you to gradually snap back into phase. Anyone looking at you while this occurs will experience it as blurred vision and a moment of forgetfulness, much like a dream that escapes your recollection the moment you awake."

"What are the other destinations?" she asked.

"Number two is your bedroom at Deborah's house. The third is a room we have assigned to you at the farm in Virginia. The others give you options. I have a couple of destinations in mind, but they are — how shall I put it — yet to be confirmed."

"This is the same device you used to escape from Garrick Stamford," she said.

"That's right."

"But that disc burnt out after just one use — Stamford showed it to me."

Tavon nodded. "That was by design. Made for a single-use getaway to ensure the portal closed behind me. Your network is more robust."

"I'm sure Stamford has boffins poring over that disc, trying to understand how it works."

"They won't get far with it. Was Garrick angry I left?"

"Yes and no," she said. "Recalibrating the saucer's operating system has given them a lot to think about. He flew me home, I guess he can't have been too upset."

There was another knock at the door.

"Is that the other you?" she asked.

"That," said Tavon, "is Sherman Adams."

Edna looked at him in amazement. "You knew he was coming."

Tavon shrugged. "I wanted to be here when he arrived."

There were no conventional means by which Tavon could have known the President's man would turn up today; they didn't know one another. But Edna had only begun to scratch the surface on the Outherians' ability to predict the future.

"He has a proposal for you," Tavon said. "But before you answer, I want you to know you can stay in this apartment indefinitely. I own it, so you don't have to worry about rent. You're my guest. Remind me later to show you the wall safe — Clarence has plenty of money."

A few more pieces of the puzzle snapped into place. "You've been helping him make money." Lee Tavon just smiled. It made so much sense. Clarence was a disillusioned priest; he had no interest in money. Until this moment, she hadn't stopped to ask herself how he'd managed to trade in gold so successfully.

She almost laughed when she opened the door to discover Adams wearing a trench coat, trilby, and dark glasses. The grey coat and brown hat were oddly mismatched. Edna guessed he'd thrown the outfit together in a hurry. Upon seeing Tavon behind Edna, the President's man was taken aback — he'd obviously assumed she'd be alone.

"Would you like to come in?" she asked him.

"Perhaps it's best I come back another time," Adams suggested.

"I'm amazed you've come at all," Edna admitted. "But there's no need to be shy, this is someone you'll want to meet."

Adams stepped inside. Lee Tavon introduced himself and Adams shook his hand.

Edna watched with no small degree of amusement at the wonder and astonishment washing across Adams' face. "You're the infamous Lee Tavon," said Adams. "You look remarkably down to Earth for someone from another planet."

"That's because I am both these things at once," said Tavon. "It's how I hide in plain sight."

Adams finally remembered why he'd come and turned his attention to Edna, offering her a profound apology for not getting in touch sooner as he removed his coat and sunglasses. "I had to wait for the press to lose interest. Though I did see two G-men out front," he said, smoothing his hair back into place as he took off his hat.

"I hope that doesn't worry you," she said.

"J. Edgar is nothing if not predictable," Adams said. "It's why I dressed incognito."

"Probably safe to assume they'll identify you in photo analysis," said Tavon. "But there's no need to worry, we have another way to get you safely out of here." He gave Edna a wink.

"What would that be?" Adams asked. "A spaceship on the roof?"

"Not exactly," said Tavon. Though space travel of a sort was certainly involved. "It's more of a secret passageway. Now, you two have your talk; I'm going to make a pot of coffee." He wandered off towards the kitchen, already well aware of the topic of conversation. Edna urged Adams to take a seat on the lounge, aware there was more to this than an apology.

"I was impressed with how you handled the lion's den," Adams began. "I want you to know neither the President nor I will forget it."

"Forgive me for not taking a great deal of comfort from that. You left me to fend for myself."

Adams nodded. "We did. It's one of the harsh realities of politics. You can't always help your friends. But that's why I'm here. We want you to come back and work for us. On the down-low."

"Sherm, my name is mud. How would you ensure that didn't come back to bite you politically?"

"Quite simple, really. We'd give you an entirely new identity," Sherman Adams offered. "We need to kill Edna Drake."

FIFTY FIVE

Sunday September 6, 1953

"All we need to do is fake your death," Adams explained.

Edna screwed her nose up in horror. "I could never do that to my parents."

Adams nodded. "No, no, I guess not. I take your point. All right then, what if Edna flees to Mexico or Argentina?"

It was odd, hearing him talking about her in the third person. "That could work," she admitted. "But Mexico would be her preference. Edna's always wanted to visit Acapulco."

"All right, good. That's settled. She flies down for a holiday and decides to stay for good. She'll be out of the FBI's reach and officially, as far as the US Government is concerned, Edna will remain there forevermore. Blending into the expat community, and drowning her sorrows in gin cocktails by the waterfront."

"Meanwhile I become somebody else."

"All you'd need to do is make the odd appearance down there to maintain the ruse, then return to America in the guise of your newly minted self," he said.

"I think, with Lee's help, we can go one better than that. But you'd need to make sure we have the CIA on board," Edna insisted. "I wouldn't want James Angleton trying to undermine me."

"Already taken care of," Adams assured her.

"But why now?" she asked. "Why couldn't you do this for me to begin with?"

Adams smiled grimly. "You needed to die before you could rise again."

She laughed heartily. "Don't let Bill Donovan hear you talk like that. Likening a woman to Jesus Christ? That's blasphemy."

"I say it merely to make my point," Adams said. "I've read the report you sent me on the FS-1 operation and your experiences in the underground hangar. Remarkable work. The President has noted your concerns about that power in the hands of Verus and Lockheed."

"It seems wrong to me that these things have been happening without the President's knowledge," she stated.

"You're right. Mr Eisenhower and I would happily place the entire Verus Foundation operation under your control, were that within our remit."

Edna thought about this. Verus was an autonomous organization; Truman had made sure of that while he was still president. Menzel might be the man in control, but there were still ways to have an influence over his behavior. "There must be someone else in MJ-12 who shares our concerns," she said. "What about Roscoe Hillenkoetter, or Hoyt Vandenberg?"

Adams shook his head. "Hoyt is dying. He's about to go into hospital. I'm afraid he won't be coming out."

Edna was shocked, but not surprised. "I'm very sorry to hear that." She'd liked Vandenberg from the moment they'd met; he was a straight shooter.

Now that she was thinking about it, it occurred to her that a front-on assault was not the solution with a man like Menzel. There was a better way.

"Roscoe Hillenkoetter is in favor of opening Majestic matters to public scrutiny," said Adams. "He and Menzel differ on that point, and I'm not sure the art of gentle persuasion is one of Roscoe's known attributes."

"No, you're right," she agreed. "The person we need is Gordon Gray. He and Donald are both intellectuals. Gordon is well capable of helping Dr Menzel gently shift course."

"What does that mean?" Adams asked.

Lee Tavon delivered them coffees on a wooden tray and then made another tactical retreat. As usual, he'd appeared at precisely the right time. With a single glance, he confirmed to Edna he knew what she was about to propose, and that he approved.

"We can control the purse strings," she said. "Clarence Paulson has become something of a necessity for Verus. He trades in gold. In fact, I strongly suspect he has a stockpile of it. All we need to do is ensure the money keeps coming, through Clarence. He who controls the money, controls Verus."

"You're talking about a man who's about to be deported," Adams pointed out.

She thought of the black box handed to her by Lee Tavon, and the spare destinations remaining on the dial. Edna grinned. "I don't think will be much of a problem. But tell me, what exactly is it you want me to do for the President?"

Adams stared at her intensely. "We want you to help us work toward full public disclosure. Let's get these secrets about unearthly visitors into the open."

That caught Edna entirely off guard. "Sherm, do you understand what you're saying?"

"I do. More importantly, the President understands."

"There are many powerful men who will do everything to stop you. To say nothing of the visitors themselves. There are some whose motivations remain far from clear," Edna warned.

Lee Tavon chose this moment to reappear. She knew he'd been listening in, or reading their minds. Or both. "The Outherians would fully support your plan," Tavon said. Edna wasn't surprised. It was the Outherians who had orchestrated the Big Flap — the saucers that appeared over Washington D.C. for two successive weekends the year before.

"What about the churches?" Edna asked. "Or the stock market? This would need to be done very carefully."

Adams nodded. "You're right. It's why we need to conduct a test."

FIFTY SIX

Wednesday, September 23, 1953

Ernst 'Teddy' Stauffer was a handsome musician who looked like he was born for the silver screen, though his star quality had dulled the moment he'd opened his mouth. Not that this was his fault. It was due to his German Swiss accent, which was decidedly out of vogue at the box office.

This Germanic confidence that oozed from every pore, combined with his Aryan good looks, meant Teddy came across like a Nazi poster boy when Edna had first met him. Germany was where he'd begun his career, playing American swing music with his band the Teddies. In the 1930s, he was regarded as Germany's King of Swing. But the war drove Stauffer back to Switzerland — the Nazis never trusted jazz. It wasn't deemed to be good German music. From Switzerland, Teddy emigrated to America, and thence to Mexico where he had built for himself a lush and lucrative life.

Teddy Stauffer was the manager of the Casablanca Hotel in Acapulco. The grand iconic landmark sat high upon a hill, a haven for America's rich and famous. Its suites and public spaces offered unparalleled views of the Acapulco waterfront. Teddy had become a close friend and associate of Washington bar owner and businessman Lee Tavon, and happily agreed to do him the favor of hiring Edna.

He'd made a pass at Edna by way of an opening gambit. She'd taken a great deal of pleasure in turning Teddy down; she'd heard the casting couch was his standard hiring tactic. Thus, he'd blithely assumed he would have his way, because men like him almost always did. His look of shock at her forceful rejection was worth Edna's trip to Mexico all on its own. He'd hired her anyway, as she'd known he would. They had both been happy to put that first awkward meeting behind them, and had since become firm friends.

In the short time he had been running the Casablanca, Teddy had attracted many of the biggest names in Hollywood to his lavish playground south of the border. For them, the promise of a getaway — free from America's relentless scrutiny and bothersome morality — offered endless allure.

Teddy had nearly become a celebrity in his own right. In 1947, he'd been Rita Hayworth's lover while she was between husbands, her heart broken by Orson Welles but still valiantly playing the field. The affair didn't last long. Later, Teddy married actress Hedy Lamarr, but it was over between them inside two years. That's Hollywood, folks.

For Teddy, fame and fortune had their attractions, as they did for anyone, but they were by no means the only way to his heart. He simply loved to love. But Edna couldn't afford to be just another one of his conquests. She needed his respect and, more importantly, she needed him permanently on the hook to support her cover story. Teddy hired her as deputy manager of Casablanca's rooftop nightclub, Ciro's. It was supposedly her job to be on call for the nightclub's performers, and to hand out party invitations to VIPs: a job that might take her anywhere in the city or abroad. As such, Edna's prolonged absences raised no eyebrows.

Teddy's cooperation had been secured by none other than the charming young Senator John F. Kennedy, while he was honeymooning in Acapulco with his new wife Jackie. The Senator had paid Teddy a discreet visit at the behest of Sherman Adams. Sure, he might have been a Democrat, but Kennedy had no problems with delivering a letter from the President. Had he known what it was about, he might have thought twice, but thankfully Senator Kennedy was happy to act in the service of his nation, no questions asked. The letter offered Teddy the promise of reward from the leader of the free world. It didn't stipulate the nature of this reward, but the promise was enough to ensure Teddy instantly became Edna's greatest fan.

She had spent a week learning the intricacies of the nightclub business, so she could talk about it convincingly when the occasion called for it. For the most part, it was pretty breezy and fun. There was the mundane side of ordering food and beverage and organizing staff, but the hotel itself was like heaven on Earth. Ciro's was an open-air nightclub. Her evenings were spent surrounded by stars above and below as she played hostess to the glamorous, wealthy, and famous, while they partied long and hard into the wee small hours. She loved Teddy's taste in jazz; he had hired some of the best in the business to play at Ciro's.

One day, Edna though she might be happy doing all this for real. Meantime, she was free to come and go between Mexico and America as often as needed.

"You need to leave," Teddy insisted that morning. "Don't come back for at least a week."

"Why?" she asked.

"Rita's coming," he said.

"Rita Hayworth?"

"It's the perfect time for you to make your exit. Once Margarita is here, nobody will notice your absence. She's all anyone will be talking about."

"Isn't she getting married again?"

"Fourth time lucky. So she thinks," said Teddy. "The wedding's tomorrow, in Las Vegas. They're coming here for the honeymoon."

"She's spending her honeymoon in her ex-lover's hotel."

"Dick Haymes is a terrible man," said Teddy. "I hear he's flat broke. In Hollywood, they call him 'Mr Evil'. You can bet he's marrying her for money. Poor girl. Still making bad choices."

Edna held herself back from pointing out the obvious. "Why would she come here? Are you still... friends?"

A term with its own special hierarchy of meanings in Hollywood circles.

"No," said Teddy. "Maybe. I don't know. These things are never clear with Margarita. No doubt she'll have Jack Kennedy back in here. I've heard he likes movie stars. You don't want to be around for any of this, things could get complicated. Rita treats her men like father figures, and it brings out the worst in them."

Edna reluctantly agreed it was a good time to leave. "But you call me if you need me. This is my world too now."

"You should pray I don't take you up on it."

Acting against the express wishes of Mr Adams, Edna had taken Teddy into her close confidence. She'd demonstrated to him the means by which she moved to and from America. Her hotel room had become another destination point on the dial of her little black box. Adams believed Teddy Stauffer couldn't be trusted to keep this information to himself. But Edna's recent experiences told her the opposite was true. Who could he possibly tell, and what could Teddy say to make such a tale sound convincing? That he'd hired a spy with magical powers? She'd told him his life would be over if he breathed a word of it to anyone. Teddy believed her.

Edna's best protection was the sheer strangeness of it.

Teddy made all the predictable noises about fortunes in the offing and how they could put the airlines out of business. But when Edna pointed out this was precisely the reason they couldn't go public, he understood. In Edna's mind, this was her first tentative step along the road ahead. Teddy was her everyman; her sounding board. In return, she would never be more than an hour or two away if she was needed at Ciro's, or if strange men in the service of J. Edgar Hoover started questioning her whereabouts. All Teddy had to do was pick up the telephone, and she would return.

For her American alias, she'd gone with her middle name, Jean. Her father had often called her "Edna Jean" or "Jeanie" when she was a kid, and she instinctively answered to the name. Her new surname, Gellhorn, was a nod to novelist and journalist Martha Gellhorn, who'd been a profound influence on her life during their time together in Berlin in those terrible days at the end of the war. Gellhorn was why she'd become a journalist.

There was no real need for Jean Gellhorn to have a passport, but Adams had made sure she had one anyway, in case she ever needed to travel more extensively. She also had her own social security number and a convincing cover story, which was anchored in reality. Jean Gellhorn was a badged Treasury special agent, reporting directly to the head of presidential security, Elmer Deckard. It was enough to ensure compliance from whoever crossed her path, no questions asked.

Of course, in the event questions *were* asked, Deckard would back her to the hilt. She took a great deal comfort and satisfaction from the irony that, as she set out to end UFO secrecy, her own tracks were being zealously covered up by the Secret Service.

FIFTY SEVEN

S aturday September 26, 1953

Coffee and cigarette in hand at the red formica kitchen table of Deborah's house at Arlington Forest, Edna Drake set her order of attack to paper.

There were two important considerations. First, they must decide upon the number and the makeup of their group of test subjects. Each of these people would need to be approached delicately to gauge their interest in serving their country, yet they could not be told ahead of time the nature of the task they were being called upon to perform. This could only be revealed on the day of the test.

The idea was to expose these test subjects to all the collected knowledge and evidence of interplanetary activity on Earth. It would be made clear their safety was assured, though this might ultimately offer little or no comfort in the face of such a shocking reality. But there would be no point excluding people who they thought might react badly — this was the very reason the test was necessary.

Who and how many to pick for this group required a great deal of consideration. A glance at the latest US census information offered an almost endless array of options upon which to base their choice. Edna felt strongly that black and Latino people should have a place in the assembly. But there was also religion to consider, along with political opinion. This brought into question levels of education and socio-economic status. Then there was a question of age — there had to be a range of ages, if they were to go anywhere close to reflecting the breadth of public opinion.

Normally, taking this many variables into account would necessitate a group of several hundred people, but they simply couldn't involve that many people. Each member of the group would need to be vetted (definitely no Communist sympathizers) and sign vows of secrecy. Edna decided they should go with a group of twelve people. This was the number chosen to serve on a court jury and, in the end, a verdict was what they needed here. Six men and six women chosen across a spread of ages, backgrounds and beliefs. Not perfect, but good enough.

She committed this note to paper and delivered it personally to the White House for consideration. Another of Tavon's transport discs allowed her to travel to and from the President's private residence unseen. She would leave a note in a small bathroom attached to a bedroom, periodically used by Sherman Adams. Either Adams or Eisenhower himself then retrieved her notes without anyone else knowing. It dispensed with the risk of communicating over open telephone lines, which could be bugged by the FBI. She was getting used to the momentary confusion brought on by the dimensional gateway; doing several jumps in one day no longer bothered her. Delivering her note to the White House took less than thirty seconds; she was always relieved to get in and out without terrifying the cleaning staff when she materialized from thin air.

It was dark outside by the time Edna arrived safely back in her room at Deborah's house. The letdown from the adrenalin rush of the delivery always left her feeling weak and hungry. But she knew an empty stomach would probably be best for what the rest of the night had in store. They were returning to the Monongahela National Forest, in the hope of speaking with the Zeta Reticulans. If they appeared, she expected the experience to take a physical toll.

She'd suggested traveling to the forest alone, arguing this might be the best way to establish her own rapport with the visitors. Tavon pointed out that they were the ones who had first come to him, and he doubted they would appear merely because Edna alone willed it.

The shift in temperature between the two locations was immediately apparent. It was cold in the forest, and eerily quiet. The air was still; the atmosphere damp and earthy. Not a creature was stirring, as the old story went. The best part about that was the welcome absence of mosquitoes. Welcome but odd, nonetheless. Where had the insects gone?

Tavon flicked a torch on and off, the signal to indicate their presence. Edna was pretty certain the Grar knew they were there. There was no immediate response. After almost an hour of inaction, Edna was pretty sure they weren't coming, but Tavon urged patience. Half an hour later, she was shivering with cold, parched with thirst, hungry and dying for a cigarette, when a light appeared above them.

From a glowing red sphere the size of a small car, a cone of light shot down to the ground. The night air was alive with charge and Edna felt a buzzing in her ears. Two of the Grar appeared at the bottom of the shaft of light, looking much as they had before. It looked like they were wearing jumpsuits of blue or silver, but their shapes were strangely ill-defined. She moved to take a step closer, but found her legs wouldn't budge. She was glued to the spot and knew somehow this wasn't of her own doing.

Her body was under their control; Edna tried not to panic. "Thank you for coming," she said.

"We have a question for you," said Tavon. He took a step forward, apparently untroubled by whatever it was keeping her legs frozen to the spot.

"Will you let me come closer too?" she asked. "You can surely see I'm no threat to you."

We know what you want.

It was an odd voice, beamed right inside her ears and head, though not through the air.

"Will you come? Will you help us?" she asked.

Why?

"So you don't have to live your lives in secret."

There is safety in secrecy. There is also freedom.

The red light holding them in place pulsed a deeper red. It looked like an umbilical cord; Edna sensed they needed to remain within its light. "Why would you feel threatened by us? It seems to me your science is way more advanced."

You fear us.

"No..."

Look deeper within yourself. It is your natural animal response. You cannot help it. You fear us because you do not understand us.

"But I'm trying to get to know you better," she said, almost laughing at her own choice of words. It sounded like a bad pickup line.

What if we said the Grar defy human understanding? Our worlds are utterly separate. Where once we shared a language — long ago — these days are gone. The most basic tenets of our existence are at odds with the very nature of human consciousness. This was true ten thousand years ago, and it is the case more than ever now. We move about in states unbound by physical form.

Edna made an effort to step forward. To her immense surprise, her leg moved. She kept going. One step, then another. "Thank you," she said.

Are you afraid, Edna Drake?

She thought about that. She was ready to say no, but it wouldn't have been an honest response. "Yes," she said, "I am frightened. But less frightened than I was a minute ago."

Confronting the truth has a cost. To demand payment is easy when it is another who pays the price.

"Nothing about this is easy," she said.

The Grar stood their ground for at least a minute before responding. She looked up, trying to get a clearer line of sight on the craft that had brought them here. It was triangular, and there were lights set into its hull. As she watched, the lights pulsed through different shades of red and orange, but it was so bright she couldn't be sure this wasn't simply her eyes playing tricks on her. A noise sounded, high above them, like a bell. A single chime that hung in the air, like the forest was an echo chamber.

We will consider your proposal.

Amid the strangeness of it all, their response was almost mundane. It occurred to her the words and the phrasing were her own. The Grar somehow had been using her own words as a framework for their communications.

A moment later, they were gone. Within seconds, the normal sounds of the forest returned. Crickets chirped. An owl hooted as it buzzed over their heads. A swarm of mosquitoes descended on them like they were the only warm-blooded creatures for miles. As the full moon poked above the horizon, a wolf began to howl.

FIFTY EIGHT

Saturday September 26, 1953

Edna was awake and lonely in her room on the top floor of Deborah's suburban hideaway, unable to sleep. She didn't have a clock, but she knew it was late. She felt like a drink. But more than anything else, she didn't want to be alone.

Then she remembered Mexico. She opened the drawer on her bedside table and pulled out the black box Tavon had given her. She set the dial for Acapulco, hit the blue button that set this bedroom as the automatic return point, then pushed the red button to activate the portal. With two steps she travelled two and a half thousand miles to her room at the Casablanca.

Staff rooms were on the lowest level, meaning there wasn't much of a view from the window. But the room was bathed in a beautiful shimmering blue hue from the lights reflecting off the water below. It always made Edna feel like she was underwater. The hotel itself felt like a cruise ship, far removed from the troubles of the outside world. She pulled on a black frock, set her hair back in a bun, and made her way across the lobby to the elevator that rose straight to the rooftop nightclub.

At Ciro's, events were in full swing. She stared up at the stars that hours ago entranced her for entirely different reasons, half a continent away. Here they seemed magical, romantic. Utterly human. Acapulco

Bay shimmered and sparkled. As the band finished its number, the masts of a hundred yachts rang like tiny bells from their cables catching the wind. She took herself behind the bar, threw ice into a tall glass, and poured herself a Tom Collins.

"Edna! You're back." Teddy Stauffer patted her on the shoulder and offered a weary smile. "I guess you heard."

"No... heard what?" she asked him.

"Rita and her husband didn't come. They're staying in Las Vegas. Rita never bothered to cancel the booking. She apologized profusely and promised to pay, which was kind of her, though I can't help feeling disappointed. Having her here would have been good for business."

Edna knew it wasn't all she was good for in Teddy's eyes. "Now that you mention it, I did read something about police investigating a threat against her daughter. I guess they wanted to stay closer to home."

"Dick has a nightclub gig in Philadelphia on the 28th. They were never coming," he said ruefully.

"Guess that means I can stay," Edna said. But a face had appeared behind him, one that made her gasp. "Teddy," she whispered urgently, "is your top drawer still fully loaded?"

"Of course. But..."

"Good," she said, immediately shifting her attention to the woman now staring at her across the bar.

Nina Onilova looked pale. Maybe even scared, though she was trying hard not to show it.

"Sister Josephine. Out of uniform, I see."

"Edna. It is you." She sounded relieved. "Then I really am in Acapulco."

"You've been sticking your nose in where it's not wanted. I ought to turn you in to the FBI," Edna threatened.

"I don't think they have a field office in Mexico," the Russian replied, trying hard to laugh, but stopping as it caught in her throat. She was close to tears. Terrified.

"You don't know what's happening, do you?" Edna said.

"Pour me a drink. A big one."

Edna grabbed a tumbler, threw in a few ice cubes, and filled it with vodka. Onilova downed it in a single gulp. Edna poured again. The place was busy, but Edna pointed to where a couple were just leaving a table at the back of the bar. "On the house. Go take a seat, I'll be over in a moment." The Russian looked skeptical. "Go on — what choice do you have, Nina?"

Onilova had done her best to pull herself together by the time Edna sat down beside her. "Nice place you have here," she said.

"Let me guess what's happened here," said Edna. "You broke into my apartment in Washington. Am I getting warm?"

Onilova stared out across the water. "If I'm not back by morning, they will think the worst."

"You just travelled the best part of three thousand miles in a heart-beat," said Edna. "I think we can have you back by morning."

Onilova looked at her in astonishment. "One moment I am in your lounge room, the next I am in tiny bedroom somewhere else entirely. Still in Washington, I think. But when I move toward the door, I find myself here in this hotel. I am afraid to try again. I see a door and I open it. Then I find you here."

When Edna had turned on the portal in Deborah's house, she'd left it open. But by designating her bedroom at Deborah's as the hub, Nina couldn't return to Paulson's apartment once she'd left it, not without resetting the destination dial on the black box. The device was back in Edna's room at Deborah's house — the last place she wanted to take a Russian agent. It was bad enough that Nina had already been there once.

"What could you have possibly been hoping to find by breaking into that apartment?" Edna asked her. "You must have known I'd left."

"That day you had so many visitors," said Onilova. "I knew something was strange."

Because the Russians had the place bugged. They must have deciphered some of what Tavon had said and gone looking for a black box. Luckily, Nina hadn't found it yet. But the moment it was revealed to her, Onilova would do everything in her power to steal it. And Edna didn't have the skill to take on a trained killer at close quarters.

"You had me totally fooled in Rome, you know," Edna said. "You make a very convincing nun."

Onilova shrugged. "Not so hard. They are simple creatures. Kind hearts, but weak of mind. Easy to manipulate."

"Like us Americans?"

Onilova eyed her warily. "Now it is you who has advantage, no?"

"It's not like I wanted you to find me here," Edna pointed out. "But somehow you knew we would come to Rome. You were waiting for us. You were too clever by half. You had Paolo wrapped around your finger."

Onilova smiled. "I hear he misses me."

Edna lit a cigarette and offered her pack to the Russian. Nina accepted one gratefully and Edna lit it for her. "You've given him entirely the wrong idea about nuns," said Edna. "He thinks they're sex slaves for the priests. Of course, he's a bit old-fashioned."

"Take me back to Washington," Onilova said pleadingly. "I will forget this ever happened." It was a bald-faced lie, but at that moment Nina almost sounded like she believed it.

"Why should I?" Edna asked.

"We can help one another. Compare notes."

"You want to defect?"

"Maybe," Onilova said, though it clearly wasn't what she'd meant. "Yes, I can do that. I can work for you."

"Could you persuade your people to stop listening to my private conversations?"

"I could tell you where the bugs are hidden. You fix them yourself."

Edna smiled. "All right. I think we might be able to work something out."

Onilova finished her drink and got to her feet, eager to leave.

They said nothing as Edna led the way back through the hotel. It was late, or early depending on your point of view. The more determined drunks were huddled together at tables in the foyer bar. At the front desk, the night clerk nodded at Edna as they passed. Edna led the way around a corner in the corridor that led to her room. They passed Teddy Stauffer coming the other way. He apologized to Edna as he bumped into her, brow furrowed like he had something on his mind. "Good night."

Onilova watched him leave. "Strange man, your boss. He says nothing when you bring a woman to your room so late at night."

"Hotel managers never ask those sorts of questions."

Edna turned the handle on the door to her room. She never bothered to lock it, because there was nothing in the room worth stealing. She ushered Onilova into the room and stopped her just short of the portal — the disc itself was hidden beneath the carpet.

"Let me grab the control box," Edna said. "It's under my pillow."

As Edna turned around, the Russian must have realized something was wrong. She leapt at Edna like a cat, but Nina Onilova was a moment too late. Edna fired twice through her pillow, hitting her in the head and chest. She fell on top of Edna, who swung her fists wildly, throwing Onilova to the floor. Edna pulled the gun up to fire a third time, but saw Onilova was already dead.

The room was flooded with light from the corridor as the door opened.

James Jesus Angleton looked genuinely shocked as he took in the scene. "I heard shots," he said. He looked back along the corridor, then stepped into the room and closed the door.

Edna sat down on her bed, the pistol shaking in her hand. "I should have known you'd be lurking out there in the shadows."

"You're full of surprises, Miss Drake. Here's me thinking you're working for the Soviets. Do me a favor and put that gun down."

Angleton's needle was stuck in the same groove. Edna unclenched her hand and dropped the pistol on the bed, but couldn't stop the hand from shaking. "So, are you here to help me or hang me?"

Angleton smiled grimly, surveying the scene as he weighed his options, but there was sympathy in his eyes. "Will you be all right?"

Edna could feel her heart pounding beneath the sound of her own frantic gasps for air. She realized he'd asked her a question, but she hadn't been listening. "I've never shot anyone before."

He sat down beside her. "No, I thought as much."

"I had to... I was terrified. She's a killer...was a killer. She caught me by surprise..." Edna began to see it must look bad. "I'm no communist."

Angleton took her by the hand and gave it a squeeze, firm but somehow tender at the same time. "You did what you had to do. It's over now."

"She knew too much," said Edna, looking searchingly into his eyes. "I had no choice. She found out..." She was rambling; she stopped herself just in time before mentioning the portal.

Angleton's head tilted quizzically. "Found out what?"

Edna looked away. "Who I really work for."

Angleton rose to his feet. "And who precisely is that, Miss Drake?"

Edna looked at him with sudden disdain. "Don't play dumb. The wind will change and you might stay that way."

Angleton nodded. "OK, I deserved that. Don't shoot me."

Edna let out a nervous laugh. She felt strange. Grateful to have come out on top, and at the same time not at all sorry she'd pulled the trigger. "They killed Helen Barber — just because they saw it as a way to get to turn me against Menzel. And it almost worked."

"Go throw some water on your face, we need to get this cleaned up," he said.

"I take it you have people outside who can help."

Angleton nodded. "Whose gun is that?"

"It belongs to...a friend."

"I don't think your friend will want it back."

"What do we do?" she asked.

"We take a little cruise. We're gonna need a boat."

"I can ask Teddy. He'll know how to do that."

"You trust him?" Angleton demanded.

Edna looked down at the gun. "With my life." She lifted her shaking hand to her face and wiped away a tear. "We need blankets. There's a utility cupboard two doors down. Can you go and grab some? I'd probably just drop them at this point."

Angleton quietly backed out of the room, closing the door as he departed. She leapt to her feet unsteadily, figuring she had about a minute. Nina Onilova's body lay sprawled across the floor. Her feet were missing. She had fallen down at the edge of the portal and now her legs were in two countries at once. It was sheer luck Angleton hadn't noticed. Not wanting to touch the body, Edna jumped over it instead and fell through the portal into her bedroom at Deborah's house.

The air here was different. Fresher and cooler. No smell of death, though there was a pair of disembodied feet on the floor. She wondered what would happen if the portal was turned off now. Would those feet would remain here?

Edna picked up the black box from her dresser and stepped back through the portal to Mexico, then urgently kicked at the dead woman's legs until her feet reappeared. She hit the red button to switch off the portal, then shoved the black box in the drawer of her bedside table.

Her hands were still shaking as she adjusted her hair in the bathroom mirror. Edna took a deep breath and told herself to get it together. She had to tell Teddy Stauffer he was an accessory to murder.

FIFTY NINE

Saturday February 20, 1954

The jury of twelve arrived in a plain gunmetal grey bus at the floodlit gates of Plant 42 just after dusk. Edna was waiting for them at the front gate. She made a point of climbing aboard the bus to welcome them as it stopped at the security checkpoint. The project psychiatrist had said it was important they saw familiar faces ahead of what was to come. A dozen faces stared back at her in nervous silence. Had it been like this for the whole trip from LA?

Operation JD — shorthand for Judgement Day — had been conducted like an operation run by the French resistance. Information had been strictly compartmentalized. At each step of their journey, the twelve were handed off by one courier to another. Thus, the woman who met them at LA Airport with the friendly efficiency of a tour guide had handed them over to another friendly female face who took them through reception and dinner at the Biltmore Hotel. After issuing them with written instructions that breakfast would arrive via room service and to stay in their rooms until further notice, she too had vanished. Just before ten o'clock the following morning, a ticket for the bus to the Palmdale Philately Convention was stuck under each of their doors. The journey to the base had taken about ninety minutes. Time enough to develop a healthy dose of regret.

The twelve were unknown to one another, as would be the case with any jury. But these jurors had been gathered both from various walks of life and from vastly different parts of the nation. The process of selection had been quicker and less rigorous than Edna would have liked, but they were limited to a time schedule dictated by the President's future movements. Today had been the only day they could make Ike disappear for several hours with a believable cover story.

The end result of the selection process, following weeks of argument between her and Adams, had proved satisfactory to all. They were a suitable cross section of American life, with the sole exception of Teddy Stauffer, who had been included at Edna's insistence because he was already in the know about Verus operations and Outherian technology (to say nothing of being an accessory to the murder of a Russian spy). He was one more person Edna could count upon to act as a voice of reason if members of the group became deeply agitated, or hysterical. A few others had similarly been selected for reasons of expediency. Edna and Adams both knew this was her attempt at shortening the odds on a positive outcome, but she doubted it would make much of a difference in the end. Getting them here was what mattered.

Teddy, like everyone on the bus, was told nothing of why they had been chosen or for what reason. All any of them knew was that they would carry out an important task in the service of their President, one for which they would be remunerated, but that demanded utmost secrecy. They must never, ever speak of what they saw to another living soul. That point had been earnestly underlined on several occasions, and this alone had been enough to prompt three people to walk away before today, prompting a hasty search for candidates to replace them.

They were six men and six women, ranging in ages from twenty-one to sixty-six. Brown University English lit major Philippa Keen was the youngest of the group, while there two people in their sixties— Brooklyn Catholic priest Father Albert Peters, and housewife and grandmother Colleen Sprite from Detroit, Michigan. Miguel Romero was a youngish Hispanic doctor from San Diego. Sergeant Patrick Horton was an ageing and world-weary cop from Chicago who thought he'd seen it all.

There was San Francisco nurse Lucy Hernandez, along with two people from Washington D.C. — USAF staffer Therese Williams and black barman Beverley King. Office secretary Josephine Johnson hailed all the way from Savannah, Georgia. Then there were the two people who now held each other's hands like star-crossed lovers — assistant bank manager Francene O'Leary from Boston, and Hollywood stage hand, Justin Cavitt. They had shared a bottle of bourbon the previous night, and one thing had led to another. Edna wondered if they understood they would never be able to see one another again after today.

Garrick Stamford, and most of his Lockheed personnel, had been told to take a hike. Only one or two remained to help run the operation. The main Skunkworks hangar was bathed in light, but its regular personnel were absent as the bus drove in through the main hangar door.

Sherman Adams stood waiting in the middle of the hangar floor. He shook the hand of each person in turn exiting the bus, thanking them for their service. None of the jury members appeared to have any idea they had just met the President's right-hand man. With everyone out, the bus headed back out through the hangar door, where a short distance away a small twin-engine Piper Apache had just appeared. It taxied inside, and pulled up about fifty feet away from them. Elmer Deckard threw open a door, stepped down to the floor of the hangar and flipped his seat forward. The President emerged from the plane's rear seat, stepping gingerly to the ground using Deckard's hand to steady himself. Several of the group gasped as the magnitude of the moment hit them.

Ike was officially on holidays in Palm Springs. He'd fled from his holiday home an hour earlier on the pretext of a toothache, claiming he urgently needed to find a dentist. He gave a wave to all assembled and walked over to join them. "Thank you all so much for being here today," he said, nodding and smiling as he shook hands. The looks on their faces would have warmed the hardest of hearts.

"Now folks, we are here today," Adams began, "to reveal to you all that your government has come to discover about flying saucers and visitors from other worlds." A ripple of surprise died down quickly. Several of the group had already guessed as much by this point.

"I knew it," said Beverley King, who must have been harboring plenty of unanswered questions after his years working with Lee Tavon.

"First," said Edna, "can I please ask everybody to step over this way and behind that yellow line on the floor."

With everyone safely in the designated zone, the floor of the hangar began to vibrate. A large crack opened, and two massive concrete panels slid apart to reveal the cavernous underground section of the hangar. From here, Flying Saucer-1 rose slowly. It glowed pale blue and hung pulsing in the air for a few moments, before skipping right over the President's plane and out the hangar doors, to the runway and the desert beyond. The group watched in awe as it performed a sequence of extraordinary low-altitude aerial maneuvers, then reentered the hangar, stopping in midair at the edge of the opening in the floor.

"Oh, my Lord, that was incredible," cried Josephine Johnson, clearly delighted and excited by the spectacle.

A hatch in the saucer appeared and Lee Tavon descended the stairs to meet them.

"Lee? That you? Damn," yelled Beverley King.

"Hello Bev," said Tavon, tossing a disc onto the floor just in front of him. Edna checked her watch. The others would be here in five minutes.

"Does anybody have any questions so far?" Tavon asked.

"Is that saucer one of ours?" asked Sergeant Horton.

"It is now," said Adams, "but we didn't build it. It's the handiwork of people from another world. More specifically, a people known as the Ryl who have lived on Earth for more than six thousand years."

Lee Tavon took up the story. "In the Old Testament, the Ryl were known as the Sons of God, the mighty men of old. The Sumerians called them the Anunnaki, and at one time they lived openly among us. Their blood is also your blood. What you see before you here is literally the origins of Man."

"Oh, my Lord," said Father Peters, crossing himself. He began muttering a prayer to himself, as if seeking protection.

Right on cue, Paolo Favaloro materialized before the group, at his full eleven-foot height. "This ship once belonged to me," he declared proudly. "I am Utnapishtim, the last antediluvian king of Sumer. I am of Ryl and human descent. I have been alive on Earth for more than six millennia."

Teddy Stauffer didn't know where to look. "Is he for real?" He stepped forward and over the yellow line, reaching out toward Paolo. His hand passed straight through him.

"Holy shit," Sergeant Horton exclaimed. "Did anyone else see that?"

"Please step back behind the line there, Teddy," Edna urged.

Teddy's mouth hung open in complete bewilderment. "Is that some sort of trick? He can't be real."

"I assure you, I am as real as you are," Paolo replied.

Francene hit the deck in a dead faint. Lucy Hernandez rushed to see she was OK, as Justin lifted her head off the floor and patted her cheeks. It was a momentary distraction from the reality confronting them, because Lee Tavon quickly drew everyone's attention back to the show.

"I too, am not of this world," Lee revealed. He stepped forward and touched Teddy and Horton on the arm. "Physically, I am human. But mentally and spiritually, I am of an alien race known as the Outherians. We travelled here via meteor in a journey we believe took thousands of years. We came in the form of a virus that allowed us to take human hosts."

Everyone took a few steps back.

"Don't worry," Lee added cheerfully, "it's not catching!"

"Shit, Lee," said King. "I always knew there was something strange about you, man."

"Bev, as they say in the movies — you ain't seen nothing yet." Tavon pointed grandly to the floor. From a portal to his farm in Virginia, six more Lee Tavons stepped into the hangar, as if from thin air. They were followed by seven Deborahs and the groups of two of her daughters. The Deborahs spoke together all at once. "We are both many and one, of like mind and body, sharing each other's experience to vastly enhance our mental and physiological capabilities."

Father Peters fell to his knees and began loudly retching and vomiting.

Francene O'Leary, who had just been revived, screamed like she had woken to a whole new nightmare.

"Please, there is no need for panic," President Eisenhower assured them.

"Please, everybody, calm down!" yelled Edna. "You are safe. No harm will come to you here."

But an air of panic had begun to take hold of people. It wasn't just about feeling physically threatened; the world as they knew it had come apart at the seams. Philippa Keen started to run toward the desert with a look of abject terror on her face. She was joined by

Francene and Justin, who were staggering like drunks; their terror had thrown them off-balance.

Colleen Sprite held her head in her hands and kept repeating, "No, no, it's not real, it's not real..."

Beverley King was just shaking his head. "Shit man, this is so fucked up."

Dr Romero had crouched down to put his arm around Father Peters, but the priest looked catatonic. He was deep in the grip of an intense emotional and spiritual crisis. Teddy, and Horton the Chicago cop, were bent down and talking to Deborah's daughters, touching them gingerly like they might be booby-trapped.

At that moment, Philippa, Francene, and Justin ran back in through the hangar doors. The looks on their faces could almost have been taken as amusement, but they were actually in deep distress. "They're here," Justin yelled, his arm around Francene as they made their way back to the rest of the group.

A reddish light appeared at the door of the hangar and into this light the figures of two Grar took shape. Lucy, Colleen, and Josephine, who had started holding hands, now began to recite the Lord's Prayer together to ward off the evil.

Sanity had left the building.

"That's enough," Sergeant Horton yelled at Eisenhower and Adams. "You need to stop this. You're scaring the life out of everyone, can't you see that?"

Eisenhower stared back grimly at the policeman, then finally nodded. "Wrap it up, Edna."

Edna caught the attention of one of the Deborahs and gave her the signal, then walked quickly out toward the Grar, focusing her thoughts on them and doing her best to offer her thanks and urge them to leave. She could only get so close before fear or involuntary muscle spasm forced her to a stop. She stared out at them, trying to offer an apology and ignoring her own growing sense of apprehension.

Her ears were ringing and it kept getting louder, to the point where she couldn't stand it anymore, and then they were gone.

Edna stood frozen to the spot, staring out at the desert in sheer relief. The only sound she heard now was the sobs of a terrified Hollywood stagehand, and the persistent prayers of three women clinging to one another like their very lives depended on it. Edna made her way back to them.

The Deborahs ushered their daughters back through the portal, then began to move through the group, touching each of the twelve gently on the back of the head. Edna didn't know how this worked, whether it was hypnotherapy or a form of telepathy, but the end result was all that mattered. The Outherians made it all go away, tucking the trauma deep down into the folds of each person's subconscious. Moments later, as the Deborahs themselves departed, everyone was smiling.

The FS-1 craft remained in midair right in front of them, but now it might as well have been invisible; nobody saw it. In their minds, it was no longer there. To Edna, this was more profoundly disturbing than anything else they had witnessed, yet at the same time it was vastly preferable to the alternative. It was better for these people that they didn't remember anything.

One by one, the Tavons quietly slipped through their portal and vanished.

SIXTY

M onday February 22, 1954

Verus Foundation headquarters on Church Street was deserted. There was a "For Sale" sign on the wall beside the front door. Edna climbed the stairs to the main entrance and noticed the front door was hanging open. She gave it a push. The foyer looked as run-down as ever, except now the absence of furniture added to the air of neglect. She stepped inside.

The door to Menzel's office was ajar. He'd always kept it locked; entry was by invitation only. The book shelves lining the walls of the old study were empty, save a single copy of *Flying Saucers,* a book written by Menzel himself the previous year in an effort to debunk every known avenue of inquiry into unexplained flying objects. She was sure it had been left behind deliberately as a message for her. She was out in the cold. Left behind. The doors to this building were open to her, but the doors to Verus itself had been slammed in her face.

Sherman Adams had this morning succinctly summed up their experiment as "a complete failure". There would be no public disclosure, no mea culpa, no revelation of the grand conspiracy. People just weren't ready for it. To say nothing of the institutions and the businesses that kept the wheels turning. Disclosure was just too much of a risk to life as they knew it.

Nevertheless, Adams had offered her a job as a special envoy to the President. It was a good offer; one that would resurrect her career. But it would inevitably become steeped in politics, and after what had gone down with McCarthy, Edna didn't trust them to have her back.

"We're going to shut McCarthy down," Adams had assured her. "The President is determined. And I've been talking with Ed Murrow. He's getting ready to tear McCarthy apart live on national television."

"I'm pleased," she said. Somebody needed to stand up to that man.

"We feel real bad about what he did to you. Let us do the right thing. Come work for us."

She had told Adams she'd think about it. They both knew what that meant.

Lee Tavon was waiting for her on Church Street as she exited the building. "I have a counter offer for you," he said.

She smiled. Damn mind readers.

"Come work with us. I'll pay better than whatever Adams is offering. There's a project I need your help with."

"I don't have much of a head for technology," Edna confessed.

Lee waved his hand dismissively. "When we built our space-time matter translator..."

"You mean the portal?"

"Yes, the portal. To build it, we had to refine the design of what we call a crystal valve. Also known as a transistor. We have engineers working inside Philco on research and development. They've come up with something called a surface barrier transistor. It's going to revolutionize communications."

"I understood about a quarter of what you just said," said Edna.

"We need to put more of a human face on our business. This transistor will be crucial in helping us miniaturize the matter translator and a whole bunch of other tech. There's something else that might be of interest to you," Tavon said, smiling knowingly at her. "We want to expand into the UK. I see a trip to London in your near future. Perhaps a chance to hook up with an old friend?"

Edna grinned. "You know Lee, this might actually be the start of a beautiful friendship."

They started walking back toward Dupont Circle. "Of all the gin joints in all the world," said Tavon, "she walks into mine."

She grabbed him by the arm. "I don't want you turning me into one of you. No alien mind soup. No more Ednas running around. You hear me?"

"Crystal clear," he promised. "Crystal clear."

"I suppose I'd have to travel to Britain via traditional means," Edna realized.

"Yes, but it'll be so much quicker coming home again," Tavon assured her.

"Or maybe I could hitch a ride on a flying saucer."

"I don't think so," said Tavon. "Last time I was in the cockpit, I reset the controls to the way they were."

She glanced sideways at him. He was poker-faced as usual, utterly unconcerned by the trouble he had caused. "You're a sly fox, Mr Tavon."

"Having that ship in the air would tip the balance of power too far. Bill Donovan's right, it would start a war."

But international relations were not the sort she had on her mind. "If I go to England, I may want to stay a while — assuming I'm welcome. Any thoughts on that?"

Tavon just kept staring into the middle distance. "Sorry kid, you're on your own there."

She laughed and shook her head. "Why did I know you were going to say that?"

After all that had gone down, it seemed odd to feel nervous about what lay ahead. But somewhere deep in her gut she knew it was one more risk she needed to take.

Made in United States
Troutdale, OR
08/09/2023

11929906R00148